I0659828

Taking Care of Business

The Richard Jackson Saga, Volume 10

Ed Nelson

Published by Ed Nelson, 2024.

Table of Contents

Other books by Ed Nelson

The Richard Jackson Saga

Book 1 The Beginning

Book 2 Schooldays

Book 3 Hollywood

Book 4 In the Movies

Book 5 Star to Deckhand

Book 6 Surfing Dude

Book 7 Third Time is a Charm

Book 8 Oxford University

Book 9 Cold War

Book 10 Taking Care of Business

Book 11 Interesting Times

Book 12 Escape from Siberia

Book 13 Regicide

Book 14 What's Under, Down Under?

Book 15 The Lunar Kingdom

Book 16 First Steps

In the Richard Jackson World

Mary, Mary

Stand-Alone Story

Ever and Always

Cast in Time Series

Book 1: Baron

Book 2: Baron of the Middle Counties

Book 3: Count

Book 4: Earl

Book 5: Earl of the Marches

Dedication

This is dedicated to my wife Carol for her support and help as my first reader and editor.

Thanks to my editors, Ernest Bywater, Lonelydad57, and Old Rotorhead.
Also, the Bellefontaine High School Class of 1962 just because.
Professionally edited by Janet E. Rupert

Quotation

That's the way it happened, give or take a lie or two.

James Garner as Wyatt Earp describing the gunfight at the OK Corral in the movie *Sunset.*

Copyright © 2021

Chapter 1

After the Holidays, I flew back to England to start my new term at Oxford. The first thing waiting for me at the mail table, sitting in The Meadows entrance, was a stack of telegrams.

Every one of them was from my brothers and sister. Each telegram reminded me that I was seventeen years old. During my birthday celebrations, I made the mistake of saying I was eighteen.

Why I made that mistake I don't know, but my wonderful siblings weren't going to let me forget it. Something about not being as perfect as I thought I was.

Maybe I was getting forgetful at my advanced age; who knew? I might forget to buy them Christmas presents next year.

Speaking of Christmas, when I arrived at The Meadows it was Christmas all over again. Nothing big, but Grandmum had knitted me a sweater.

It was dark blue with the Oxford logo in grey. The logo was offset on my left side. It was really neat looking.

I had bought her a one-hundred-pound gift certificate from Harrods. I know I should have picked out a real gift, but I had no idea what to get a lady of her age.

She seemed very happy with it. To her, she would be getting her shopping for free!

I also had Mr. Hamilton purchase cufflinks for the male staff and a brooch for the females. I gave him a matching tie clasp and cuff links from Tiffany's in New York.

Having staff all over the world was very convenient for running errands.

The staff chipped in and gave me a new set of riding clothes. I thought that strange as I didn't have a horse in England. That is until I was handed a card from Mum and Dad.

A riding horse they had purchased was waiting for me at a local stable. It would be kept there, as we couldn't justify supporting a stable at The Meadows.

I was glad to see that while money was no object, the family was still mindful of spending.

My first class at Oxford was part of a business course. I had given up on a formal program leading to a specific degree. Instead, I was taking those courses that would help me in general and sounded interesting.

This business course was part of the MBA program. I thought I would have an easy A, but that I would learn a few things along the way.

I had a rude surprise about the easy A.

The don introduced himself and then told us the course requirements. Besides the normal reading requirements, there was a live business case study.

The course was run over two terms so we would have six months to complete the case study. We had to start a business and make a profit. Our grades would depend on the gross profit made.

We would start with funds of 50 pounds each. If by the end of the second term it had made 500 pounds, it would be a C, 1000 pounds for a B, and 2500 pounds for an A.

That seemed easy enough to me. We had a choice of going it alone or combining it with other students. If we combined it would scale up, for two people 100 pounds, but 1000 pounds for a C, 2000 pounds for a B, etc. Three people would have 150 pounds and would need 1500 pounds for a C.

I thought it would be easier for me to go alone.

It turned out I had no choice in going it alone. After the don explained the terms, he continued.

"We have a special case in class, Sir Richard Jackson. For any that may not be aware, Sir Richard is very wealthy.

"As such, this assignment would be nothing for him; I'm proposing a challenge especially for him to level the grading curve in the class."

Crikey, he's set me up. I have to accept whatever is coming or I will be blamed for a bad grading curve in the class.

"Sir Richard's challenge is that he will start with 10,000 pounds. To get a C, it will take 100,000 pounds, a B 250,000 pounds, and an A will be 1,000,000 pounds."

Oh well, I can use Jackson Enterprises as support, not that big of a deal.

"He must do this from scratch without using any of his current company resources."

Arrgh, can I drop this course? No, he has me cornered. If nothing else, my pride won't let me do it.

"What say you, Sir Richard?"

I can accept, accept under protest, refuse the challenge, or drop the course.

"I accept."

"Capital. I wish your sister Mary were in this course. I would love to see what she could do."

"You seem to know a lot about my family."

"It's called business intelligence. I research the backgrounds of all my students. You will have to learn to do the same in the business world."

Someone in the back of the room asked about my sister. Is she rich?

"Miss Mary Jackson is worth a million in her own right and from what I understand is about to receive a royal patent to purvey clothes to Her Majesty."

"Hey Rick, is anyone shagging your sister?"

I didn't think I could move that fast. Several men in the crowd pulled me off the guy before I could do him harm.

"Sir Richard, please sit down. If you are going to do violence, do it outside of the lecture hall. I should have mentioned that his sister Mary is six years old."

That set up an uproar in the room. Half the class wanted to help me kill the jerk, the other half wanted to know how she did it.

The jerk wasn't completely stupid; he left the room and dropped the class. For all I know, he fled the country, as I never saw him again.

After the room settled down the don added one more thing.

"Some of you will have a letter from me in your mailbox. As I told you, intelligence is important. I know some of you are under extreme financial difficulty, and I'm sending you fifty pounds for your business."

"I'm like any other businessman and want to make a profit. I expect my money back with ten percent interest from your first profits. That won't count against your grade count.

"If you lose all your money, then I will be out mine, just as in the real world. I'm making an unsecured loan. For all the years I have been doing this, I've ended up in the black every year."

After that, there was a long question-and-answer period. While that was going on I thought about what I would do. To raise that amount of money in a six-month run would be difficult.

The only way I saw to accomplish that was to invent something and license it out. I would have to give this some serious thought.

My losing my temper over Mary had one positive effect. Normally at the end of the class, I would have been inundated by the girls who wanted to know the rich guy and possibly marry him, and guys wanting to be a friend of the rich guy.

They all left me alone. This was good and bad; good as I didn't want false attention, bad because it prevented me from having real friends. This problem has plagued me since my first movie.

One neat thing happened. While I was in class a message was left for me. The restoration of the Ferrari I had won from that Arabian jerk of a prince was complete. I could pick it up in London at any time.

Instead, I called and asked for a price to have it delivered to The Meadows. It seemed reasonable, so I agreed to the amount, and it was due on Wednesday.

While I was at home at Christmas some old business had come up. The new R&D center for Jackson Personal Products had been scheduled to open last October.

New requirements put in place by the State of California delayed the opening. If they kept doing this, we would have to give serious thought to moving operations out of the state.

The new opening date was in late January, so I had to sneak a trip back to the States for the ribbon cutting. At the same time, I would try to corner Mum on what she was doing in Morocco during the war.

I had tried to corner her at Christmas, but she always seemed to drift away. One thing I noticed—Dad was never present when she would even use the word Morocco.

I had to find out, inquiring minds, you know.

Another thing that I was behind on was doing voiceovers for the documentary about the new container business. I just wouldn't have time to get it done while in the US.

I made a mental note to contact Mr. Monroe and see if it could be done at Pinewood Studios. That was another thing. I had to give a definitive answer about the two movie scripts they had sent me.

I was inclined to do them as they fit the criteria I had given them. They both seemed like fun comedies.

Then I had to get up to London sometime and review the proposed flying uniforms for the new division of the Queen's Messengers. I hoped they would be practical.

I reviewed my list of fun things to do: I had to take delivery of a Ferrari and at the same time arrange for pictures with a pretty girl on the hood. I was hoping to get Nina from Switzerland some weekend. Perhaps she would like to be the "hood ornament".

Then I had to fly to the States for a ribbon-cutting, do voice-overs for my documentary, and, oh, yes, sign up to appear in two movies.

I almost forgot. I also had to select a uniform for the Queen's Messengers.

Then I had to keep up with my classwork, and I suppose I should check with the queen to see if she needed any dogs robbed.

Oh yes, and invent something that would make a lot of money in the short run. All in all, it sounded like an easy term coming up at Oxford. Well, easy as compared to running for my life from the KGB and the Stasi.

Being a logical person, I took care of the important issue first and called Nina to see when she could come over for the pictures with my new Ferrari. She was busy catching up with things this weekend but the next would be grand. I would fly over to pick her up on Friday and get her home on Sunday.

Even though it was dinner time in the UK, it was still work hours in California, so I put in a call to Mr. Monroe. He wasn't available, so I left a message for him to call me at his convenience.

I mustn't upset the girlfriend's dad.

All this and it is just past dinner on Monday.

grandmum and I had tea and coffee after dinner. She told me that she was having dinner with John on Friday. For the life of me, I couldn't figure out who John was.

I must have had a puzzled look because she said, John Norfolk, the Duke of Suttonham,

Egads and little fishhooks, my grandmum going on a date with a duke! I was at a loss for words. I mean they were both adults, but Grandmums weren't supposed to go chasing after men at her age. At least, I didn't think so.

"That's nice. Where is he taking you?"

"We are having dinner with the royal family at Windsor."

Things became a little clearer; Queen Mum Elizabeth might have a hand in this.

"Is he picking you up?"

"Oh no, I'm picking him up. It's on the way."

What a modern Grandmum I have. Who would have thought?

"It will be a long drive back."

"I know. That's why we would like to borrow your suite in London."

"Certainly."

I need some brain floss. The pictures I'm getting are not normal.

Again, my face must have given me away.

"Richard, what nasty thoughts you have. Mr. Hamilton is driving us and staying, and we are being accompanied by Pamela and her new boyfriend."

As the Alka Seltzer ad says, "Oh, what a relief it is."

"Good to know."

"I'll 'good to know' you, you nasty boy. Women of my age don't bed men on the first date; it usually takes about three."

Oh my God, let me out of here.

Grandmum started laughing like a loon.

"Oh, Richard, the look on your face was priceless. We don't act like that at all."

"You frightened me. I'm just not used to thinking of you as a woman. You are my grandmum."

"That's all right Richard, my lad. By and by, we don't count the dates. It's by the number of presents."

I fled to my room, coffee untouched, routed horse and foot. I thought Mum was a holy terror, but now I knew where she got it from. If it passed down through the female line, the world would come to an end when Mary grew up.

Well, maybe not an end, but the place of females in the world would change. I tried to go to sleep but it evaded me as I thought of Mary changing the world.

When I decided it could be a good thing, I was able to drift off.

Tuesday had me up early and running. I had increased my run to ten miles a day. East Germany was still fresh on my mind.

As I ran, I thought about my economics class project. I could object and have it changed, but I did agree to it. Besides, it sounded like a fun challenge. The question was, what could I invent, patent, and license out in a short time frame? I didn't come to any conclusions.

After cleaning up and eating breakfast, thankfully missing Grandmum, I went to the library to type a paper that would be due by the end of term. My typing had greatly improved, but I still would clash and occasionally stick the keys.

While easy to do on the old mechanical typewriters, it was hard to accomplish on the new electrics. That's when it dawned on me; why did we have these long levers with letters on them?

It made sense with the original typewriters, but the new electrics could work in different ways. I would have to think about this.

I also decided against attending the economics class. The other students would be all over me for the wrong reasons, fame and fortune. I could avoid this by skipping most of the classes.

The don was one of those who stuck closely to his notes, so I could just keep up with those. If I had any questions, I could schedule an appointment.

One problem solved. Now I hoped the rest of the day went as well.

Chapter 2

Driving into Oxford for my first class of the day, I thought about the typewriter idea I had yesterday. If I eliminated keys, how would the letters be struck?

I was still thinking about it after I parked my Aston Martin in the garage and was walking to class. I passed a toy shop on my way. In the window was a toy typewriter.

It was made by Marx, a large toy company. What struck me was that it was supposed to be a fully functioning typewriter, but it had no keys.

There was a dial on top which had to be turned into position for each letter by hand, then the head depressed—well, slapped, to print the letter.

It would be tedious to type a letter, to say the least, but it could be done. Now, if there was a way to motorize the operation it would be a great improvement over the current keys.

I was on to something; I would have to think about how I could get an electric signal sent by touching a letter on the keyboard and translating it to mechanical action.

My lecture was okay, but I didn't feel like I learned anything, just confirmed what I already knew. While a certain amount of this was helpful, I would hate for every class to be like this. I needed new information.

I had lunch with my escorts; they were still ever-present in uniform. Their being with me tended to keep other people at their distance. Today I was with an army major from New Zealand and an army captain from Australia.

Since I had been to both countries, we had an interesting conversation. Granted, for me, it was only one business trip.

The major loved my story about the "tall" mayor. The man had a reputation that was not the best. He was thought of as a bully, so the major was glad to see him put in his place.

The port project in New Zealand was stalled by continuing union problems, so I avoided that subject.

Australia on the other hand was growing its seaports like crazy. The container business had opened up new markets for their companies, and they were taking great advantage of it.

It was good to get unbiased thoughts on how things were going. If you read my company's internal reports, things were glowing except for New Zealand. It was good to get confirmation of the accuracy of our company reports.

That made me wonder if I should have an independent group tracking my company's progress in each market.

Our reporting chain was typical for American companies. Each unit reported to a manager upstream who in turn reported to higher management.

This was all well and good unless one of the report sources was problematic. They could report everything was fine, and we had no independent checks around the individual reporting.

If we had a weak manager reporting to a weak manager, things could become buried and fester until they became a major issue.

That bothered me enough I called Dad that evening and asked him his thoughts.

"Rick, your managers should have their boots on the ground. Not just take their subordinate's word but go out to the job site and talk to the customer to make certain everything is okay. This needs to be done at every level in the corporation. Your management needs not only to talk to the people below them but sample the staff that reports to them. This is especially true when the manager may be in one country, his direct report in another, and the working staff in a third."

"Is that being done?"

"I have no idea; it's your company."

Ouch. Following the logic I had just agreed to, I had to visit my direct reports and their directs to make certain nothing was being bottled up.

How would I make the time to do this? Those in the US would be difficult but doable. However, I had people spread out all over the world.

I would have to give this serious thought. I wanted an education but not at the cost of everything I had built up in the last several years.

I went to my room and had some hard thoughts. I had too many irons in the fire. How could I make movies, go to school, do that economics challenge, and take care of my real business?

Also, there was my role as a Queen's Messenger, plus my having a life that included dates with Nina. Something had to give. The problem is that I wanted everything.

Well, not everything. That business challenge had been forced on me. I could back out of it completely or find another way to accomplish it.

I had made no movie commitments yet, so I could slow that down. Then I could talk to Mr. Norman about only taking on serious messages.

Then I had forgotten I had to do a narration of the documentary on my container business. Plus, there was property in Spain that I had never visited.

Criminently! This life stuff was difficult. I was going to have to make some hard choices, and they would affect my future directions in life.

I dithered about what to do for hours. I finally got to sleep at one in the morning. I woke up feeling like I had a hangover.

Even my morning run didn't help that much. I felt like I had the weight of the world on my shoulders and didn't know how to set it down.

I drifted through my classes; I'm not even certain why I bothered to go. If I hadn't purchased the notes, I would have been lost.

As soon as I got back to The Meadows, I called Nina. She answered her phone. The posh school she went to allowed each student to have a private line in their room.

I spent the next two hours telling her about my woes. She was supportive but didn't pretend to have any answers.

We talked about the business challenge and in explaining it to her I had a realization. Nothing prohibited me from hiring a prototype firm to translate the Marx toy typewriter into a real working typewriter.

It would cost a lot, but it would save me a huge amount of time and effort.

After I gave my tale of woe, I spent another hour listening to her problems. They were all social, as in relationships at school and who was in the in-crowd.

I listened and said the right supportive words in the right places. She deserved it for hearing me whine.

My only real contribution to her problem was to observe that social status at her school was defined by either title, fortune, or fame.

She was barely holding on in the title division by dating me, a lowly knight. While well off, she didn't have a fortune, though again I lent her some help in that area.

Fame seemed to be the one thing that she didn't have that was doable. I suggested she earn fame by being an actress.

At first, she was cold to the idea. She knew too much about the inside of the industry. I countered that by pointing out that she had a built-in advantage. No creepy director or producer would try to get her on a casting couch with her father being a power in the industry.

Besides that, she had me. Without any facts being public, my reputation now had an undercurrent of violence. I didn't know how that got started, but it was out there. It went beyond my Death Wind role.

She told me she would think about it. I thought she was making much about nothing, but I would support her no matter what.

I called Jim Williamson in the US and asked him to look up prototype developers in the Thompson Directory. Those huge green books had every company in the US in them.

I didn't think using Jim to look in the directory was abusing the business challenge. If it was, they could stick it in their ear.

He found a company that had offices in New York and London. This was perfect. In England, they went by D. L. Prettyman, Ltd. I called and made an appointment with them for Thursday afternoon.

I could attend a morning lecture and then fly to London. When I landed in London, I spotted a DC-8 with an unusual paint scheme. It was in the colors of the House of Saud.

It was in the private plane area, so I got a good look while I was filing a return flight plan and seeing what the weather would be like later in the early evening.

I asked about the aircraft. It was a wonder. While none of them had been inside, they related how it had full-sized beds, bathrooms, and living room-type seating areas.

While riding in a cab to town, I thought about that. If I had to go all over the world, maybe I needed a plane decked out like that. With an office set up, I could keep up with my schoolwork as I went.

I wondered if I could lease a 707 and have the interior redone to my liking. It would take too long to have one built from scratch. Mum and Dad had been trying for two years now. Of course, they kept selling their place in line.

At Prettyman's they welcomed me; they had called my bank and knew I had money. That always helps.

I sat down with a sales type and an engineer. When I described what I was trying to accomplish the engineer started nodding his head.

He had just read about a device called a whiffletree linkage. It would translate a binary input (electric), to analog (mechanical). Each key on the typewriter would send a signal to the whiffletree which would extend out connecting to a specific key on the disk with the letter face.

We discussed it for a while, and instead of a disk as on the Marx typewriter, we would have all the letters on a ball. It would be about the size of a golf ball, so we started calling it that.

The ball would tilt and rotate to the correct position using a shaft. Another shaft would give case shifting and spacing.

It all made sense to me, so I signed a letter of intent with a contract to follow and left them a five-thousand-pound deposit.

I left there feeling good about the business challenge I had been given. IBM would snap this up in a heartbeat.

I had planned to stop at the palace and check in with Mr. Norman, but the time at Prettyman's had run longer than I planned. I headed back to the airport just in time to see the Saudi jet take off.

I had to look into that. I certainly had spent enough hours in the air just sitting there or trying to work with people looking over my shoulder.

Nina arrived at Heathrow on Friday evening. I was waiting at the gate. This was the most time-efficient way for us to have a real weekend. From there, we went to my suite at the Plaza as we intended to do dinner and a play tomorrow evening.

It had not been said, but I knew tomorrow afternoon would be shopping. We walked to my favorite fish and chip shop for dinner.

It was wonderful, as always. It would be a good restaurant to make a franchise. Maybe I should talk to Mr. Treacher about that.

We had a nice evening eating, walking, and doing nothing. Well, not quite nothing, but we shan't go into that. I will say there was no chance of any issue from our evening.

Saturday morning, we had a late breakfast. It was a pleasure being able to sleep in. I didn't even bother to go for a run.

We did talk about Nina appearing in movies. She was, at her best, lukewarm to the idea. She had seen too much of the industry and just didn't want the lifestyle.

As I feared, the afternoon was spent shopping. My job was to be a mule. I also had to nod and say that everything looked wonderful. I must say that the new-style dress she tried on did look wonderful.

They called it a mini dress. That, coupled with a pair of boots, got my blood racing. I didn't have to fake my enthusiasm for the outfit.

Nina bought several of the dresses and several wide belts, along with two more pairs of boots. Next, she had to pick out a selection of blouses to wear with them.

She spent a lot of time in the backroom with the sales assistant. I heard a lot of giggling. When she came out to show off the complete outfit, I thought it was neat.

When she turned and her whole front moved, I realized she wasn't wearing a bra. My mind froze up. I only had one thought, let's get back to the hotel.

Nina and the salesgirl looked at each other and nodded.

Nina said while smirking, "Yep, it works."

A guy never had a chance.

She changed back into the clothes she had worn to the store but assured me I would get another look at the hotel.

Not only at the hotel, but she also wore the outfit to dinner and the theater. It's a wonder there weren't car accidents when we got out of the cab at the restaurant.

I had made reservations, so there weren't any problems getting to our table. Well, other than that one guy who thought he had his wine glass to his lips when he tipped it. What a mess.

The maître d' must have approved because he gave us a very prominent table. After a nice meal, we left for the theater.

Someone must have called the press because photographers were waiting for us. My approach to these matters was to keep my head down, my mouth shut, and get into the car as quickly as possible.

Nina posed and strutted for the photographers for a good five minutes. She was having a ball. I wonder what her father would say when he saw the pictures, as I was sure he would.

I asked her about it and got a laugh. "He understands publicity, no problem."

When we got back to the hotel there was a message waiting at the front desk. Would I please call my sister Mary?

Strange. I only have one sister.

I called Jackson House and Mary was brought to the phone. I even quizzed her about the message.

"Oh, I thought it would be more professional if I identified myself."

"Then you should have left your full name."

A big brother has to give his little sister a hard time.

"Don't be silly, Rick; I called you for a reason."

"What's that, squirt?"

"We are going to expand my clothing line to older girls. We need a model. We want a fresh new face, not the same old tired ones that are out there. Do you think Nina would be interested?"

There was so much in that sentence that I had a hard time processing it. Instead, I handed the phone to Nina and told her, "It's for you."

The girls talked for half an hour or more. I did pick up that Nina would be modeling and that the photo shoots would be in Switzerland, so they wouldn't interfere with her classes.

When she hung up, Nina was ecstatic. She now had a paying job and points in the social game.

Chapter 3

After Nina calmed down a little, she gave me more details on her deal with Mary. Well, it was actually with the ad agency for the company that made Mary's clothing collection.

With a lot of adult help from Mum and Susan Wallace, Mary retained control over how her collections were presented. Using one of Mary's approved words, there would be nothing slatternly in her image. At least until she was older, like maybe fourteen. At the time, I didn't argue with her, I figured Mum would handle that.

Anyway, Nina would have to meet a photographer in Zurich to build a portfolio for the ad agency. While Mary had the right to submit and approve models, the agency also had the same rights.

I didn't think it would be a problem for Nina. She had the slender height that was getting to be the new fashion for models.

I had a brilliant thought; of course, it was brilliant, and it was mine. I called Denny. He had taken a lot of candid photos of Nina and me over Christmas. I asked him to look through and see if any were worth submitting. He thought there would be some. He would airmail the photos to Nina.

They had his studio watermark on them, so they would be sure to get the credit. It might open a new door for his studio.

The work would be well-paid, but she wouldn't end up wealthy. However, she would be invited to all the best parties and events if this came to pass.

I was glad I wasn't a girl with all these pressures.

Sunday evening, I saw Nina off at Heathrow. She was to call me on her safe arrival. When she didn't call at the appointed time, I began to worry. She called two hours later. There had been a mechanical delay at the gate at Heathrow.

On Monday during a break in my classes, I called an aircraft leasing firm that was stationed at the Oxford airport. I had learned to play the Sir Richard card immediately on any business deal in the UK.

It got me through to the managing director. I asked if they leased 707s wet and if the interiors could be modified.

I quickly learned for enough money I could have training wheels on the wings if I wanted them. I passed on the training wheels and described the interior I was looking for.

It would be no problem. All it would take is time and money. They could meet my March 20th requirement. This was the beginning of the three-week break between terms. I then made an appointment for Tuesday afternoon to put down a deposit and settle the details.

I sat through my economics class feeling a bit smug as I thought I had the business challenge under control.

The don must have read the look on my face, as he called on me.

"Sir Richard, do you have anything to share with us on your project."

"No, sir. Other than I have had an idea and turned it over to a prototyping firm to build a proof-of-concept model."

"Capital!"

Class let out and I was walking to my next one when one of the army officers came running up to me.

"Sir Richard, they need you at The Meadows immediately."

"What for?"

"I don't know, something about the police. We just got a call at the Hall a few minutes ago."

I ran to my garage and fired up my Aston Martin. It was crowded in there as the Ferrari was also parked inside.

I took off in a flash. Fortunately, no dogs or small children were on the road as I sped along. One cyclist was shaking his fist at me when I roared by him.

As I was turning onto the road to The Meadows, I saw a caravan of police cars heading toward my garage, at least that's what it looked like.

I did a sliding stop at home; there must have been ten police cars in the yard. At the front door, Mr. Hamilton was standing like Horatio at the bridge.

The crowd of coppers split apart as I approached the door. I called them coppers because they weren't dressed as bobbies on the street but like they were going to war. There were several men in suits.

I asked, "Mr. Hamilton, what do we have here?"

"Sir Richard, these gentlemen desire to have a conversation with you. They have a warrant with your name."

The way he said gentlemen left no doubt that he considered them anything but that.

Pushing his way to me, a senior officer, I think an inspector if I read his credentials correctly, asked, "Are you Sir Richard Jackson?"

"Yes, I am."

"We have a warrant to search the premises for a longbow and hunting or war arrows."

"May I see the warrant?"

About that time one of the men in suits said, "We don't have time for this; get on with it."

The inspector handed me the warrant saying, "Sir Richard is within his rights to see the warrant before it is executed. It's not as if it was for high treason. It is only murder and in another country at that."

That told me a lot right there.

I perused the document, then said, "I don't understand. I did kill a man in Germany in self-defense, but it was with my bare hands. I don't know what this has to do with a bow and arrows. I will concede the warrant is legal, but I will contest the grounds. Detective, please follow me."

I led them to the back of the house to the weapons room. There racked were the estate's shotguns and hunting rifles. Also, my bow and arrows were there.

"Please notice inspector these two bows are not longbows, and the arrows are field points."

The guy in the suit asked how we could tell if it were a longbow.

The inspector answered, "Any longbow used by Sir Richard would be almost as tall as he is, much taller than you.

"As far as the type of point, these are very distinctive field points, as opposed to hunting or war points. Those are designed to rip and tear flesh, both going in and out. These will not."

"Confiscate them anyway."

I spoke up, "Inspector, I would like a receipt for anything you take."

"Certainly, Sir Richard."

"Be very clear that these arrows have the fletching and markings of the Shawnee Indian Tribe."

"How can I tell that, Sir Richard?"

I led him and his entourage to the library, where I pulled out one of my books which described the arrows used by the various tribes.

The inspector was meticulous in writing down the author, title, edition, and publisher of the book along with the description given.

"These arrows match the description."

The guy in the suit spoke up again, "Enough of this. Toss the house, is how I think you say it."

The inspector got a very pained look.

"Sir Richard, I'm afraid we have to do a thorough search of the premises, as Mr. Ramsey has stated."

"Just who is Mr. Ramsey?"

"He is with the Home Office; they are acting on instruction from the Foreign Office."

I finished for him, "And they are acting on a request from the East Germans."

He nodded.

"Inspector, did you get a chance to read this warrant thoroughly."

"No, Sir Richard, this was sprung on us this morning."

"Please read the part about what search is authorized."

He read it, and with a barely contained smile, told the man from the Home Office, "This warrant specifically states a search may be made of the weapons storage at the estate known as The Meadows."

I thought the man from the Home Office was going to have a fit, but the inspector would not budge.

The Inspector, speaking to me asked, "Sir Richard, do you own a longbow and arrows with hunting or war points."

"Yes, I do."

The man from the Home Office jumped at this, "We got you! Where are they?"

"They are in storage where I always keep them."

The inspector had to ask, "Where is that?"

"They are kept in the Yeoman's Armory in the Tower of London. I'm certain that when you check you will find they have not left the armory for some time now. I have been delinquent in my practice."

I thought about the actual bow I had used in Germany. It was broken and buried in a ditch in the forest. The fletching was pulled off the arrows and drifted in the wind. The war points were at the bottom of a pond. The wooden bodies of the arrows were in another ditch.

The man from the Home Office gave a nasty laugh, "If we are lucky, they will be in his garage, which has been searched by now. They will have torn the place apart.

"If you have a car there, they will have dismantled it."

When you don't want to show weakness, you pretend indifference.

"It is only a Ferrari. I'm sure your department can have it repaired. I know of a good shop in London."

The inspector looked like he had swallowed a green apple. Mr. Ramsey turned red in the face. Several of the bobbies in the background had to stifle their laughter.

I was given a receipt. The police then packed up and left. I noticed that all the police had wiped their feet so they wouldn't mess up the carpeting. Mr. Ramsey didn't. Just one more item on his debt.

I drove back to the garage. The police had searched the place but hadn't damaged the car. I mean, where could you hide a six-foot longbow and yard-long arrows in a Ferrari?

Chapter 4

Tuesday morning, I skipped classes and straightened up my garage. The police hadn't destroyed it, but they had dismantled anything that looked like it might conceal a longbow. Well, I would have to buy a new couch as they had ripped out the seams on the back.

I also called everyone that I could think of who might be interested, everyone but the press that is.

Mr. Norman was the most interested. He spent time questioning me about Mr. Ramsey. He thought he knew who he was. From the direction of the questions, I got the impression he didn't have too high of an opinion of the man.

He told me he would file a complaint with the Home Office on my behalf about issuing a warrant with no grounds. He wanted to keep stirring the pot, plus put them on warning the palace was interested.

Mum was home; Dad wasn't. She told me to keep to my normal routine and watch my back. She didn't doubt that I was being followed.

"They are out to get you, Rick. Have no doubts."

They are the Soviets and their partners. What had I ever done to them, except upset their plans for world domination?

In the afternoon I kept my appointment with the aircraft leasing company. They were very amiable and ready to accommodate my every wish. I wondered about that because every serious business I had dealt with before had balked at my youth and possible ability to pay.

When I mentioned that, the managing director chuckled.

"We get enough people trying to con us out of an aircraft that we automatically run a check on them. It was easy to find out who your bank is, and from there, a simple phone call told us we wanted to do business with you."

I thought that was a wonderful approach and wished more would practice it.

He walked me through how they would approach my request. The interior of the aircraft would be done in modules bolted to the floor. Very much like my cargo handling containers.

When I expressed that thought he said, "Exactly. We copied your idea. It's a series of your containers set up as each room.

"To accomplish this, we have to lease an aircraft that was built to serve as a cargo aircraft or a passenger line, depending on the needs of the moment. That's the only way we could set it up to get the prefabricated interior modules in more or less intact."

"The lease of the aircraft will be different than the containerized rooms. Those you can buy outright for your reserved use, or you can lease them from us, and we will lease them to others at request."

"I will purchase them upfront. That way they won't get damaged from others using them."

I also privately thought, and no one would be able to place spy devices in them.

"When not in use, I will want them sealed and placed in a bonded warehouse."

"We can do that. I think I understand what you are implying, and that is an interesting perspective. We could sell some units based on that concept. Some people are very concerned about their privacy."

He then invited an engineer and an interior designer to discuss the specifics of what I wanted.

I hadn't given it any thought beyond the functional items, bedroom, office, kitchen, dining area, and sitting area.

Working with a long narrow aluminum tube was somewhat limiting, but it all could be done. I remarked it would be nice if someone produced a wide-body jet. They agreed it would be nice but didn't know of any in the works.

As far as the interior design went, I asked the designer to tour my suite in London at the Plaza. It would give him an idea of what I liked. He thought that was a great idea, so I called the hotel then and there to put him on the allowed visitors' list on a limited basis.

They assured me that they could have everything in place by the required term break. I had explained I had to do a quick trip to many worldwide locations but didn't want to get behind on everything else while doing so.

The engineer asked, "Where do you want your secretary's office and quarters?"

That question floored me. I had never had a secretary who would travel with me. I had a secretarial pool in California but not a dedicated person who went with me.

A picture of a pretty female flicked through my mind, then Nina's reaction. This was followed by a motherly and then a grandmotherly type, with my reaction to them. A fine-featured man appeared and disappeared, with me almost shuddering.

"I don't think I will need one. I haven't needed one in the past, so I don't want to start now."

We played around with configurations for another hour. It ended up from front to back first a general first-class seating area, then a sitting room adjacent to a dining area, followed by a kitchen, then the office, and after that my bedroom

The office would have hookups that could plug into local phone systems.

Wednesday was a day of lectures. I enjoyed the learning and the company of people my age. I was jealous of the time it took.

I spent Wednesday afternoon typing up papers that would be due later this term. I had a real advantage over most of the other students in that I had my library, so reference books were available at need. I didn't have to chase books down that might be loaned out, or wait in line for them, or have them restricted to library use only.

The copy machine was a wonder. How did we work without one in the past?

As I typed, I wondered how Prettyman was doing with my prototype. It would do no good to call them, as all they could say was that it was in process. If there were any problems, they would contact me.

I called Nina in the evening. She was all excited because her pictures had been taken, and Mary's production company had approved her as the lead model.

The key to that statement was "the lead model." It turned out that they wanted her help in picking out other girls to model with her.

Talk about social power. She could recommend classmates. They would have to fit the criteria, but she got to put them forward.

They wanted all sizes and looks so that girls her age would identify with one of them.

Paybacks were going to be hell. Her words, not mine. I asked her if she had talked to Mary about this. She had; Mary had given her the term. Patty was really in the doghouse.

Thursday and Friday were school days. It felt strange doing nothing but going to class or doing homework. You would think I was a student or something!

Saturday, I spent at Pinewood Studios. I was doing the voice-overs for the documentary on the new containerized shipping business and what it would do to world trade.

It was strange sitting in a studio and reading a script without any pictures to go with it. Some of it was hard to put together, but I managed. At least I managed to read the script smoothly without odd stops and starts.

At one break I was asked to stop by the office to talk about the scripts they had given me. I expressed interest in the bookstore owner part and playing the young prime minister.

We talked about the fact a stir would be created by a "Yank" playing the part of a British prime minister. It gave us a chuckle and we all agreed that it would give the movie a good buzz.

They would send contracts for the two movies to Susan Wallace for her and legal to review. If all went well, we could start work next week on the first one with a preproduction meeting. That would be *Edgware*, about the bookstore owner.

From Pinewood, instead of returning home, I drove on into London and spent the night in my suite. For some reason, I was more relaxed there than at The Meadows. It may have something to do with never knowing what my grandmum and her expanding circle of friends might be up to.

It is very disconcerting to walk down the backstairs in your underwear to grab a midnight snack and walk into a roomful of old ladies performing a séance.

Later I was told that I had been the highlight of their evening and that I could prance around like that anytime I wanted.

No, thank you.

Sunday after a late brunch, I drove over to the Tower and asked to be let into the armory. The duty sergeant had my name, so he retrieved my bow and arrows.

I checked that the arrows were all there and nothing had been tampered with. I explained what was going on to the sergeant, and he made a note that no one was allowed to see, much less touch them, without my express approval.

If someone showed up with a warrant, they were to contact Mr. Norman at the palace. I added that they could feel free to keep that person in the dungeon but was told the dungeon no longer met prisoner housing requirements. No telly.

We laughed about that. There are no real dungeon cells as we thought of them in the Tower.

Chapter 5

I drove back to The Meadows late Sunday to be ready for school on Monday. There was a small package waiting for me in my office.

I opened it to find an invitation to the inauguration of John Fitzgerald Kennedy as the 35th President of the United States of America on Friday, January 20th, 1961. There would be a ball at the Willard House that evening. I and one guest were invited to the function. RSVP.

Wow! I had just barely met the man. I certainly would be going. I filled out the RSVP at once and got it ready to mail. I did make a copy of everything for posterity and to make certain I relayed the details correctly to Nina, whom I planned to invite as my guest.

Almost as an afterthought, I called Jackson House for Mum and Dad. I relayed the exciting news. They congratulated me. Then they let me know they would be attending the inauguration ball at The White House.

I didn't know there were multiple balls that evening. It seemed there were seven of them. My parents were invited to the most prestigious; I was invited to number two. I asked how you got invited to each level. They didn't know all of them.

They did know that the highest level was for major donors and strong supporters. My level was for people who Kennedy wanted to turn into major donors and who were influencers.

It descended to level seven. These were the people who had knocked on doors and planted yard signs. At that level, they had to pay to attend.

The president and Jackie would make appearances at all seven balls. What a hard night for them!

"I didn't know you guys were such strong supporters of the Democrats."

"That would be your dad. That is why we are invited.

"What if Nixon had won?"

"Then the invitation would have been to me as a strong Republican donor."

"So, it's both ends against the middle?"

"Now you understand politics, Rick. You have to have a foot in both camps so that no matter who wins, you have a voice."

I didn't know quite what to make of that, so I dropped that part of the conversation. Mum let me know that Nina and I could stay at their house in Georgetown.

I didn't even know the family had a house in Georgetown. We agreed to keep in contact about the arrangements.

After hanging up, I called Nina. I played it coy. I told her if she didn't have any plans for January 20th, a Friday, I would like to take her on a date.

"I would be delighted, Rick. Where are we going, so I know what to wear?"

"Not much, just an inaugural ball for John F. Kennedy in Washington, DC."

I love it when I can drop a bomb like that.

"What?! Yes, but I have to go shopping. What do you even wear to an event like that?"

"I'm sure that Mary's collection has something in it. The latest in pinafores or whatever."

"Men!"

"Or you could call my Mum. She and Dad are attending one of the balls."

I then had to explain my new knowledge of the different inaugural balls. And that we would be staying at my parents' house in Georgetown.

"Please take care of the travel arrangements, and I will take care of my outfits and ensure you have the proper wear."

That sounded like a good division of labor to me.

After that, the conversation went onto more mundane subjects of how the East Germans had connived to have my house searched for the longbow and war arrows that had killed those three guys.

She asked me what I was going to do. I told her there was nothing I could do. They had made a legal request which was honored by Her Majesty's government. I did wonder how much influence the Communists had in the government.

Nina in turn told me how the snobs were practically begging her to be models. It was so much fun. The news about the ball would be the icing on the cake.

She wondered if she could get a picture of herself with Jackie. I made a mental note to discuss this with the White House.

I just hoped her school wasn't into hair-pulling and eye-scratching.

Tuesday was a regular school day. That is, I attended my lectures. It seemed I missed as many as I attended but the notes kept me up to date on those classes I skipped. I was fortunate in that the classes I had stuck to their notes fairly well.

I had learned to be careful in picking my classes.

Wednesday, I drove over to Pinewood Studios. This was the day of the preproduction meeting. The cast would get to know each other a little. We would go over the shooting schedule and do a run-through of a draft of the script.

The movie *Edgware* didn't have a large cast. There were the male and female leads and then some supporting cast. No one could be classified as a second lead. The movie had a lot of dialog between the actress and me.

It quickly became apparent that everyone but me had worked together before. It was like an old home week for them. They also appeared to be a snobbish bunch, as they did no more than acknowledge my presence.

I had run into similar situations in Hollywood, so I didn't let it get to me. The schedule was discussed, and the director kept deferring to me as to my availability. This finally resulted in several snide remarks.

I refused to react, letting the remarks roll by me.

Their words meant little to me. Now if they had started shooting like the Russians or East Germans, it would have been different.

Copies of the draft script were handed out. We each read our part in turn. I kept my British accent all the way. It was almost more natural than my American one by this point.

One of the things we were looking for was sentences that didn't roll off our tongues. It would be easier to modify them than to try to learn them.

There was one spot that just didn't read right for any of us. At one point the actress, a young lady named Ann Briton, told me she loved me.

My response didn't ring true. As a group we all made suggestions. None of them worked. Finally, on one read-through, she said, "I love you."

In a smart-aleck way, I responded, "I know."

It wasn't meant to be serious, but it stopped the whole crowd.

The director said, "That's it."

For once everyone agreed. That was my only contribution to the script.

As the session was ending, the director asked if we could meet tomorrow. Everyone could, but a page knocked on the door and handed a letter to the director.

He looked at it and handed it to me. It was from the palace. I read a note from Mr. Norman who told me the queen requested my presence at the palace to assist her tomorrow morning.

I apologized to the director, as the queen had summoned me. She had a dog that needed to be robbed.

The only one who laughed at that was a senior stage manager who must have been in the service.

Arriving on time at the palace in full uniform, I was escorted to Mr. Norman's office. After the pleasantries, I asked what I had been summoned for.

"Not much, old boy. We recommended that you be called in on at least a monthly basis so a record could be created of your duties being more than ceremonial.

"The Crown gets criticized for having people on staff for no good reason, so we have to show that you are working. At this point, we are reluctant to send you to Europe because of East Germany.

"They don't want to give up on getting you into their custody. You wounded their pride. Even their Russian masters haven't been able to restrain them.

"One good thing that has come out of it is the orders for the warrant to search your properties originated with a group of dons that we have been watching at Cambridge. We will be watching them even closer now, and if they are Soviet moles, we will use them for false information.

"As to what you have been summoned for, Her Majesty is aware that you will be attending a Presidential Inaugural Ball. She is sending a formal note to President Kennedy but will have you deliver a personal note for her."

"That sounds easy enough."

"Sometimes it is."

"So, what else do I do today?"

"Take the day off?"

"What a wonderful idea."

I left the palace and went to the hotel where I changed into casual clothes and walked the rainy streets of London looking into shop windows. It was a wonderful day.

I flew back home late in the afternoon and listened to the latest rock and roll records. It was relaxing.

Chapter 6

This coming Friday was Kennedy's Inauguration Ball. I had to make certain that all my ducks were in a row. Nina was flying to London on Wednesday. I would meet her there at my hotel suite, and we would fly to DC on Thursday.

I double-checked with Mum the address of their house in Georgetown. The Ball was white tie, so Mr. Hamilton packed me an outfit. This was one of the few times I had luggage with me.

I went ahead and chartered a plane for the trip. I was getting used to the thought of having money that I could spend. It would only be about ten thousand dollars. Yeah, only ten thousand dollars. Watch it, Ricky; you will get a big head.

It was another 707. I wish they would make smaller jets for groups of ten or so people.

Anyway, Nina came in on Wednesday, and we had a nice evening in London, going to a play.

It was called *Beyond the Fringe*, at the Fortune Theater. I liked the lead guy, Dudley Moore. I thought he would do well in the future.

In the morning, we went out to Heathrow's general aviation area to catch our flight. I had had the hotel take our luggage to the plane the evening before. I did think to ask if it made it okay. It had.

Nina had never been on a charter of a large jet before, so she was amazed at how empty it looked. The charter company had a deluxe package of meals and refreshments aboard.

For the price, they should have. That said, it was a smooth flight to Washington, DC. We both had schoolwork to do while we flew. The booth with a table in the first-class cabin helped.

We took a break and had a wonderful meal. The hostess offered us wine or beer with our meal, but we both declined. I drank beer in England occasionally. I didn't want to make it a habit.

I think Nina may have been following my lead.

We touched down on time in DC. The plane would be there to take us back on Sunday morning. It would fly to Switzerland, drop Nina off, and then take me to London.

They had another trip the next day, so the plane wouldn't sit idle.

A limo had been arranged by Mum to take us to Georgetown. I was glad. Washington traffic was bad on a Thursday night. I guessed that it would be any night. It would help when the interstate around the city was complete, as there would be no traffic congestion then.

Mum and Dad were there. The kids were still in California with Mrs. Hernandez. Mum had promised her a trip to Spain if she would put up with them for the weekend.

She would have done it anyway, but Mum and Dad were always trying to find ways to give her something nice. She was a loyal member of our family.

I asked Mum if Mrs. Hernandez was seeing anyone. It appears Mrs. Hernandez was the hit of the Latin community. It helped that she had Jackson Charities, Mum, on her side. She was being escorted to an event every week.

I got the impression these events could take several days. Go for it, Mrs. Hernandez.

The first order of business was to get Nina and me settled into our bedrooms; no sharing in this house! Mum believed in appearances.

From what I had picked up from Grandmum, it was "Do as I say, not as I do."

At least when she was younger.

Now that she was a Mum herself, things were going to be different.

We didn't burst her bubble.

Mum went to help Nina settle in, leaving me with Dad. I think there was a scheme at work here.

"Rick, how serious are you and Nina?"

"We aren't planning to get married anytime soon if that is what you are asking."

"I guess I was. You used the word soon; does that mean you have plans?"

"The only discussion on marriage we have had is that we are too young to even think about it and that we will not have children before we are married if we get married, that is. Answer enough?"

"Don't get snotty with me, young man. I'm still your father and can knock your block off."

Dad and I eyed each other. After looking up at me, he backed down first.

"I think I could knock it off, anyway."

"Dad, I don't think we will ever find out."

That was very gracious of me, as I knew he could knock my block off. As a captain in the MPs, he had to fight some tough characters. The fact of the matter was, I would stand there and let him hit me before I would fight him.

"Rick, your Mum and I have watched you grow up fast in the last few years, and we want the best for you. Nina may be the woman for you, but as you said, you are both too young to decide. We do worry you know."

We had a few more words of no import, and I went to change for dinner. It was a suit-and-tie event with a combination of businesspeople and politicians. Twenty of us sat down to dinner in my parents "small" Georgetown house.

There were seating assignments, so Nina and I were separated. I was in between an overweight senator who droned on about some bill and a recent twenty-some-year-old divorcee. She was on the hunt.

I found the senator's bill on imports to be fascinating.

After dinner, Nina and I hid out on the open back porch. She told me about her grilling from Mum. I shared my experience with

Dad. We both had been consistent in our story, so that should take care of that for a while.

It did allow me to ask, "Would you marry me?"

She jumped up and hugged me and said, "Oh, yes, Rick, I will marry you!"

I almost fell off the back steps I was so flustered.

"I didn't mean it that way. No, I meant at some future date. No, I don't know what I meant."

"Silly, I knew exactly what you were asking, and yes, you are on my shortlist."

"How short is your list?"

"You are the only one right now, but who knows what the future may bring?"

This was my night for talking me into problems. I think it was that word "marry" that was throwing me off my stride.

"Rick, I like you a lot, and maybe even love you, but it is too soon, and you know it."

"Yes, I do."

"Good, now kiss me good night."

Some instructions I can follow very well.

The next day was a rush. The ball was that evening, so the ladies had to have their hair done and all those other mystical things that women do.

Dad and I watched our new president being sworn in. He and President Eisenhower seemed to get along.

Dad told me that Ike had thought JFK was too young for the job, a whippersnapper who had got elected on his daddy's money. After Ike talked to him, he thought JFK was brilliant.

The conversation didn't give me a chance to ask Dad how he knew this. I had thought he and Ike didn't get along.

The ball that Nina and I attended was almost anticlimactic. It was a crowded hot room full of smoke. The president and Jackie made an appearance. They walked around the room greeting people.

They did stop at our table, and the photographer accompanying them took pictures of us together. At least Nina would have her evidence for her school friends that she met Jackie.

For her part, Jackie was very nice. She acted impressed when she asked when Nina was flying home. I guess saying our chartered jet was leaving in the morning said something.

I had a chance to pass the queen's note to the new president. He did a double-take when he saw the royal crest.

"I had forgotten about your connections, Sir Richard, or should I say colonel?"

He may forget some things but not many.

"Rick will do, Mr. President."

He smiled at that, "It is nice to hear that. One could get used to it."

When the president and first lady left, so did Nina and me. Our limo driver was with a bunch of others in a special parking area. When we went to retrieve our coats and our car was called, I noticed the attendant had a pillbox hat like the first lady. What a spy ring the women had. I was glad I only had to fight the KGB or the Stasi.

The next morning, we had breakfast with Mum and Dad, who from their good cheer had had a successful evening. From there we went back to the airport and flew back to Switzerland for Nina, and then I got dropped off in London, from whence I then flew myself back to Oxford.

What a weekend. I loved the word whence and tried to work it in when I could.

Chapter 7

Monday started as another boring school week. I had taken to eating lunch at Rawdon-Hastings Hall or RH as it was becoming known.

The food was good. The only thing that I had to dodge was dinner invitations. I found out that a dinner invitation was a polite way of saying, "There is this girl we would like you to meet."

These invitations were given at the direction of the various wives. It appeared there was nothing more frustrating to a young married lady than that an eligible bachelor was out there, and he might get away from her perfect friend.

I started carrying a picture of Nina in her miniskirt around and showing it to all the guys when any hints of dinner were brought up. I finally realized these poor guys had no choice in the matter. If they didn't issue an invitation, they would have a miserable weekend.

They were off the hook if it was issued in front of witnesses, and I declined. This quickly became an unspoken game between us guys. They had a duty to perform, and they did it.

Other than that, the lunches were fun. I got to meet a lot of guys around my age. If they were American, we talked about sports. Everyone else I quizzed about their country and military establishments.

One hot topic of conversation was that the Dutch army was considering unionizing. We couldn't visualize how this might or could work. Trying to imagine a wildcat strike in the middle of a firefight was mind-boggling.

We made many a joke about that. No Dutch soldiers were attending Oxford to our knowledge. We decided that while it was fun to joke about, it would never happen, and if it did, it would be a disaster.

I ran into my drinking buddies, Tom, Steve, and Bill at the Dog and Crown after lunch on Friday afternoon. I had decided to skip the afternoon lecture. The prof was an absolute slave to his notes. I could read in twenty minutes what it took him an hour and a half to lecture on.

We all bemoaned the fact that the English weather was so damp and cloudy. We would have loved to see some sunshine.

I think we all had the thought at the same time. The city of Nice is nice! Let's go to the Riviera for the weekend!

We all headed back to our respective digs and packed for a casual weekend. Being the cautious sort, I also rolled up a sports coat and tie in case something a little more formal came up.

I called The Meadows and left word where I was going, and that I would be back late Sunday or maybe Monday if the weather were nice in Nice.

We met at my garage, where Bill Benton picked us up in his four-door sedan. On arriving at the airport, I had to check over the aircraft and file a flight plan.

While I was doing this, the guys were in the Flight Center flirting with the hostess. I knew she was married but let them have their fun. She seemed to be enjoying it.

We were in the air when I told them she had three kids at home. That didn't seem to faze them at all.

We had a good flight, exchanging jokes all the way. We refueled and had a pit stop in Paris but made it as quick as we could. It was still daylight when we landed in Nice, but not by much. After landing, I called home to Mr. Hamilton, who told me that his mission was successful. He had reserved a suite for us at the Hotel Negresco.

When we checked in, we were welcomed by Jeanne Augier, the owner. She had bought the place in 1957 and was turning it into a work of art, a museum in its own right.

Someone yelled, "Hey, Tom and Rick!" as we were getting onto the elevator. It was Paul from the Beatles; I had met the band in Liverpool with Tom. I had briefly owned some of the rights to the band but had given them up. That was beginning to look like a mistake.

That was water over the dam. The band was here to play a special request for Princess Grace. They would have stayed at the Casino Hotel in Monaco, but they were banned, something about two goats and a llama.

Some things you are better off not knowing.

After dumping our stuff, we met in the bar. One thing about the Beatles was that if they were there, the girls were there.

We had a good time; I made certain I was never in a compromising position. The last thing I needed was for Nina to see my picture in the paper with some floozy.

The next morning was hard on my crew. They had partied hard. I got smart and had only drunk a couple of beers. I went to bed around eleven. They went out to the historic old town area of Nice and found a bar L'Oxford. Of course, they had to close it up. 5 a.m.!

Since they all had on their Oxford sweatshirts, they drank free most of the night. They had a good time if they could only remember it. All I heard were groans when I got up. No one wanted to run with me!

The band was still up when I left but must have kept saner hours, as they were in the lobby when I got back from my morning run.

We went to breakfast together. John joked about how I had missed making my fortune by selling my share of the band. I replied that I would bear with it. Some of us had to take what life gave us and if being poor was to be my lot, so be it. I tried not to smirk when I said that.

I received a breakfast roll up the side of the head from Ringo for that remark. They had a pretty good idea of my worth. It had now been in almost every newspaper in the world. My days of anonymity were over.

They invited me to go with them to check out their setup at the palace in Monaco. Having nothing better to do and knowing my friends wouldn't be up until dinner time, I agreed to the trip.

The band's road crew had set up the equipment yesterday. All they had to do were some sound checks for their later performance.

I sat in the back of the room while this was going on. I called it a room, but it was more like a miniature concert hall in the Grimaldi Palace.

As the band was tuning up, two children came in, a girl about four and a two-year-old boy following her. It didn't require much brainpower to figure out the young royals had escaped from their nanny.

I invited them to sit down and listen to what was going on. Princess Caroline informed me that we hadn't been introduced so she couldn't talk to me.

Not talking didn't include not sitting next to me. Albert, the two-year-old held up his arms, so I picked him up and set him in my lap.

It took the prince about two minutes to fall asleep.

Princess Caroline thought this was enough of an introduction that she confided in me that she thought Paul was rather good-looking. I didn't see it myself but who was I to argue with Her Grace?

Speaking of Her Grace, the Royal Mum herself appeared, hunting for her children. She held out her arms for Albert, who I gladly surrendered. He had slobbered all over my shirt.

Princess Caroline thanked me for my hospitality, took her mother's hand, and left. Less than a minute later a beefy-looking guy in a suit and tie sat down next to me.

"That was nice of you to look out for the children. May I ask your name?"

"Sir Richard Jackson. I'm here at the invitation of the band for their setup."

"I thought it might be something like that. Thank you for being cooperative."

I didn't give it another thought, but the telephone must have been ringing off the hook. The band finished up, and we were back in the hotel within the hour.

Waiting at the front desk was an invitation to the prince's palace for a performance by the Beatles this evening.

The dress was a sports coat and tie, very informal. My packing the same turned out to be genius. Well, lucky, anyway.

The boys were up and having a late lunch in the restaurant, so I joined them as I hadn't had anything since breakfast.

They wanted to know if I wanted to go to L'Oxford with them this evening. I told them I had another engagement so couldn't join them.

They wanted to know who she was, so I told them it was a young lady named Caroline. They fell for it hook, line, and sinker. I couldn't wait until the trip home.

Chapter 8

I had to take a cab separately to the palace for the performance because the band wanted to double-check the setup. One thing I admired about them was their work ethic. To many, they appeared to be a classic drugged-out group, but nothing could have been further from the truth.

When they partied it was hard, but when they worked, they were professional.

My invitation got me into the palace with no problem. I had to wait a few minutes as guests assembled.

I was really glad I had packed a sports coat and tie. I fit right in.

Five minutes before the concert the royal family walked in. They were dressed like the rest of us, except for Princess Caroline. She had on a Feed-the-Puppies t-shirt.

I was on an end seat in the aisle, so she walked right by me.

I said, "I love your t-shirt."

"This is part of the Mary Jackson collection. She is the absolute best."

"I think so too."

Her Mum was standing right there and made a sound of disagreement.

"What's wrong with the Mary Jackson Collection?"

"The clothes are very nice and well made, but they are not what a young princess would wear on many an occasion. But if it isn't from Mary Jackson, Caroline won't wear it."

"What types of clothes aren't in her collection?"

"What a young lady would wear on a formal occasion."

"Hmm, I'll talk to her about that."

A wide-eyed Caroline, who had been listening to the exchange asked, "You know Mary Jackson?"

"She is my little sister."

About this time the band was ready to start, so they moved on, but I knew that I would be hearing more on the subject.

As soon as the band had finished for the night a four, almost five-year-old, came running up to me.

"Are you her big brother?"

"Yes, I am."

"She is the neatest! I love her ads on 'Feed the Puppies.' Her clothes are the bestest."

"I will tell her that."

Princess Grace caught up with her child.

"Your Majesty, I have had a thought that I would like to discuss with you."

"What is that?"

"Maybe Mary needs a Princess Collection. To do that, she would need some royal motherly advice."

"I would be glad to comment if it would get Caroline into proper clothes. However, I cannot commercially endorse anything."

"You wouldn't have to. In my experience, that sort of thing comes out anyway and is all the better for being a 'discovered' secret. I also know another princess who loves Mary's clothes."

"Who would that be?"

"It would be Princess Anne of England."

"I'll ring up Elizabeth, and we will see what we can do."

"I will let Mary know of the opportunity. She can talk to her clothing company to see if they would be interested. I don't see it as a high-volume line, but more for the prestige."

"I think you will be surprised about how many young ladies would love to wear clothes that princesses wear."

"I will call Mary tonight, as it won't be her bedtime when I get back to the hotel. Thank you for inviting me for the evening. I have enjoyed it very much."

At that time Princess Caroline asked for my autograph. I pulled out one of my publicity pictures and signed it, "Sir Richard Jackson, Mary's big brother, to her fan Princess Caroline."

I knew who got top billing on this one.

Returning to the hotel, I called the US. It was midnight here and three in the afternoon there. I told Mary where I had been and who I had met.

Being the little business shark she is, she immediately started talking about the possibilities. I gave her Princess Grace's number and told her I was now out of it.

She thanked me and then asked how much of a commission I expected. I pretended I was wounded that she thought her big brother would charge her for help.

I had forgotten that Mary was only six. She immediately started to cry. At first, I thought she was faking it, and then realized I had upset her.

About that time Mum stepped in, and I had to explain myself. I received a lecture on the tender sensibilities of young ladies. She also thought the Princess Collection was a wonderful idea and would make certain that Mary followed through.

Knowing the shark as I did, I wasn't concerned about her following through. I still wasn't convinced she wasn't faking the whole thing. I know the upshot was that there was no more talk of a commission. Dang! I wanted a new car cover for the Aston Martin.

I was asleep for less than an hour when the phone rang. My good buddies needed to be bailed out of jail.

It appears after a night of drinking they decided to get some souvenirs from Monaco. They thought a license plate would be nice. They were rare as there weren't that many cars in Monaco.

There had been so many stolen over the years that they didn't use the normal method of attaching the plate with screws. They mounted them with pop rivets.

My good buddies didn't know that, so messed around making enough of a racket that the police were called. They were now in custody.

They needed someone to come down and post bail for them, or they would be stuck in jail until Monday morning.

I gave serious thought to letting them sit but realized that they would have no way to get home, and they didn't need to miss Monday's classes.

A taxi dropped me off at the station. I requested the driver wait while I bailed my friends out. The desk sergeant, or whatever his title was, had questions for me. Like was I with them and got away?

"No, sir, I wasn't with them this evening."

"Where were you?"

"At the palace attending a band performance."

He took the time to call palace security to confirm my story. He also wanted to look at my identification. My diplomatic passport settled the issue. I was allowed to post bail.

Steve, Tom, and Bill were brought out. What a sad-looking group. I hustled them into the waiting cab and got them back to the hotel.

I wasn't the happiest person in the world right then, so at four in the morning, I told them to be packed and ready to go to the airport for the trip home. No one argued.

They were sitting in the lobby when I came down at nine o'clock. I had my sleep out. Did I mention that I wasn't happy with them?

There were no complaints. They knew they had screwed up. I walked over to the concierge's desk and paid for a package they had waiting for me.

Returning to my chums, I opened it and gave each of them a coveted license plate cover that had been purchased this morning at a local shop.

We then started for the airport. We had to delay leaving the hotel as Bill had to make an urgent trip to the WC to throw up.

They wouldn't forget last night for a while. At the airport, among my preflight items, I double-checked that we had a dozen air sickness bags on board.

They were needed before we got back to England. It seemed that we had to go through every bumpy cloud along the way. Did I mention I wasn't happy?

As they dropped me off at my garage, they all apologized. I accepted the apology but told them they still had to pay me back the bail money.

It was only like twenty-five dollars American, so they could afford it. It was very much the principle of the thing.

Heads hung low, they promised. I then asked a question that I had wondered about on the trip but didn't ask as I wasn't speaking to them.

"Did you have a good time at L'Oxford?"

This livened them up as they assured me, they had a wonderful time. I was asked about my evening and told them it turned out to be a business deal for my little sister.

They looked bewildered and nodded at that, but they didn't follow up.

I drove home to The Meadows and took a nap. After lunch, I called the US and talked to Dad. He told me that they would be contacting me for Mary's company and meeting Nina and the other new models early Monday. A trip to Switzerland in two weeks was being put together.

The trip was a combination of business, meeting models, and putting together the Princess Collection with some professional princess advice.

I was invited as I was the one person who knew all the major players. It promised to be an interesting meeting.

Chapter 9

The school week was a normal boring week. The highlight was when my friends came to apologize and repay their bail money. I let them off easy. No Way! I lectured them until Tom poured a pint over my head. All was well in our world.

I skipped classes Friday and headed out to Switzerland.

Friday afternoon I landed at Flughafen, Zurich. Mary and company were already there. I knew it as I taxied in. There was a DC 8 parked there with huge letters, Feed the Puppies, on its side.

I caught a cab to the hotel we were all using. As I walked into the front door, I was attacked by a wonderful armful of Nina.

She had me checked in, so we headed right for my suite. After our reunion, she helped me unpack. After that, we headed down for dinner in a private dining room. Mary, Mum, and about thirty other people were already there.

Family hugs all around. We were barely settled when in walked Princesses Grace and Caroline, accompanied by their entourage.

We went through all the greetings only to have Queen Elizabeth and Princess Anne walk in. It was quite a crowd.

Again, it took about fifteen minutes for all the greetings to occur. The new people I met were the president and some of the staff of Mary Jackson Clothing. The original company had changed its name since Mary's collections were by far the mainstay of their business.

Numerous introductions passed right by me, photographers, business agents, marketing people, and many others. They were the working portion of this whole clothing business.

Nina was also accompanied by five young ladies who would help model the collection.

I noticed that Princess Caroline and Mary had hit it off at once. The odd one out was Princess Anne, as she was eleven or twelve and didn't fit with the younger girls.

I nudged Nina and quietly pointed this out. She immediately brought Anne into the circle of older girls. From her face, this was the right thing to do.

It was almost amusing to watch the dynamics of the girls surrounding Nina. She was the social influencer that they now looked up to. I was happy for her.

I just hoped she didn't get a swelled head. Of course, I could always burst that bubble. All I had to do was remind her of a bra lost one night parking in Hollywood.

It had her name embroidered on it, and she was scared that someone might find it. I had trashed it ages ago, but it was still fun to bring it up occasionally.

All I had to say was, "I wonder what happened...."

The meal was fun with all the talk around the table. It was such a mixed group. Imagine two very young girls seriously discussing the plight of puppies in war-torn Africa, next to a gay photographer discussing the cost of perfumes with the Queen of England.

You could tell the queen had no idea what he was talking about. I knew that she had her fragrance made and reserved only for her. This would be ordered by the palace and she would have no idea of the cost. Still, she was polite. Comes with the territory, I suppose.

As dessert was being served, a man burst into the room holding a camera and snapping pictures like crazy. Security people who had been discreetly standing at the sides of the room had him in hand, the film out of the camera, and him out of the room in a flash. Ah, the life of a papa-rats-eye.

After dinner, everyone split up to go to their rooms. I had the ridiculous hope that Nina would be able to go to mine. One look from Mum had Nina and me say good night to each other before she returned to her dorm.

"Rick, I'm not ready to be a grandmum yet."

"Yes, Mum."

What else could I say?

The next morning the groups had a buffet breakfast and then split up into their working teams. There were three basic groups: those taking pictures for the older girls' collection, Nina and her friends; then the princess group, the royals, Mary, and several designers; and finally, the business team from the dress company trying to put all of this together.

About the only one with nothing to do was me. I had made the original introductions and now was at loose ends.

I went back to my suite and went over the lecture notes of those classes I had missed in the last week. It seemed almost a bother to attend class anymore. I had given up on a degree, though I supposed it would happen. I was now learning for the sake of learning.

It would be business classes for my future, and other stuff for the fun of it. Because of this, none of my classes seemed like a chore. I could dig into each one as deeply as I wanted.

I went down for lunch but found it to be an empty room. The various groups either were having working lunches or skipping them altogether. The only one I saw was the gay photographer from last night, and I had no desire to talk about perfume prices.

I heard a bit of a commotion out in front of the hotel, so I went out to see what was going on. A fashion shoot had been set up with Nina and her friends.

The police had set up barricades around them to keep back the watching crowds. I found a good spot next to the hotel entrance to view the proceedings.

A guy next to me said, "So, the Ricky Jackson Circus is in town."

When I got a good look at him, I realized he was with the press.

"No, this is the Mary Jackson Extravaganza, never to be confused with a Rick Jackson Circus. Notice, this is grace and beauty. If it were my production, it would be brash and over the top."

"May I quote you on that?"

"Please do."

"I see what you mean about grace and beauty. I didn't realize you meant Grace and beauty."

Princess Grace had chosen that moment to step out of the hotel to look at the modeling.

I had to chuckle at the fortunate timing.

"Yes, and I suppose I should have added Her Majesty."

"I thought the princess was referred to as 'Your Grace.'"

"She is. A wonderful play on words, I was talking about Her Majesty," as Elizabeth and my mum joined Grace.

They were almost the same age and looked to be as thick as thieves. I hated to think about what they might dream up for me.

It didn't take long as I was summoned by Her Highness, Mum.

"Rick, the girls need a male to play off of. I'll have your clothes brought down so you can change outfits as needed."

I boldly stated, "Mum, I only brought a few casual clothes for the weekend."

Well, it came out more like a squeak.

"You are so predictable. I had Mr. Hamilton ship the wardrobe that is being prepared for your chartered airplane. That is a very good idea by the way."

Cornered like a rat, I whined and whinged but knew I was lost.

I hadn't noticed it, but the girls would change outfits in a luggage closet right at the entrance. I wondered where I would change. I found out quickly.

The clothes racks were pushed into a small square and I was expected to change there. Any modesty I may have had was lost that afternoon.

I hated every minute of it. I would never want to do this for a living. It would take a stupid boy to do so.

Like all things, this came to an end. I had to use all my acting skills to keep a smile, but I managed. Nina and her friends were over the moon about the day.

From what I could make out, half the people in the crowd were from their school eating their hearts out, the beauties because they weren't having their picture taken, the snobs because they couldn't hobnob with a queen and princesses.

I did get a chance to talk to Mary. I asked her what she liked most about the day.

"Caroline and I got to sneak off and take a nap."

I was glad to see her priorities were in the right place.

Mum told me that the Princess Collection was going to be real. The royals all thought it would be fun. They were even going to model some of the clothes. Their portion of the profits would go to Feed the Puppies.

I tried to picture the queen in a Feed-the-Puppies t-shirt, and it didn't work. As far as I know, she never wore one, even though she loved her corgis.

Chapter 10

From everyone's point of view, the weekend was a rousing success.

The royal mothers had their daughter's clothing under control. It would also put them up in the royal snobbery sweepstakes as the guiding force behind the clothing all self-respecting princesses would now wear.

The princesses had clothing they and their mothers approved of. I was surprised about how normal the clothing looked that they ended up picking. It looked good but wasn't over the top.

Nina had established social status in her school. She was the arbitrator of who would get to model Mary's older girl collection. That seemed an odd phrase, "older girl." Well from Mary's perspective, they were older girls. I suspect the clothing company would come up with a better name.

Mary's company had kicked off two new collections which would be money makers. There will be bonuses all around this year.

Mary herself now owned one of the strongest fashion brands in the world. No hungry puppies now. I was proud of my little sister for not forgetting her true mission, feeding puppies. Everything else was just a means to an end.

For myself, I had a happy sister and girlfriend. Even Mum smiled when she looked at me. What a great weekend!

I left Zurich in enough time to make it back to Oxford just as the last light was fading.

Monday started as a normal day but went to heck quickly. At 8:30 as I was leaving for class, I had a call from Prettyman's, the people doing my prototype.

They had run into a snag and needed more money to proceed. They wanted another forty-eight hundred pounds. This would put me down to two hundred pounds on my class budget. I had no choice but to tell them to proceed.

I would be coming to London later in the week to get an update on the project.

My first class was Economics, and of course, the don wanted updates from everyone. I bit the bullet and told them that I was now all in on my project. It had to work, or I was lost.

The don rather snidely said, "Pride cometh before a fall. One should be careful about erring when one is human, as the divine may not forgive."

So, he was a friend of the don that I had put down over the Wicked Wasp of Twickenham. I had been set up for a fall.

Rather than react I kept a straight face and ignored the comment. Let him think I didn't get his allusion. The stakes in this game had just been upped.

I don't know how I would win this contest, but I would.

Tuesday was a normal day, other than I took a different route on my morning run. I remained on our property but looped out into the woods without a trail.

I hadn't gone very far when I stumbled on a rock, or what I thought at first was a rock. Since I was lying face down with it within an inch of my nose, I got a good look.

It was a man-made material with some design in it. I pried it up and took it with me. I was curious as to what it might be. It was twelve inches tall and another five on the other dimensions. It weighed a good twenty pounds.

When I got back to the house, I took it to the kitchen to wash it off. The cook wasn't pleased. Mr. Hamilton came upon the scene as it was being explained to me that dirty great rocks weren't welcome in her kitchen.

Since she was waving a meat cleaver as she talked, I listened carefully and nodded my head in the right places. I agreed that I was a gormless idiot.

I'm not certain what gormless is, but I must be to get myself into this predicament.

Mr. Hamilton saved me by offering to take the miscreant off her hands and get what she described as, "the bloody great boulder" out of her kitchen.

Whatever we paid him wasn't enough.

He led me out to a shed near the greenhouse. The shed had a table and a sink with running water. Who knew?

I rinsed most of the dirt off with water and then scrubbed out the inscriptions with a worn-out brush from the horse barn.

Now that I could see what was inscribed, I could tell that it was in Latin, and said, "Welcome to our house."

Did we have an old Roman villa on our property? That was enough that I promptly ditched class to go back to the area with a shovel in hand.

I spent all morning there because there was a villa there. All that was left was the outline of the foundation. Inside the foundation line, were there remains of the flooring? It consisted of multicolored tiles that formed a mosaic.

Leaving the shovel in place, I returned home for lunch and picked up a stiff broom. Returning to the ruin, I briskly swept the mosaic clean.

The complete mosaic didn't look like what you would find in a normal house. The pictures were of Capricornus, Pegasus, and Mars. In an arc, over all of them, it read Home of the Second Augustan Legion.

It appeared that I had found a military headquarters. There should be many other buildings nearby. A quick search of the area confirmed my thoughts.

This was a major find. I would have to notify experts to have this place excavated carefully. How does one find experts to excavate old ruins?

I suspect someone at school would know the proper people. I went home, cleaned up, and changed into more suitable clothes. I didn't think a fedora and leather jacket were the proper clothing for Oxford, at least in the better offices. Maybe in a pub.

I started at the bursar's office with my inquiries. It turned out a good thing that I did. There was a huge archaeological department, and like most organizations, a lot of crossing of lines. If I started in the wrong department, I would never get anywhere.

The bursar wanted to know who owned the property. I told him that it was in my mum's name, Viscountess Jackson, and I didn't see any problem getting her permission for a dig.

He suggested I call her, which I did from a separate office he provided. Mum was all for the dig, provided I paid for it. I thought they would do it for free. Silly me.

Also, I was to have a contract where the family retained all property rights, and I specifically was to have title to any treasure trove found. She thought since I was paying, I might recoup some of my cost.

She told me she would have her legal people in London draw up an agreement. After we said our goodbyes, I relayed this to the bursar. He was agreeable; especially when he found out I was willing to bear the costs.

He took me over to a faculty lounge in one of the colleges that specialized in British archaeology. We met with the department head there, and they had an arcane discussion about who should get the project and all the associated glory.

While they were doing this, I was looking around at what was going on in this den of higher learning. What I saw was a bunch of old men taking naps.

Chapter 11

There was one group in the corner having a meeting.

It must have been lively because the guy I thought was the leader pointed at one young man and told him, "Get out of here. I told you not to take any credit in that paper; it was all to go to me."

The young man stood up and left the group. He had to pass right by me.

I asked, "Did I hear right? He was mad because you didn't give him credit for your work?"

He looked at me dumbly and nodded yes.

"What does that mean to your career?"

"It means I'm done here at Oxford; I will be doing good to get a professorship at a second or third-rate school."

"What is your area of expertise?"

"The Romans in early Britain."

"Ever hear of the Second Augustan Legion?"

"Of course. How do you know of it?"

"My family owns the land where their headquarters, or at least one of them, is located."

"Where?"

"Near here, a few miles."

He got an excited look and told me, "There have always been stories about one near here, but it has never been found."

"Well, it has now."

He looked excited but then slumped his shoulders. "I have been sacked; I have lost my stipend, so it doesn't matter."

"Come with me."

I took him over to the Department Head and the bursar.

"Gentlemen I have found the man who will lead the dig."

The department head got a horrified look.

"That's not how things are done here. We have rules."

"I have a rule also: 'He who has the gold makes the rules.' This man will lead the project, or I will find someone at Cambridge."

I had heard the crude term, fart in an elevator. Now I knew what it was in real life. He stuttered a bit, but there was no doubt of the outcome.

The leader of the group, who had just fired my young friend and whose name I didn't know, spoke up and said, "Well, Randel-MacIver, you can't beg your way back into my graces or use any influence you think you may have with our department head."

"I'm not. I have a new project and sponsor."

"And what would that be excavating, kitty litter?

"The headquarters of the Second Augustan Legion near here."

"Nonsense! I would know about such a find. And how would you find a sponsor so quickly?"

I then spoke up, "He stumbled over me after you fired him. He has what I need, so I hired him."

The snotty don (I wasn't worried about his name anymore) came back with, "You're just a kid! You can't have that much money."

The bursar spoke up, "I'm afraid Sir Richard has more than enough money for this project."

Snotty Don then tried to backtrack and convince me I needed someone with experience.

"The problem I have with you taking over is I heard you try to take the credit for someone else's work. How do I know you have any experience? That is not even considering your lack of ethics."

The room got very quiet at that point. The department head told Snotty Don that they would have to have a private conversation.

Meanwhile, I learned that my new head of the dig was named David.

"David, would you like to go see the site?"

"I would love to! That will give me an idea of what we are facing in the size of the team and cost."

We stopped at The Meadows for me to change clothes again. David didn't have to change as he was wearing fieldwork clothing. That was a good sign; he wasn't afraid to get dirty.

We went to the site. It took us over two hours to walk through it. It was enormous.

"Rick, this will take years and cost into the millions."

"That's fine. I want this done right."

"You are wealthy, aren't you?"

"I never have understood it, but I'm one of the richest people in the world right now."

"Oh, then we can do this right."

"That's what I want."

After rambling around for several hours with David taking plenty of notes, we headed back to school. After dropping him off, I headed back to the site. I was intrigued, to say the least.

I wandered over to what we thought was the back end of the site when I realized there had been other buildings. I pottered around with my shovel, seeing if I could get an idea of what was there.

I almost did myself in; my shovel broke through to an underground room. I managed to throw myself backward or I would have ended up down there. I couldn't see a bottom, but when I dropped a rock, it didn't fall very far, maybe ten feet or so.

I returned to the house and picked up a torch, what Americans call a flashlight, and about fifty feet of three-eighths inch manila rope. Back at the site, I was able to shine the light in the hole; my guess of ten feet wasn't off by much.

I tied one end of the rope off on a stout tree trunk and used the other end to walk down the wall into the hole.

Once down below, I could see that it was manmade underground storage. In the opposite corner was a stairway, but it was blocked at the top.

The room had storage shelves, and, on each shelf, there was a wooden chest. Each chest was stout with bronze around each edge. They had a bronze lock. They were all locked, but keys were on hooks next to each strongbox. I tried to lift one of them, but it was too much. It would take at least two men to carry one.

I couldn't resist and used a key to open one of the chests. It was hard to turn but I was able to do it without breaking the key off in the lock.

Holding my breath, I lifted the lid. Inside it was full of coins. They took my breath away; they had the shine of real gold. They looked like they had been minted yesterday.

I went into a frenzy of opening chests. There was another with more gold, about a dozen with worn silver coins, and one chest of bronze.

After I calmed down and started thinking rationally, I relocked each chest and kept the fifteen keys with me.

Using the rope, I got out of the safe room, then rewound my rope, and did my best to cover the hole with deadwood branches. It wasn't a very good job but the best I could do.

I went back to the house and called my new expert, David, who had left me his number. I told him I had been thinking, what if there were gold or silver coins on the site? He explained the Treasure Trove law to me. At this time anything found under the ground to be retrieved later, and whose owner couldn't be identified, was considered a treasure trove and belonged to the Crown.

That told me who I had to work with. I made two phone calls, one to our legal people in London asking them to form a company, Treasure Trove, PUC. I chose this because of the limited reporting requirements and the low risk of insolvency.

My next call was to my mentor, Mr. Norman. I asked him who handled the treasure trove for the crown. His response was a groan.

"Rick, what have you found?"

"Roman coins, lots of Roman coins."

"Oh, that isn't so bad, the bronze coins aren't worth that much."

"What about silver and gold?"

Another groan came over the phone.

"Tell me it was only a few of them."

"It wasn't that many, only two chests of gold and twelve of silver."

It got quiet on the other end of the line, no more groans. Now all business, Mr. Norman told me that the chests had to be taken into custody and given to the British Museum as soon as possible. When news of the find got out, people would be all over the area looking for more.

We arranged to meet at the museum tomorrow morning. I called David and invited him to come with me.

I then called Jackson House and talked to my parents. We agreed to play this one straight down the middle. The coins would all go to the Crown, and any reward would be returned to the British Museum in my British grandfather's name. He had been an amateur coin collector and would have gotten a kick out of it.

The next day, the result of our meeting with the museum was that I would get security on the site as soon as possible.

After talking about it for a while, it was decided that a road would be put in, scraped at first then graveled. It would circle the site. This would make access easy for later exploration.

Chapter 12

For security, Mr. Norman recommended Securitas AB, a Swedish firm. David had seen them used on other projects, so I agreed to go with them. A whirlwind meeting with them had me signing a contract.

While I had financial responsibility, they were to work with David. He and I both signed a statement to this effect. These people knew what they were doing.

While money isn't an object anymore, I did choke up a bit while signing the papers. It was to be around the clock, seven days a week. There would be patrols with dogs, checkpoints, even a guard shack at the entrance, and towers at each corner.

The entire site would be fenced. They were able to justify this to me by past sites they had guarded. When the news of the find became public, we could expect a full-out assault by both amateurs and professionals.

The most important arrangement was for an armored truck and escorts to be on site the next morning to take the chests with the coins to the British Museum.

SAB, as I thought of them, told me they would have local reporters there along with David and anyone he wanted there to witness the removal. That would reduce the danger somewhat, but there would be others hoping to find something we missed.

All of this would start tomorrow morning. I made a point of letting Grandmum and Mr. Hamilton know what would be going on in their peaceful world.

Mr. Hamilton took it with his normal reserve. Grandmum became excited; what an adventure. She was on the phone with her confidants in minutes. I suspect the news would be in the morning papers.

I called the US to keep Mum and Dad in the loop. I was informed that my sister Mary had already decided to do a fashion shoot on-site.

In the morning, it looked more like a military convoy, rather than moving cash from a store to the bank.

I watched the start of the process but had other commitments to keep. I drove down to Pinewood Studios for the next step in preparing for the movie.

This trip was for a wardrobe. I had to try on everything to ensure it fitted. Then they would take pictures to see what the camera thought. If that all worked, I had to stand next to people wearing the costumes the other actors would be wearing to make certain they didn't clash with each other, that is, if they weren't intended to clash.

Of course, everything wasn't perfect. Some items had to be changed, which required a repeat of the process. Some had to have a nip or tuck taken. By the time it was done, I had spent the whole day, and the only food I had was a dry sandwich from the Pinewood canteen.

Their canteen could have some lessons from Warner Brothers. I didn't tell them that though. I had to come back again.

When I got back to The Meadows, the place was empty. I asked the lone gardener where everyone was, and he told me they were at the dig.

I changed into some rough clothes, donned my leather jacket and old fedora, and hiked back. I was stopped by guards twice and had to show identification. This was a good thing.

At the edge of the site in a clearing, a huge tent had been set up. It was the sort you would see at a large garden party. This is where I found Grandmum, the Queen Mum, Mr. Hamilton, and most of our staff. They had set up tables with refreshments of all sorts. These were intended for the guards and David's staff.

It seems Grandmum had decided to take care of all her visitors in style. Looking at the way David's people were putting it away, you would think they were starving students. They will love to work on this site.

Grandmum was having a wonderful time, and I hoped she would stay with it rather than that duke. No luck there, she asked me if I could supervise here on Friday, as she had a dinner date with his dukeness; my words, not hers.

Of course, I would.

I was back at Pinewood Studios the next day. This day would be a run-through of the script. All the principal characters were there. The woman playing the part of the famous actress was new to the acting world.

She was gorgeous and had a wonderful voice. I could see why they picked her for the part. The only negative was that she had a pretty high opinion of herself.

While I could work with her, I doubted if we would ever be friends. The last straw was at a break where she started complaining about the cost of the royal family and that the institution was archaic and should be done away with. Who would have thought that American me was a Monarchist at heart?

I wasn't ready to give the colonies back, but I favored the British setup for Britain. It was probably due to my close relationship with the royal family.

After lunch, we continued with our lines. At one point, she stopped the reading and told the writers that here was a wonderful place to put in a line about the redundant royal family.

I had to ask if a comedy was the place to put in a political statement. The writers didn't have any problem adding her line.

That got me up on my high horse, so when I had to respond to her screed, I made a pro-royal statement. That brought some tension between us that was reflected in our body language for the rest of the afternoon.

At teatime, the writers left us and had a conference. When they came back, they told us that our disagreement about the royal family was exactly what was needed.

It gave a reason for us not getting together until we made up at the end of the movie. I asked how we would resolve our disagreement. It turned out that she as the actress would get a part in a Hollywood movie, and we would move there to live happily ever after.

I objected as I would have to give up my bookstore. This got me some weird looks as there wasn't a bookstore; it was a prop in the movie.

I explained that my character had been built around being a bookstore owner and that is what attracted her to me in the first place. It didn't seem logical for me to walk away.

We reached an agreement that Foyles would buy out his bookstore and that he was looking to buy a laid-back bookstore in the US.

Thus, the royal family issue became a moot point, as we weren't going to live in England, at least as the movie ends. I still didn't care that much for the girl.

We were going to have to kiss several times during the movie. This meant we would have to have hundreds of kisses on set. Well, she was good-looking. I would just have to man up.

When I got back to The Meadows in the evening, it was a right mess. There were vehicles parked everywhere. There must have been several hundred cars on the property.

The word about the treasure trove find was out. After changing, I went out to the dig. I drove along the newly made gravel road. I took one of the estate cars. No way was my Aston Martin going on that gravel.

I had to show identification to get past the SAB people, which was more than fine with me. Grandmum was at her tent with another group of her friends. I didn't know there were that many silver-haired women in England.

They were feeding the guards and students. The guards were there in small groups, eating like normal people. As one of the ladies said, the students were like gobbling gannets.

I did find David, who had set up a large tent of his own. They were still in the preparatory stage of the dig. This included developing a map of the site. He told me this would be the most significant find in a hundred years.

He had seen the chests delivered to the British Museum and had delivery receipts for them. It would be several weeks before there was an official valuation, but he was told that it would be in the millions. Since I had agreed in writing to donate any reward to the museum, they wanted a high valuation to excite the public. Interesting how that works.

David told me that he was going to give a tour of the site to reporters, once they had it mapped out and had walkways staked. He asked if I would have any objection to a BBC crew filming the dig at various stages, with the idea of making either a movie or TV series out of it.

I told him that was a wonderful idea and that we wanted to charge them to offset the costs. My accountants were going to love the new mess I had created for them.

Chapter 13

I gave a press conference at the dig on Saturday morning. David asked me to do it, as he was getting pestered all the time. I knew there was no escaping it and that I just should do it and get it over with.

The questions were all predictable.

"How did you find it?"

"I stumbled across it on a walk. I tripped on a root and noticed a stone with inscriptions."

"How much was in the chests that were removed?"

"We won't know until the British Museum values them."

"What do you think about all of it going to the Crown?"

"That is the law."

"Normally a reward is given. Do you have any idea how much you will receive?"

"It doesn't matter. My company has already donated it back to the British Museum."

"What company is that?"

"Treasure Troves, PUC."

On it went until they were repeating themselves. Finally, I said, "One last question."

A man in the back raised his hand; he hadn't asked any questions until now.

"Is it true you are the wealthiest person in the world now?"

"I have no idea; the Sultan of Brunei and others don't share their financial status with me. Yes, my companies are worth a lot of money and will earn more in the future. It's not about the money though, but about what you can do with it."

"And what will you do with yours?"

"Build a company that helps businesses and through them, the people."

"Wouldn't it be better just to give the people money directly, letting them decide what to do with it, instead of you thinking you know what is best for the world?"

"I don't know what's best, but I hire smart people to advise me and manage my businesses so that I can hire people and improve their lot in life."

"You are a filthy capitalist!"

"And proud of it. This press conference is over."

As I turned, a shot rang out. I looked back; security guards were all over the last man to question me.

No one was hurt except that the man who had fired the shot would have a tremendous headache where he had been coshed.

The SAB people held him for the police. Of course, all the reporters who were at the press conference were asking me and each other questions.

The shooter kept yelling nonsense. Well, it was nonsensical, but it was finally figured out he was a true believer of Marx and Engels. He was going to kill the filthy capitalist.

Lucky for this filthy capitalist, he was a poor shot.

I thought it was luck that had security right there. It turned out they were suspicious of him from the start. His press credentials were good, though from a communist newspaper, so they let him in.

At the same time, they kept several people close to him. As soon as the pistol came out of his pocket, two guards were on him. When he fired the gun, they had forced his arm pointing straight up in the air.

Hiring SAB proved to be a good decision.

The local bobbies showed up and took statements from all present, at least all that had not left the scene. It was funny watching all the press interviewing each other.

David wanted to know if my life was always like this. Thinking about the last three years, I told him, "Pretty much."

"Sucks to be you."

"There have been some very good times to offset the bad."

"If you say so. How many times have you been shot at?"

I thought about it, "I haven't kept count."

"If you don't mind, I'm not going to be sitting next to you at any public events."

"Only if I don't have to defend you in any faculty meetings."

He pondered, "Maybe getting shot at isn't so bad after all."

We had a good laugh and went our way. I liked that guy.

Grandmum had all the details before I got back to the house, so I didn't have to explain all of it. She wanted to know why I hadn't hit the rotter. I told her I hired people to do that.

She thought that was an excellent idea. This explained Mum's attitude to the world more clearly. Hit someone in our family and we hit back harder.

Sunday I was out watching the dig, at least for three hours. After a while, I realized this was like watching paint dry. They were being meticulous like I had never imagined.

Everything was being marked, photographed, and documented before even a leaf was disturbed. From watching their work, I began to understand the time and money a project of this size would take.

I realized I needed to have the accounting people work with David, so he would have the money he needs. From what I understood, archaeologists were always underfunded and trying to save a ha'penny. This project did not need to be done like that.

I made a mental note to let him know that I wanted this to be the best dig and restoration the world had ever seen. That guy who tried to shoot me had one valid point. What use is money?

Monday, it was back to class. I thought people would be asking me questions about the find and attempted shooting. University students like to think they are too sophisticated to ask questions.

That is, except for Tom, Bill, and Steve. They were all over me wanting the gory details. So, between lectures, I shared them as I saw them.

At home that evening, I had a note to call the Prettyman Company in London. They needed to talk to me. From the way the message read, it was urgent.

I called before heading out to class on Tuesday. It turns out they were having trouble getting the whiffletree linkage to work correctly. They decided to call the author of the paper.

They tracked him down to his company. IBM! He was reluctant to talk to them because IBM was doing work in that area. He did let it slip that it involved typewriters.

Well, there went that idea down the drain along with my development money. Prettyman's wanted to know where to proceed with the project. I asked if there were any funds left on the account. They told me no. As a matter of fact, I owed them one hundred pounds for work done beyond the budget.

I told them I would see that they got their money, but the project was dead. I was mad, mad at myself. The one lesson I should have learned in the Economics class was business intelligence. All I would have had to do was read the biography of the author of the whiffletrees article, and I would have known that IBM was ahead of me.

I contacted my London office, which had just opened. It was attached to the freight forwarding business, but Jim Williamson had set up a small office just to handle my affairs.

They would handle all my cards and letters that I needed to sign rather than ship them to me from the States. An accountant there handled my financial matters as opposed to company matters.

I called him and explained that Prettyman's would be sending a final bill for one hundred pounds and that we would pay it. After that, the project was finished and was to be used as a tax write-off.

I gave some thought as to how I was going to handle the Economics course project and grade. As far as the don knew, I was failing at this point.

What he didn't know about was Treasure Troves, PUC. I had set it up out of personal funds, not company money. Depending on the British Museum's evaluation, the find would meet the requirements for an A.

He had set it on gross profit, not net. Since I was donating the money back to the museum, a large sum would flow into the company and then back out. To hype the find to the public, it was in the museum's best interest to value the find as high as they could. It would cost them nothing to do so.

This would give me another personal tax deduction, which accounting informed me I needed desperately. The only question was whether I should let the Economics class know now, or surprise everyone later.

I was inclined to let it wait, as the don was being a jerk about things. It would be cool to set him up and then shoot him down. Not very adult of me, I know.

After thinking about it some more, I decided to update the class on the project now. I could savor the thought without taking the action.

It would look like I was taking a high road while getting to enjoy the low road thoughts. It was the best of both worlds. Was I growing up, or growing cynical?

I did call the museum and asked when the evaluation would be complete. They thought it would be another couple of weeks. They gave me a ballpark figure of ten million pounds, give or take a few million.

Yeah, I could savor some thoughts while doing the right thing.

Chapter 14

Thursday morning, I set up my trip to Spain. I had a map book of the region my new properties were in. The main ranch was near Granada in the Andalucia region.

I had to change planes twice to get there, but they were good connections, and the flights were all on time.

I was flying commercial and could have chartered a flight but had second thoughts about doing so. I didn't want to end up like Howard Hughes. Afraid of everything and everybody.

Considering it was winter, the weather was sunny, cold but sunny. On the trip down I read the Spanish newspapers that had accumulated at The Meadows.

There were two of them, *ABC* from Madrid and *Ideal* printed in Granada. *ABC* had been subscribed to at my request ever since I started school at Oxford. The purpose was to keep my Spanish up to speed.

I had gotten lax on reading the daily edition, but I usually got caught up on the weekends with binge reading. What I like about *ABC*, they were always pushing for the royal family to come back into power.

I'm not a royalist in the general sense. I take the American stance of rooting for the underdog. With Franco in power, they were the underdogs. I suspected it would take Franco's death for anything to happen.

The newspaper *Ideal* was Mr. Hamilton's idea. When I obtained the property from the duke, he suggested I keep up with local issues at least until I knew what I was facing.

The only item in *Ideal* was about the land being sold that would contain the intersection of 902 and 44. There had been big development plans, but they were now on hold. These were two major highways.

I paid attention to all the names in the article. They meant nothing to me right now, but I bet they would soon.

The writer of the article didn't seem upset about the developer not being able to proceed.

I also had a copy of the quarterly reports that the duke had received from his agent. The income amounts were within what one would expect. I had my accounting staff review them to make certain.

They thought the rents were a little low and that I might consider raising them. I wasn't going to do anything until I had visited the site.

I had dressed very casually for the flight. That meant I had on boots, jeans, a polo shirt, and a sports coat.

I had let the people who ran my new house know that I was coming. I was told that I would be met at Armilla Airport.

My last flight was a puddle jumper. Since it was a Cessna 320, I could have flown it. There was one other passenger on board. He slept most of the one-hour flight, so I had time to wonder what was waiting for me.

I would never have guessed. I had a Hartmann soft duffle bag for my two days of clothes. I intended this to be a quick trip, one I really shouldn't even be making with so much going on.

I needed to see what I had bought and see if there were any issues.

Waiting for me at Armilla Airport was a guy about my age and his younger sister. She must have been fourteen. A nice-looking girl but not beautiful in a fashion sense, normal in other words.

He was holding a sign with Richard Jackson on it.

I identified myself with them. We piled into a station wagon made by a company named SEAT. I had never heard of it before. It was a rough-riding car without much attention to detail, unlike cars from America or other modern countries' cars.

I asked and was told it was made in Spain. Due to the driver's tone, I didn't say anything negative about the car. It was the best they had.

I was only half paying attention when I was asked a question in Spanish by Alejandro, so didn't hear it. In English, I asked him to repeat his question.

He did so in pretty good English. The little girl Elisa said to her brother in Spanish, "I guess he doesn't speak Spanish."

She continued, "He looks like Rick Jackson, the American actor, but he is big and has a British accent so can't be him. Besides, everyone knows that American actors are short. They have to stand on boxes to kiss the leading ladies."

Poor Alan Ladd. He had set an image for American actors that wouldn't be lived down for a long time.

Alejandro replied, "I don't care who he is. I just hope he isn't here to raise our rents. We are barely getting by as it is."

Now that brought me up short. I had been considering raising rents based on my accountant's recommendation. What was going on here?

I asked in English, "What is life like on the ranch?"

I avoided using *la estancia* or *la hacienda*.

They gave me a basic description of what I would call farm life. Elisa told me about her school. What she described sounded pretty dilapidated to me. This was strange as the duke's records listed a large amount being used to modernize it.

I asked about how expensive it was to live on the ranch, thinking that they would tell me that rent was included in their pay for working the ranch. The money sent to the duke would be an accounting quirk to show the purported income from the estate.

Instead, the amount being charged was twice what had been sent to the duke.

All of a sudden, my quick trip didn't look so quick. I had questions that needed answers.

After an hour's drive on Route 902, we came to a huge intersection where Route 44 merged with it in a three-way tangle. I later learned that there was not a modern limited access expressway in all of Spain, which was a backward country compared to the rest of Western Europe.

There was plenty of open land on the feeder roads. I could see why it would be a natural spot to put a truckstop and other roadside facilities.

I asked about the truckstop land. The kids, as I thought of them, told me that a big fight about that land had been going on for a long time. It was hoped as the new owner I would get it settled so jobs would be created in the area.

Arriving at *la hacienda* was an experience. To get to it we left the main highway on a private road and had to drive two miles to the main house. I called it the main house, but it was a small village in its own right.

I could see a small general store with gas pumps, a school that had no evidence of recent work done, at least on the outside, a small church, and there was a cantina.

Alejandro drove up to the front door of the main house. It was old-looking. When I asked how old, Elisa proudly told me that it had been built in 1895 but the buildings had been updated only ten years ago.

That was before the duke owned the place. There had to be a story here.

On the trip, I learned that the ranch grew olives, grapes, almonds, walnuts, cherries, apples, quinces, and wheat. It was more of what I thought of as a farm rather than a ranch.

The surrounding land looked very familiar to me. It looked like the California foothills in the summer. All brown hillsides. I bet in the spring everything would green up.

That made sense as all of the early settlers chose land that looked like home because they knew how to work it. This was true of English, Spanish, and Scandinavians, or anyone else you could name. It made a lot of sense.

Well, until you got to the Louisiana bayou. That area never made sense to me, but the natives loved it.

The kid's mother greeted me at the door. She was a widow who was the housekeeper for the main house. I didn't see how she could be charged any rent to live there.

I made a mental note to ask her about it as soon as I got settled in. As the new owner, I was given the master suite. It hadn't been used for a long time but was elegant. I suspected it was last redecorated in about 1920 by someone who loved Rococo.

Over the top is the best description I have. It could have been used as a stereotypical Spanish bedroom as a movie set. The movie would have had to be a period piece. As I looked around, it kind of grew on me. It was so ugly that it worked.

The room had been dusted and the bedding changed so it was fresh. I didn't have to worry about bedbugs here.

There was no telephone in the room. The only one I had noticed was on a table in the hallway. It might be the only one in the house.

I later learned that there was one in the office that served both the ranch and the house. It was a large room built with solid walls. This could have been used to stand off an Indian raid.

Chapter 15

I went back downstairs and was formally introduced to Senora Echerivera, mother of Alejandro and Elisa. She was a nice-looking woman about my mother's age.

After exchanging pleasantries, she asked if I wanted a tour of the ranch. I told her yes, if she would accompany us. The family and I then set out on a walking tour of the main buildings surrounding the main house.

My initial impression was correct; it was like a small village. As we walked, I asked various questions like how many people lived on the ranch. Around two thousand, I learned.

After several of these, I asked her what her rent was for living in the main house. She told me a number that was twice what the accounts gave as the in-kind amount the ranch was charging off the books. She was not supposed to be paying anything.

I then asked if we could speak to the priest in charge of the local school. That was easy as we were just standing outside of the building the local priest lived in. I think it is called the Diocesan House. Fra Tomas was right there; I think he had been watching us out of a window. I asked him for a tour of the school.

He gave me a short tour of the four-room building; it also had a central auditorium. No money had been spent on the building or classroom materials in many years.

I tried to innocently work in questions about the man who handled the ranch's books and bank accounts. I would have thought it would be someone working on the ranch.

Instead, it was a local accounting firm with offices in Granada. It was run by Senor Francisco. I asked what he was like. Instead of telling me about him as a person, I was told that he was a cousin to the local chief of police.

The way Fra Tomas answered me, I knew I wasn't fooling him a bit about what I was thinking.

After finishing up the tour, I asked if there was a phone I could use in private. That is when I saw the office. It was big and had a lot of possibilities, though I would be spending little time here.

I called Jim Williamson and asked him to put together a team of accountants to go completely over the ranch's books. There had been fraud on a major scale. He was to put the team together but do nothing until I contacted him.

I then called Mr. Norman and asked him how I would go about getting official help in Spain when I thought the local police chief and accountants might be crooked.

He told me that I should go through the British Consulate to contact the *Cuerpo Nacional de Policia* (CPN) or National Police. They handled the investigation of crimes that may involve the local authorities.

He gave the number of the consulate in Madrid. I would call them tomorrow as it was getting late in the day. I returned to my room and lay down for a few minutes.

An hour later, Alejandro woke me up, knocking on my door. It was dinner time. In the country, they didn't eat as late as in the city, but it was still eight o'clock in the evening.

At dinner, they all spoke English with me. Little Elisa told her mother in Spanish that the Mary, Mary Collection had some new dresses out that she would love to have.

They had to know sooner or later so I replied in Spanish, "Do you know she is my sister?"

You talk about looks. Mum was surprised, Elisa gasped, and Alejandro looked mortified.

"I'm sorry, but this morning I got cut off before I could say I speak Spanish. Then Elisa made her comment about American actors having to stand on a box, and I just had to get even."

Mum asked, "Get even?"

"I'm the actor who she said was so short I had to stand on a box to kiss the girl."

Elisa ran from the table wailing at this point. I always had a way with girls.

Her mother left the room to try to calm her daughter down. I was starting to feel bad about my little joke.

Alejandro started laughing, "Serves her right. She is always making assumptions, then blaming the world for her mistakes."

"Still, I shouldn't have let it go on for so long."

"I know how you can get back in her good graces."

"How?"

"Your little sister."

And that's how Mary got a Spanish model for her collection. It worked so well her people started recruiting girls from all the different countries and ethnic groups they could. It did get me out of the doghouse with Elisa after I called Mary and told her I needed her help.

She told me she would do it, as she still owed me for the East German kidnapping. Man, she keeps score like no one I know. I would have to arrange her kidnapping regularly to stay ahead.

The next morning, I called the British Consulate and explained to the *chargée d'affaires* what I suspected. He arranged a conference call with the CPN, on a Saturday no less. I was impressed.

Within two hours after I hung up, two plainclothes men were at the ranch. After explaining what I saw and showing them the duke's summary of the ranch's finances, they talked to Mrs. Echerivera and Fra Tomas.

A tour of the school was the final straw. They then told me they had been trying to get the goods on the police chief and his cousin for some time. This would put them away.

I wrote personal checks to Mrs. Echerivera and Fra Tomas, Mrs. Echerivera's to reimburse her for her rent since I owned the ranch, the Fra's a much larger one to start fixing up the school.

I also asked them to start looking for a person to keep the ranch books who would live on-site.

That was when I learned that Mrs. Echerivera was a degreed accountant who couldn't find work locally since her husband died.

I immediately hired her to keep the business side of the ranch under control, and she was to hire a housekeeper. Neither of them was to pay rent. I also asked what the going rate for an accountant was and paid top end for that.

It is good to have money and be able to fix some wrongs. I couldn't fix the world, but I would do what I could.

I addressed one last piece of unfinished business.

"Who should I contact about building facilities on the *autovía*?"

She didn't know but had a cousin who would. I had to remember that different countries had different methods. In Spain, the family came first. I asked her to call him tomorrow to start the process.

I told her that the work would be bid out and that also there would be several accountants from my home office to check out the true financial condition of the ranch and help her set up the books.

She told me that I should also hire a business manager to replace the one the accountants in town were using. The business manager would sell the ranch's products, but they were never told what the profit, if any, was.

The same people refused to let them buy new tractors or any other equipment. I could see that this would probably be a financial sinkhole until everything was updated.

At breakfast Sunday morning, I asked a question that had been at the back of my mind since I arrived.

"Everyone calls this the ranch. I thought most estates like this have a formal name."

"The duke had a chance to rename it but never bothered. Would you like to give it a name?"

That's how Jackson House España got its name.

Alejandro and Elisa drove me back to the airport for my flight back to England. By this time Elisa had talked to Mary, so I was in her good graces. She was excited by what Mary proposed.

I told her I hadn't thought of it before, but the next time she talked to Mary, suggest they do a photoshoot at Jackson House España.

It would be neat if they did, especially when I presented Mary with the bill for using my property. Teach her to cheat me at Monopoly!

Of course, I would tear the bill up, but it would be fun to see the look on her face.

The flight home was uneventful, thank goodness. I had enough going on in the last two days to last me for a while.

I slept most of the flight home. I dreamed I was in a movie with an actress so tall I had to stand on a box. Would you call that a nightmare?

Chapter 16

I got home late enough Sunday that I went straight to bed without talking to anyone. After my morning exercises and run at breakfast, I updated Grandmum and Mr. Hamilton on my trip to Spain.

Grandmum wanted to know if my actions would have the Spanish National Police knocking on the door. I told her I didn't think so. I was the good guy this time. Wait, I'm always the good guy.

It seemed Mr. Hamilton had spent some time in Spain during his army career. He told me that I should consider how I was doing business there.

It would be best if I had a partnership with some locals. Despite the way the ranch ownership was set up, there still could be questions about foreign ownership. Foreigners were not allowed direct ownership of property.

The company setup got around this, but it would be best if I had some Spanish partners. I told him I would give this some thought.

I decided to go out to the dig and check on things rather than attend my first class. It was Economics class, and I didn't feel like facing that today. I was becoming a real college student, any excuse to cut class!

Once I got past the security at the dig, I caught up with David. He took me over to a tent set up for the security team and got me a badge. It was cool; they took my picture with a Polaroid camera and laminated it, and I could wear it around my neck on a cord.

There was no change in the appearance of the site as they were still doing the preliminary survey. He was particularly excited about one area.

The area looked level but when they started probing, they found it was a large depression that had been filled in. There was a good chance it was the camp dump. For an archaeologist, it would be a treasure trove.

I liked the treasure trove I found better.

I asked if many people had come nosing around. It seems they had come in droves. Yesterday they had so many visitors that he set up a display in the field out front, showing what the area looked like and examples of what they had found so far.

Except for the treasure that is; that was safely in the British Museum. They even had come up with an empty chest like those I had found.

I asked him how much they were charging to park cars and the per-person admission. He looked at me like I was crazy. I guess there hadn't been this notorious of a dig this close to civilization before. They weren't used to the idea of making money.

I also suggested he get plans made for a VIP tour of the actual site, as that would occur whether we wanted it to or not. We might as well get out in front of it. I had an idea on that point.

It would be a wonderful outing for Prince Charles's class. Of course, we would have the press there. I was going with my instincts on this. There was no real reason to want all the publicity, but it seemed like a good idea.

I left there thinking I had done all the damage I could. When I got to Oxford, I made a long-distance call to the British Embassy in Madrid. My business with them was still being talked about, so the ambassador took my call.

He updated me on the news in Spain. It seems the chief of police and others in Granada had been arrested on numerous charges, fraud, embezzlement, and tax evasion among other charges.

The embassy was in good standing for its part in bringing these guys down. It appeared the Franco government had been after them for some time, and this was what they needed to nail them.

He then asked me what my call was about. I explained that I had concerns about my sole ownership of the Spanish ranch and thought that I could use some local partners.

Did he have any suggestions? Oh, boy did he. It seems Her Majesty's government could make a lot of political capital from this. We talked about possibilities for a while.

The result was that several very high-profile officials were going to be asked to build a truckstop and associated facilities at the intersection of 44 and 902.

They would own the facilities outright. They would rent the land that it was sitting on from my ranch at a very favorable rate, this to be determined later.

He gave me a list of potential buyers. Most meant nothing to me, except one jumped out: Colonel Frade, an Argentinian who was allowed to own land in Spain through his wife.

Could it be? In the hope that it was, I asked that he be included. It was too choice to pass up.

I then called Jim Williamson and let him know what I had set in train. He was a little grumpy. I realized that I had caught him opening the office in California, and he hadn't had any coffee yet. I apologized, and he forgave me because I kept things interesting. That was without me even bringing the good colonel up. He did not need to know that story.

After that, I called Spain once more. This time to the Jackson House España, letting Mrs. Echerivera know what was going on. She was still to contact a builder, as we would be presenting the buyers with a completed truck stop.

She told me that things were already changing for the better at the ranch. Bills that were behind were now caught up. That was better than taking out an advertisement in the newspaper.

She was getting all sorts of phone calls from friends, family, and busybodies. They all wanted to know if it was true that a famous short American actor had bought the ranch.

She giggled when she used the word short.

I didn't think it funny at all but saw where it had come from. Her only problem was the fourteen-year-old diva who had taken over her daughter's body.

I was glad I was in England right now.

While I was on a phone-calling spree, I called home in the US and talked to Mum. Dad was at his office, and the kids were in school.

I told her about my visit to Spain and the outcome. She thought I had handled it well. She made one comment that I found cryptic.

"Next you will hear from the bishop. Maybe even a cardinal."

I didn't understand what she was driving at, so let it go.

It seemed Mary's business was going like crazy. All Mary was doing was being a front person. She would appear in one of her outfits and be cute like only Mary could. The clothing company did the rest.

All she cared about was how many puppies were being fed. There were a lot of puppies in pounds all over the world.

The clothing company had already grabbed the idea of having girls of all ethnicities around the world appear in Mary's Collection. It was the Mary, Mary Collection, but that was too much to say.

They thought if they used enough different girls around the world, Mary could become the *Time Magazine* Person of the Year, maybe even get invited to the UN, and after that receive the Nobel Peace Prize. I thought the publicity people were smoking something illegal.

Mum agreed. She was seriously thinking about reducing Mary's public appearances. She had to have time to be a little girl.

I made the mistake of asking when she was ever a little girl. This was Mum's baby we were talking about. My ears were burning by the time she was done.

After calling me a typical teenage brat, she let me off the hook and agreed that Mary had always acted beyond her age. She even relented and told me how she caught Mary out, having a pair of high heels made in girls' size six with four-inch heels.

She put a stop to that. I thought she should have let her wear them and try to walk in them. That is what I thought—I knew when to keep my mouth shut.

Other than that, things were going fine for the boys. Eddie had just made Life Scout. He would make Eagle by the time he was fourteen. Denny was a very popular photographer in the area and was making money hand over fist.

He was wondering why he should go to school if he could earn a living right now. Dad took care of that. Mum didn't say what he did, but I suspected it was a talk in the woodshed.

Dad's business was going fine. He had been asked to serve on some government business committee by President Kennedy, so my parents' contribution to both parties was paying off.

Chapter 17

Tuesday morning was a repeat of Monday, except I attended my classes. I did that every day for the rest of the week until Friday afternoon.

I had called Nina the night before, but she had too much homework to do to go on a date this weekend. So, I thought I would get a full week of school in, except for Monday.

One of the Army contingents who usually escorted me around campus caught up with my current escort. It seems Buckingham Palace was looking for me; I was to call as soon as I could. The young British officer seemed to think it was a big deal.

I had enough dealings with the palace that I wasn't going to get all excited until I talked to someone.

I repaired to my garage, thanking my escorts for their time. I certainly was safe from the KGB and company with them around.

When I returned the call, I was put directly through to Queen Elizabeth. Ah, *a dog needs to be robbed.*

We exchanged pleasantries, and then I got my request to her before she could tell me what she needed from me.

"Your Majesty...."

"Go ahead, and lay it on, Rick. What do you need from me?"

"Okay, you got me. The dig on The Meadows ground is proving very popular with visitors and not just treasure hunters. They have set up an educational program outside the dig, but I know that we will be getting VIP requests soon."

I continued, "I would like to encourage that. Do you think it would be a good idea to invite Prince Charles and his school chums on a class outing?"

"I think that is a splendid idea, Rick. It solves a problem I have been discussing with my advisors. Charles's school has a requirement that a parent chaperone all school trips. Philip, the coward, refuses to do it."

"We have been trying to come up with a trip that would limit my public exposure. This would do it nicely; so yes, let's do it. Who should I have contacted?"

I gave her David's name and number.

She chortled as she told me, "My advisors think I can only handle matters of state. They think that I'm helpless with the children. This will show them."

"That's great, ma'am. Always glad to help, speaking of which, you were the one that had me called."

"I'm pleased you remembered. I'm so excited about this class trip that I would have forgotten about what I need you for."

"I'm at your service."

"You better be young man, or I'll have you reduced in rank."

Never, ever forget who has the power here.

"Oh shudder, to be an ensign again."

"Brat."

"Seriously, what can I do for England, Your Majesty?"

"Now that's better. Rick, I need you to escort me in your full Order of the Garter regalia to the lord mayor of London's official confirmation as a baronet. Philip has other duties that day. You are the only knight I have that can bend his knees properly. The rest are too old."

It's nice to be "kneed", I thought; yes pun intended, never to pass my lips.

"When is this event?"

"Tomorrow evening."

"That is short notice. How will I retrieve my regalia?"

"It will be waiting here for you tomorrow. I wish we could have given you more notice. Prince Philip's event came up unexpectedly, but he has to attend."

I noticed she didn't tell me what the event was, and I wasn't about to ask.

After keeping awake through my lectures, the next day, I flew down to London to get ready for the lord mayor's event.

As promised, my Order of the Garter regalia was waiting for me. It all seemed over the top, but I donned the garb with assistance from an equerry.

We rode in the queen's Bentley to the border of the City of London, where the lord mayor awaited.

As the weather was typical English rain and wind for the time of year, the ceremony took place with few flourishes. The lord mayor had to hold on to his tricorne hat so the wind wouldn't carry it away.

He presented the Pearl Sword to the queen to show that she held sway.

We then bundled back into our respective vehicles and proceeded to Guildhall for the ceremony. The current lord mayor was retiring, for health reasons, I was told, so he was being made a baronet, this being the normal honor after a successful term of office.

I was introduced to the lady mayoress, who had a stressed look on her face, so I gathered this was not a celebration but a sad ending of a life.

While dancing in attendance on the queen I heard the word cancer.

As Queen Elizabeth was conferring the honor, I noticed three young men moving ever closer to the front. The one in the middle was holding something under a cloth, so I had no idea what it was.

I had a bad feeling about this.

The man carrying the cloth-covered object threw the cloth aside and reared his arm back to make a throw. It was towards the queen and lord mayor, so I stepped in front of the thrown object.

I caught the banana cream pie full in the face. The young men were quickly restrained and hustled out of the room.

The quick-thinking lady mayoress took me by the arm and led me to a small kitchen where she cleaned me up as best as possible with towels.

All the while, she was complaining about those horrible liberal students from Cambridge who tried to disrupt every ceremony they could.

When I was as clean as possible—there may have been some banana cream pie still on my hat—we returned to the main hall. There was a polite round of applause as we entered the room.

Both the queen and the lord mayor thanked me for my quick action in saving them embarrassment. The press was present and wanted an interview. I glanced at the queen, and she nodded.

"I might as well get it over with."

The questions came fast and furious.

"Sir Richard, did you know it was a pie being tossed?"

"Not until I tasted it."

"Was it good?"

"Very. I would like to get the name of the baker."

"Why do you think they did it?"

"Who knows why Cambridge students do anything?"

"It seems uncivilized of them. What are your thoughts?"

"In my opinion, the Cambridge students are doing what Cambridge students always do, that is, act uncivilized. Why would we expect any different behavior here today?"

"That seems rather harsh."

"Think of why we are here today. That is the end of questions."

I turned to leave and there was one last shouted question.

"Will the queen be awarding you a new honor?"

"I believe so, the Order of the Pie. The holders will wear a cream pie on a chain around their necks. A silly question gets a silly answer."

On the ride back to the palace the queen told me, "I ought to create the Order of the Pie just for spite. I find those types of actions despicable."

"I agree, but we can't give them credence. Mockery is better."

"It is, though it could all be solved by a few judicious beheadings."

I think that is the only time I ever heard the queen kid on the square.

The next day back at Oxford, I was cheered in the streets. I had given a blow in the eternal war between the two schools.

My escorts were on the lookout for squads of Cambridge pie throwers.

Even in class, the dons gave me special recognition. I was the man of the hour. Every class I went to had banana cream pies to share. I got very tired of them after the first three slices.

Not so tired, though, that I didn't box up my slices and carry them to my garage for later. When I got back to The Meadows, you would never guess what was waiting for me.

A banana cream pie from the Cambridge baker. It seems his business was booming. It gave me visions of the horde approaching the castle, bearing no torches or pitchforks, just pies. I expected I would dream about them that night.

I had to give a blow-by-blow description of the event to Grandmum and Mr. Hamilton. They were sitting together having tea while I told of my grand adventure. They had read about it in the *Daily Mail*. The newspaper was very unkind to the students. It appeared the lord mayor's illness was well-known and there was no good reason for such disrespect.

The last line in the story said a lot. "They are Cambridge students. What can you expect?"

I think that the KGB and Stasi had a new partner in their mission to destroy me.

I also had some fences to mend, as there were a lot of powerful Cambridge graduates who I would have to do business with. But that was a problem for another day.

Chapter 18

The rest of the weekend was quiet. Nina was still getting caught up on her schoolwork. She had lost a lot of class time recently to modeling work. Fortunately, her school loved the publicity they were getting so were willing to work with her.

I spent my weekend running and riding the horse my parents had bought me. While a good horse, he wasn't George.

I also helped out at the dig site. The only work I could do there was considered general labor. It still felt good to contribute, even if it was only driving a stake to outline a building.

There was a minor bit of excitement when another basement was found. This time it was under what was thought to be a temple to Mars, the Roman god of war.

There were spears, shields, swords, and pieces of armor. The only problem was that were they cheaply made and would not have held up in a real fight.

The interns argued about what they could have been. To me who had worked in the movies, it was obvious.

"They are props."

Once I said that, all was clear. The Roman priest would present plays about their gods to show how powerful they were. While these items were mentioned in books of the time, none had ever been found. This was another first for the site.

I had another question.

"What happened to all the stone parts of the buildings above ground?"

It was explained to me that a survey was being taken of all older buildings in the area. It was typical practice to use an old ruin like this as a quarry.

It looked like a lot of local homeowners would have some bragging rights about their buildings in the days to come.

On Sunday afternoon I received a phone call from Mr. Norman. It seems the guy who tried to kill me at the press conference had East German connections. They couldn't tie him directly to the Stasi, but it was beginning to look like they weren't done with me.

I had a choice, go into hiding, or not let the fear of them rule me. Use common sense and try to be aware of my surroundings at all times, but not cower and hide.

On Monday I gathered up all my school notes and extra books to take to Pinewood with me. It was the first week of shooting for the new movie, *Edgware*.

A good part of the week would be doing lighting checks, wardrobe checks, and script walkthroughs.

It was almost humdrum to me; I had been through the process enough times, and there were no surprises.

I had ample time for my schoolwork. I had my house trailer set up. I even requested a Xerox machine and typewriter, which were delivered with no argument.

I made sure to be polite and work with everyone on the set, even the one old bugger who worked lighting. He was a dyed-in-the-wool communist but took pride in his work.

He never missed a chance to talk about me as a capitalist pig, but he always had my lighting correct and professional. As my dad had told me a long time ago, you don't have to like everyone you work with.

I think I earned his respect when after referring to me as a capitalist pig right next to me, I turned and stated that he was a fellow traveler who would be allowed to starve to death when the first five-year plan failed.

That took him back for a moment.

"You may have the right of that, you know."

"Yeah, and people could starve if we pigs are allowed to keep all of the money."

That put us in the position of having different ideologies while recognizing that our own had weaknesses.

When we got to the final scene of the walkthrough there was one curve thrown at the director that took him aback.

Our lead actress stated that she wouldn't be kissing me. She had a boyfriend, and he was the only one she would kiss.

Since they were only doing lighting checks for each camera position, it made no difference who kissed her.

Her boyfriend stood in for me. It became apparent at once that to get the right lighting he needed to stand on a box to replicate my height. The whole crew must have wondered why I was laughing like a loon.

They kept trying to get it right, but his height just made too much difference. The director had me stand in and pretend to kiss her. If I got too close to the pretend kiss, she would shove me away.

That got old fast. She was finally told that she had no choice but to kiss me, as she would have to once the film was rolling.

"Then I quit."

At that, she and her boyfriend left the set to start their new life, anywhere but the movies. She was done.

Now I had a movie but no opposing star. Unlike the live theater, there were no understudies. There were stunt doubles. Her stunt double was a pleasant woman of about the same build, but frankly, she was far from the attractive woman needed for the movie.

I was glad she had come to terms with that as she did stand in for the lighting checks. She also was a very enthusiastic kisser. She told me she wasn't going to pass up her chance to make out with a star.

That stroked my ego until I figured out that she didn't care which star, it could have been Francis the Talking Mule for all she cared. Talk about a letdown.

After the day's work, I had a choice: I could drive an hour back home, or sleep in the trailer. I chose the drive. I was glad I did.

As I was getting into my Aston Martin, I heard my name called. It was Bond, James Bond, or as he was known, Sean Connery.

He wanted a good look at my car to see how a production model differed from his movie car. Other than no revolving number plates, an oil slick, smoke screen, machine guns, rear bulletproof screen, tire slasher, or the all-important ejector seat, it was identical.

He laughed and told me, "Well, since it doesn't have those features, I'm not interested."

In turn, I told him, "But it would be a great bird magnet for you."

That gave us both a laugh. The last thing Sean Connery needed was a car to attract women. We shook hands and parted. He to some mysterious meeting, and me for a night's sleep.

I made up the mysterious meeting. Odds are it was a late dinner by the telly. Ah, who am I kidding?

On the drive home, I got behind a lorry that was driving slowly. As it got just past an intersection the driver jammed on his brakes. At the same time, another large lorry came straight at me from the side street.

This is where Aston Martin paid for itself with its responsive handling. I had braked for the lorry in front of me when I saw another lorry coming from the side. I hit the gas and veered right onto a narrow sidewalk. Fortunately, it was late enough the stores were closed so there was no foot traffic.

Once I was safely out of sight of the lorry coming from the side, I hit the brakes again, coming to a dead stop. While I did this, the two trucks kept going.

I sat there and shook for a minute, an accident? I didn't think so. Maybe it was time to send another message.

The question was what message and to whom?

After settling down, I drove home. The next morning before heading back to the studio, I called Mr. Norman and shared my fears. He agreed it didn't look good and that he would ask some questions.

In the meantime, he reminded me of some tradecraft that I had gotten lax on. I needed to vary my routes so they couldn't set up simple traps.

I felt like an idiot as I got out a book of maps and plotted several different routes I could take. I also packed a bag so I could stay at the studio overnight.

I let Grandmum know that I may stay over some nights, but not about what I thought of as attempts on my life.

I did call Mum and let her know that I might need to borrow the sterling, as I might have to set a table. She understood my message and told me she would explore what was going on.

The trip to the studio was uneventful. The only excitement for the day was when my communist lighting friend told me that I was okay for a capitalist pig. That was after holding a lighting stand for him.

I spent the night in the trailer.

Chapter 19

I thought long and hard about the Soviets and East Germans. If one were keeping score, I was far ahead. That pun wasn't intended. Some memories are too gruesome to joke about.

Recently, they had tried to kill me twice. I couldn't prove it in a court of law. I didn't have to.

Since there had been no deaths in the last two attempts, and it was only me involved, no lethal retaliation was warranted. At the same time, I wanted them to not doubt that I was unhappy with the state of affairs.

I decided a nice fire would be the answer. I would burn the Soviet Embassy's garage to the ground, along with their vehicles.

I thought about obtaining an alibi but decided that I would have no alibi. Even though I would have a motive, method, and no alibi, they wouldn't be able to prove in an English court of law that I did it.

I wanted them to know it was me, but not be caught and convicted in a British court. The trick would be to not get caught. I wouldn't be convicted on the circumstantial evidence because the Soviet ambassador couldn't stand up and say my motive was revenge for their attempts to kill me.

As far as my weapon of choice, it would be a longbow with fire arrows. Of course, they might search The Meadows or my garage, even the suite at the Plaza.

The one place they wouldn't even think of searching was the townhouse that Queen Elizabeth had awarded to me and my family for my saving her life.

We had never used it since it had been awarded. No good reason at the time, but now it worked out.

I don't claim to be very smart but when I obtained my longbow and war arrows for my excursion into East Germany, I had ordered five longbows and many arrows, war, target, and fire. A good Boy Scout is prepared.

I had them delivered to the palace, and then Mr. Norman had them taken to the townhouse, which stood empty.

It was turning out to be more useful than the tax exemption the Crown had given me for saving the queen. I didn't have to pay any taxes on money earned in the UK. The only problem was that all my earnings so far had been in the US.

My current movie work would change that, but frankly, it would be a drop in the bucket.

I asked Mr. Norman to have a bow and fire arrows delivered to my garage in Oxford. On Thursday when they were delivered, I borrowed Grandmum's Bentley and took them into town.

On Tuesday and Wednesday, I scouted the embassy while confirming everything on a map.

There was a park about four hundred yards from the Soviet Embassy. It even had a hill on the embassy side of the park. I think it must have been a druid ring at one time as the top of the hill was surrounded by trees, but was open in the center.

I parked the Bentley in a legal spot and openly carried my weapons to the top of the hill. I had a jar of nail polish remover which was mostly acetone. I put a rag in a small bucket and poured the acetone over it.

It would make a nice slow-burning fire. Thank you, Boy-Scout stamp collecting.

Right behind the war point, the fire arrows had a six-inch sponge-like material that would burn hot. If the arrows penetrated the surface of the garage roof, the century-old wood underneath would burn.

Half a dozen of these burning on the roof would ensure the destruction of the garage. The nice thing is that the guard posts were all at the front entrances, so the fire would get a good start before being noticed.

I love it when a plan works.

In a minute, the garage was engulfed in flames. It was burning fast and furious and had no chance of being put out before the structure was lost, along with the fleet of cars inside.

I almost made a miscalculation as two people came running out of the garage in their nightclothes. Mechanics or chauffeurs slept there. Oh well, no harm, no foul.

I would have loved to stick around and see it burn to the ground but that conflicted with my goal of not getting caught.

I sedately drove back to The Meadows. I stopped at a small pond on the way and destroyed the bow and leftover arrows with metal shears and dropped them in the water.

I made a mental note to keep track of my weapon supply.

The next morning the news was all about the fire. The London Fire Brigade managed to keep the fire from spreading, but the garage and five limousines had been burnt to a crisp. Such a shame. I wondered if they had insurance, and would the insurance company have honored it. The press was reporting that it was a deliberate attack.

They knew this because somebody managed to get a picture of the roof before the arrows were all burnt. I must say, it was a nice pattern.

On Friday morning I had a message from the Soviet ambassador. Would I stop by at my convenience? I told the caller that I would be there after lunch.

When I got to the front of the Soviet Embassy, I identified myself to the guards. Standing a few feet away was the usual British policeman. I told the guards that the ambassador had asked me to come in, but I wasn't going to step foot on Soviet soil.

They shrugged; it wasn't their problem. I stood there a while and soon a man in a suit showed up. They were watching from the inside.

He asked the guards what was going on. He then asked me for some identification. I gave him a Sir Richard Jackson card. He left and the next thing I knew the Soviet ambassador came to the front gate.

To show how serious I thought this all was, I wore dungarees and a long-sleeved shirt under my leather jacket. For fun, I even wore my fedora.

Needless to say, the ambassador was not very cheerful. He regretfully informed me that a high-level East German Stasi agent had a heart attack last night. He felt that I should not live in fear for my life any longer.

I thanked him and left. What hypocrites he and I were. I didn't believe I was safe for one second, and neither did he.

Probably the only reason the Stasi guy had a heart attack was that he had failed his mission. That is assuming anyone died for any reason. It was telling that I wasn't given the name of the guy who had a heart attack.

My not going into the embassy was a last-second impulse. I had learned to listen to these impulses. Once I walked in there, I might never have come back out.

Back at The Meadows, I called Mum and then Mr. Norman. They both agreed that I should never enter a Soviet Embassy again unless under duress.

They would check through their channels to see if anyone had died. While they did that, I gave some thought as to how I could send a stronger message if needed, maybe a flaming arrow into Lenin's Tomb.

There were the little problems of getting into Russia, firing the arrow, and then getting out of the country without getting caught.

Maybe that wasn't such a good idea after all.

I went home and joined David out at the dig site. I bet it was easier in the Roman days. Send out a legion and problem solved.

Of course, I was standing amidst evidence that it didn't always go as intended. I was shown all the floor tiles that had been uncovered. The Romans loved their mosaics.

The way David raved, you would think they were the greatest thing in the world. To me, they looked like pretty pictures. Well, most of them were pretty, but some of them were ugly, and some seemed to have no point about them at all.

Maybe this was why I wasn't an archaeology student.

I even asked him what was so great about them. After looking at me like I had lost my mind, he explained that each mosaic was based on a story or legend. This find had the most mosaics ever found in one place.

By knowing the stories and legends of the community, they knew more about the beliefs and driving forces of that community.

I asked him if they had found one of them with the story of the Chuckle Lion on them. With a puzzled look, he told me he had never heard of that one.

Being the helpful guy that I am, I told him the story. In the end, he didn't say anything. He just shook his head and walked away.

I was still glad I didn't elect to study archaeology. Besides it being a boring subject, archaeologists had no sense of humor.

Chapter 20

I spent the next week attending lectures and cleaning up a few loose ends. On Wednesday, Prince Charles's school class toured the Roman ruins. One of the chaperones was the queen.

Of course, I was there for that. The kids were so excited about the venture and what they saw, in a weak moment I stated that all the school children of Great Britain should have the same opportunity.

I thought David was going to have a stroke on the spot.

"Steady, old boy, what I'm thinking is that we build a replica of the ruins nearby."

"That would cost a bloody fortune."

I didn't say anything just stared at him.

"Oh, you have a couple of bloody fortunes, don't you?"

"I do, and I'm also looking at the curator of the project."

"How will I find the time?"

I named a goodly sum that stopped him in his tracks.

"I will make the time. How fast do you want this done?

"The question is whether I want quality, cost, or speed. You can't have all three, I choose quality and speed. I will have Jim Williamson set up accounts while you find a firm that can handle the work."

The queen who had been standing there during this conversation asked:

"Are you certain you do not want a job in one of my ministries? We could use someone who can make things happen."

"You would have to have me beheaded within two weeks of my taking the job."

"Regrettably so, but it would be an interesting two weeks."

"The regrets are mine, Your Majesty, but I'm attached to this head and would like for it to remain so."

She shook her head, "The younger generation knows nothing about sacrifice."

I had no idea how to react to this, if she thinks I'm volunteering to get the chop she is crazy.

"I don't know what to say, Your Majesty, except that I'm at your service as always."

"That's the spirit, Rick, I told your Mum I could get you to agree to go to the block for me. She bet I couldn't do it."

Now I'm in big trouble. I've caused Mum to lose a bet.

"I hope it wasn't a big bet."

"It was just a shilling."

I'm dead meat. Mum only bets a shilling if she thinks she has a lock.

"Seriously, Rick, this is a good thing you are doing here. At the rate you are going a baronetcy may be in your future."

I didn't know what to say. The Queen of England was playing mind games with me? She kept a serious look for a moment then laughed that small laugh of hers.

"Rick, you are so easy."

At that, she winked at me. The Queen of England winked at me! I chose to ignore this moment of *lese majeste* practiced by Her Majesty.

After that, the royal entourage retired, or as I put it, skedaddled back to the palace.

David and I spent some time talking about re-creating the ruins on a plot of land outside of the Roman compound. We would try to make it self-sustaining by charging an admissions fee and having sales outlets on the property such as souvenirs and food.

We wondered who we could get to build and run the property. I had a bright idea. The theme park people would be perfect for this job. They had created places like Disneyland and Knotts Berry Farm and put together teams to do so. I wondered if any had teams that were available now.

When I got back to The Meadows, I called Dad at his office and explained what I needed. He had met one group several times, so he volunteered to call them.

At school the next day, disaster struck. The enemy got through my defenses and cream-pied me. They had a group create a diversion by starting a fight. While my escorts and I gawked, I got pied. They even had a photographer taking pictures of the event.

What the Cambridge pie team hadn't considered was Oxford's aversion to them. They were smothered in students. The camera and film were confiscated, and all were held by the police.

A young lady sacrificed her scarf to clean me up. Within seconds you couldn't tell anything happened. When the police showed up, they questioned everyone present about the incident.

One thing that puzzled them was that the eight students from Cambridge were standing there in their underwear. No one from Oxford had seen a thing.

The Cambridge students told their side of the story, but as one bobbie put it, "You know how they lie about everything."

Yay for the home team.

That night at the pub my gang was talking about getting a revenge team together, but I discouraged that. We didn't need the grief and besides with the talk going around campus, there would be plenty of other groups picking up our slack.

This would be known as the Year of the Great Pie War.

I was contacted by one of the tabloid reporters back in the US who wanted my side of the pie war story. I gave him a very condensed version. The war wasn't about me, other than that I interfered with their attempt on the queen and the Lord Mayor of London.

I told him about Elizabeth's joking comment on the Order of the Pie. We both agreed it was silly. This didn't prevent him from reporting it as a fact that I would be receiving the award.

The next day I had to go back to Pinewood to see how the movie *Edgware* was going. We had lost the lead actress and they were searching for a new one.

They had chosen an actress I had never met, Diana Rigg. She was very good-looking and an amazing person with a good sense of humor. We hit it off the moment we were introduced.

It was a short afternoon, so the entire cast had decided to go to a local pub. I was staying the night as part of my new security routine, so it worked for me.

Diana was going to ride with me. Well, it turned out I was going to ride with her. When we got to the Aston Martin, she held out her hand for the keys. Under her spell, I handed them to her.

I thought I knew how to drive. She had the car screaming through its gears out of the lot. Her shifting was as smooth as glass. While doing this she was talking a mile a minute about how the car handled.

We came to a stop sign where we had to turn right. She performed a power slide around the corner never letting up on the gas.

If there had been any police around, we would have been in jail. I asked her where she had learned to drive like this. She told me about a defensive driving course up in Scotland.

I decided right then and there I needed to attend that course. It would be fun and who knows, I might need it one of these days.

It was a blast eating at the pub with the group. After drinking too many beers I got involved in a sing-along. After a lot of prompting, I performed all three of my songs.

I was roundly booed by my audience which only proved that they were discerning. Since they booed everyone else it didn't hurt my feelings.

At the end of the evening, Diana told me she would see me on the set tomorrow and took off in my car, leaving me to find a ride back to the studio.

The next day I was lurking in the parking lot to see if she had damaged my car or was even planning on returning it. She brought it back and it was obvious that she had it washed and waxed. She also let me know she had put petrol in the tank.

My kind of girl. It's a shame she was six years older than me. Oops, what about Nina?

Diana was a quick study on her lines, so we were back up to speed on the movie. She brought her dry wit to the set and added some cheeky comments to the script.

She was going to spend the next two days with the wardrobe department and then we would start shooting.

The day was upbeat all around. The good feelings engendered by the pub visit last night continued. One thing was made very clear to me; I wouldn't be doing any singing in this movie. I was to consider not even singing in the shower at home.

That evening I drove back to Oxford using a new route. It was scenic and only took ten minutes longer. When I got home Grandmum showed me an article on the Great Pie War.

Things were getting messy in Cambridge. A certain baker had put on a night shift baking cream pies. He must have been making a fortune.

I made a vow to stay clear of the mess.

Chapter 21

On Monday I went to my London office to review my Spanish holdings. The audit team had preliminary findings on the ranch's status. While not good, it wasn't as bad as I thought it would be.

It was going to cost several million dollars to bring the operation into A-one condition, but it would be spread out over two years. During that time, the ranch would have income, so only a million and a half of new money would be required.

Considering the damage that could have been done, I was getting off lightly. More importantly, the lives of those living there would improve dramatically over the next two years.

Amongst the many invoices and receipts were several letters. One of them was from the local bishop of the Catholic Church in Spain. It was a request for me to visit him the next time I was in Spain. As I was spending money on the ranch's school, he wanted to discuss how I could help other schools in his diocese.

Mum had called that one. I wasn't opposed to helping where I could, but I also recognized a bottomless pit when I saw it. Maybe a portion of the ranch's profits could be dedicated to local schools. It would have to be tightly controlled as money like that was very fungible.

If I were going to do that, I wouldn't want to limit it to the Catholic Church schools. Being a milch cow for them wasn't in my plans.

I had no idea what schooling was like in Spain. This would take some careful investigation before I committed to anything.

It was getting closer to term break and my trip to the various offices of Jackson Enterprises. If nothing else, I was looking forward to having the ribbon cutting for the new R&D center.

The center had been finished for months and in operation. Due to my schedule, the grand opening kept being put off.

I contacted the firm building the components to fit in a 707. They were on schedule, and I was welcome to stop by anytime. They were down to the last fittings.

Since I was clearing up old business, I gave some thought to the Ferrari in my garage in Oxford. I preferred to drive my Aston Martin. I was going to have pictures taken of the refurbished car with a pretty girl on the bonnet and send it to the Saudi prince.

Enough time had passed that I didn't care that much, so I decided to let the issue slide. Maybe this was a sign of maturity.

Since I wasn't driving the car, I should either find another use for it or sell it. After some thought, I decided to have it shipped to Jackson House in the US.

If nothing else, it could sit in the garage and torment Denny who was getting closer to the driving age. Not so mature after all.

There was another mystery I had to clear up. What did Mum do in Morocco during the War, which was a sore point with Dad, and how did she get there in the first place?

I guessed I could ask her when Dad wasn't around, but I suspected I wouldn't get much of an answer. I wondered if Grandmum knew anything.

Something I had been putting off was coming around. It was the end-of-term exams next week. I hadn't done any revising, or studying, as we call it in the States.

All the courses I had taken this term were from dons who stuck to their course notes. I had been keeping up with the notes at odd times this term. While I had cut a lot of classes, I had kept up with the reading and coursework.

At this level of schooling there seldom was any work to turn in, just reading and understanding. One resource I had was my military escorts from when I did attend lectures. If I had any questions about the materials, I could ask them on the way to the lecture hall.

Extremely nice to have my tutors available on an as-needed basis.

It still left me with the need to go over all the material before next week's exams. The weather forecast for the next week was rain, rain, and then more rain.

A storm was moving into the area and was going to stall. Depending on how long it lasted there could be severe flooding in the area.

It would be a good time to stay in the library at The Meadows and study. I had talked to David and they were buttoning up the dig and going to indoor work for the next week.

I did stick to my revisions for the next two days, but I was getting cabin fever. I wanted out. The rain had been coming down heavily as forecast and the local streams were all at flood stage or above.

People were encouraged to stay at home or only drive on the major roadways with good bridges. This meant I had to get out and drive on a back road.

Not really, I'm not that dumb. I started on a major road intending to drive down to Pinewood Studios to see what was going on. At the first large intersection, there was an accident involving two articulated lorries. Semi-trucks to the Americans.

The police were directing traffic to a side road. We were to follow it for four miles or so and then get onto our original highway.

Traffic was bumper to bumper at about two miles per hour. I thought people were supposed to stay at home. What are they thinking?

Needless to say, I wanted out of that line of traffic. When we finally reached the next interchange to merge back onto the highway, I could see that it was also backed up for miles.

Given a choice of getting back into that mess or following the minor road which had no traffic going forward, I stayed with the minor.

That worked well for the next few miles. I was able to get up to fifty miles an hour. It felt like I was flying.

That worked well until I came to a T-intersection. I turned right as that seemed to go in the direction I needed. About a quarter-mile along the road narrowed to almost a track. The road had high banks on either side and was too narrow for me to turn around.

I would have to back up to get off this section of the highway. I decided to keep going hoping to find a spot wide enough to turn around.

The road kept deteriorating until it was nothing but a muddy track. This was a farm road, not a motorway. The Aston Martin wasn't designed for this type of driving, but it struggled on.

I hoped that I wouldn't get bogged down in the mud. It would be a long walk out of here in the rain.

Just as I thought I was in a funnel leading to hell, the banks dropped down and the road widened out. Without slowing down I turned and headed back out the way I had come.

Fingers crossed, I kept a steady five miles an hour through the muddy lane. I had to laugh at myself. I was here because I didn't want to go five miles per hour on a firm motorway.

Going back, I saw a side road I had missed going down. It was at an extreme Y to the track I was on. I wouldn't have been able to turn onto it going down. This way it was an easy turn onto the solid pavement.

The drive had been so tense that I slowed the car to a stop and just sat there for a few minutes to catch my breath. The rain was coming down so heavily now that my headlamps and windscreen wipers barely allowed me to see twenty feet ahead.

At this point, I decided that cabin fever was a good thing and that I needed to get home and enjoy it. I restarted my car going straight forward.

I had no desire to get back on that muddy track and I couldn't have turned in the correct direction anyway. I had to go slow but it was almost a pleasure since I was on solid pavement.

As I came around a bend in the road there was a truck blocking the way. It was the type that telephone company linemen used.

There was no way to pass them, so I coasted to a stop and got out. There was a bridge over a fast-running overflowing stream. It now could be called a river, an angry river.

Instead of a clear placid current, it was a raging dirty yellow. Two men were standing on the center of the bridge looking downstream.

Chapter 22

As I approached the two middle-aged gentlemen, they appeared to be very agitated.

"What's going on here?"

They turned to me.

"Look," one said as he pointed downstream.

It took a moment for me to realize what I was looking at. There was a small island in the center of the stream. On that island were six children.

My first thought was that they would be very hungry by the time the water went down, though a boat would get to them soon.

You could tell the children, about nine to ten years old, were very distressed. About that time a large chunk of the island washed away.

There would be no time for a boat to be brought in before the island washed away with the children drowning.

"We have to get them off there."

"We were just trying to figure out how to do that. We have a lot of equipment in the truck. We just haven't figured out how to get it there, set it up, and bring the children out."

I addressed the man who appeared the senior or leader, K. Tregoning from the name tag on his shirt.

"I mean no disrespect Mr. Tregoning, but this is a young man's job. I will have to go down there."

"Call me Ken and I have to disagree with you. I am fit and mature; I can do a better job."

His workmate Joe tapped his ample belly.

"Too many good meals and too many years. I doubt I would last a minute down there."

Ken said, "I think it is best if I go."

Joe started to say, "But, Ken."

Ken continued, "This is a full-grown man's job."

Again, Joe tried to say something but got cut off by Ken.

"Kid, your heart is in the right place, but I'm doing this."

Joe finally had it, "Ken, you can't swim!"

That settled that. I was the one to go.

"Have you guys any thoughts on how we can get them out of there?"

"Yes, if we can get it set up. Our truck is set up to erect telephone poles and string wire."

He proceeded to show me the large tripod which could be erected at the back of the truck. It was used to raise and set in place telephone poles.

Behind the truck was an attached wagon with a huge spool of telephone wire. It had a powerful attachment to reel in or unwind the wire.

"If we can get another tripod set up on that little island, we can reel the children up using a boson's chair. I can still set one up from my Navy days."

"What can we use for a tripod down there?" I asked.

Ken showed me three telescoping rods.

"We use this to reach high wires. They extend to twelve feet long so you can bury five feet or so and have a seven-foot-tall tripod. Using one of these pulleys and the power attachment on the wire reel and Bob's your uncle."

"I can see getting the stuff down there and set up, but how will we reel the wire back in?"

"When the tripod is set up and the first kid is being reeled in, you will have to act as a brake by wrapping the wire around your back like in mountain climbing.

"We will unwind more than twice the distance so that you can hand the loose end to the kid, and we will reel it in. From there, we have an endless pulley to bring the children and you back up."

While we were having this conversation, the children down below were yelling and screaming to be rescued. In the meantime, another chunk of the island washed away.

I went back to my auto and put my wallet, watch, keys, and other stuff inside. I also removed my leather jacket and fedora along with my half-boots.

After more conversation, a line was tied to my ankle. The other end would be used to pull the heavier telephone line to me.

All this took time. We had been planning and getting the stuff together for almost half an hour. During this time, the rain kept pouring down. The stream was really raging now.

Other vehicles had arrived, but no one approached to help. They seemed to be ghouls at a tragedy. One man approached us with a microphone in hand. That was when I realized there was a mobile TV truck present.

The jerk asked how we felt about this. Ken had the best answer when he told the reporter to, "Bugger off."

Since I was ready to go, I ignored this and stood on the bridge rail in the center of the bridge. This was to be a leap of faith as trees were randomly washed downstream. These were full-grown trees, not saplings.

One had hung up on the downstream side of the island out of the way. I just had to hope one wouldn't come through as I jumped.

Rather than overthink this I did a lifeguard jump into the water. As soon as I hit the water it was like a giant hand had grabbed me and shoved me forward. Fortunately, the lifeguard jump technique kept me from going under. This entailed me spreading my arms and legs wide while hitting the water.

I had no control of my direction in the water. I planned to jump into the water and be swept to the center of the island. Instead, it rushed me along the right side of the island. I was going to be rushed past the island.

I was saved by the tree which had hung up on the other end of the island. The water took me directly into its branches. I clung to them as I crawled to shore.

I was surrounded by six children around eight to ten years of age. They grabbed me and hung on. I thought at first they were trying to pull me out of the water, then realized they were clinging to me for safety.

I herded them to the middle of the island and told them I was there to get them off but had to set some equipment up.

The line on my ankle was still there so I undid it. Ken and his coworker Joe had tied the heavier telephone wire to the other end. They started the power reel, and I guided it to me with the lighter line.

The three telescoping poles, a quickly rigged boson's chair, and the pulley had been tied together with a loop around the telephone wire. This allowed them to slide it down to me along the wire.

It did get hung up about halfway, but since the reel was being unwound towards me, I was able to pull it in.

From there it was a simple matter of extending the poles and pushing them into the soft soil. If it had been bedrock, the plan would have failed.

I tied the tripod top together using the light line. I ran the telephone cable through the pulley and attached the boson's chair to the cable using a surgeon's knot.

Putting a little girl in the chair, I wrapped the end of the cable around my back like a mountain climber. When I was ready, I waved at Ken, and he started the reverse reel.

It worked like a charm. Little Barbara was hoisted to safety. The next four children were just as easy. I was ready to lift Billy, the last boy and the biggest of the lot, into the seat. He was last he told me because it had been his idea to go rafting.

I bet he was going to get what for when he got home, but that wasn't my concern. What was my concern was that a good half of the island chose that moment to wash away.

Ken was very alert and was reeling Billie in. As soon as Billie was over the edge of the bridge, I grabbed the still-reeling cable and started my trip to safety.

I had to hope the tripod would stand long enough for me to get to the bridge. It was not to be. I was halfway back when I felt the cable behind me go slack.

I hit the water with a splash, no lifeguard jumps this time. I went under. Hanging on for dear life, the cable reel brought me out of the water just in time for a tree to come downstream and hit me.

How I hung on I don't know. From the force of the blow, something had to be broken. I remember clearing the edge of the bridge and that was it.

What I found out later was that Ken and Joe were the only ones on the bridge. The water was over the top of the pavement. As soon as I was above the railing, they grabbed me and went for dry ground.

They made it just as the bridge gave way, taking it and their truck downstream. I was only unconscious for a few minutes. I came to just in time to see a microphone thrust into my face.

I love the press. I also learned a few new terms that Ken had picked up in the Navy. I didn't know that some baboons had striped, well certain portions of their anatomy, and that the stripes were purple.

Amazing.

An ambulance was on standby. The children had been all examined and were in the custody of their parents. They approached me presumably to thank me. I tried to rise to greet them and blacked out again.

Chapter 23

I woke up as they were loading me in the ambulance. My left arm and shoulder were a sheet of pain. I had never felt anything like it in my life. I wondered if I would lose the arm.

The medical technician who was loading me into the ambulance told me I was lucky. I only had a dislocated shoulder and perhaps a greenstick fracture of my ulna, but only an X-ray would tell. No big deal.

Not to him maybe, but to me, it was the real deal.

I knew that a dislocated shoulder was painful, and it would hurt as they reset it, but the pain would be relieved quickly.

A reporter tried to climb into the back of the ambulance to ask questions, but Ken Tregoning grabbed him from behind and set him down in the mud. Way to go Ken!

It only took half an hour to get to the hospital hitting every bump in the road along the way. I had to grit my teeth to keep from yelling. It hurt and this clown thought it was no big deal!

I started to think about that and realized that if this was no big deal then real pain must be incredible.

I asked him about it. He told me that he had been in the Medical Corps during the war and that he had seen and heard some things that he still dreamed about.

That made me think of machine-gun bullets hitting a landing craft ramp. I decided right then and there to stop being a wimp about my injuries and bear up. That lasted for a minute, but then I had to wince. Dang, it hurt!

Fortunately, we arrived at the hospital within fifteen minutes. I was wheeled into the emergency room where the doctor on duty ordered x-rays. They handled me like fine China but were still jostling me enough that my shoulder hurt like crazy.

I couldn't feel my arm. I had heard that the brain could only handle one pain at a time so the worst would always register.

After the x-rays which confirmed a fracture, I was given a shot of morphine. I had never had anything like it in my life. I was in la-la land. It still hurt but I didn't care.

The doctor put my dislocated shoulder back into place. That hurt for a few seconds, really really hurt. Before I could cry out the pain eased. Now I could feel my arm throbbing.

From a distance, I could hear the doctor saying that I needed a plaster cast on my arm. There was nothing else they could do but let it heal. The same for my shoulder.

At that point, I drifted off to sleep. I awoke in a hospital bed with my Grandmum sleeping in a chair beside it.

Looking out the window I saw that it was dark outside. I wondered how long I had been here. It didn't matter as I went right back to sleep.

The next thing I knew it was, "Wakey, wakey, time to check on you."

This was from a nurse dressed in white with a grey apron and her funny-looking cap. Grandmum was there and awake.

My mouth was dry as all get out, so I asked for water. The nurse had a glass of iced water ready for me. I sipped some from a straw.

Grandmum asked me how I felt.

"Terrible, how are the children?"

"They are all safe and sound, well except for the eldest, Billy. He won't be sitting down for a while."

I had to chuckle at that. He certainly deserved it.

In the meantime, the nurse had started to take my blood pressure and thrust a thermometer into my mouth. Whatever the readings were she seemed satisfied, as she wrote them down on a chart that was hung at the foot of my bed.

"How does your shoulder feel, sir Richard?"

"Very sore."

"That is to be expected, try to move it gently for a few days. After that, you will need to work it back to your full range of motion."

"Will I be able to play the violin?"

"That one was old when I was a girl."

Grandmum chimed in, "That was old when Stradivarius was an apprentice."

The nurse told me, "In a few minutes we are taking you down to have a plaster cast put on your arm. Do you have to go to the bathroom?"

All of a sudden, I realized I had to go urgently.

"Yes, I do."

"Let's see if you can walk by yourself."

She hovered while I stood up. I had to stand for a few seconds to make certain my balance was okay. It was.

I was able to get to the small restroom at the corner of my room and do my business without any help.

"Sir Richard, the nurse's aides will be so disappointed. They were all looking forward to helping you."

I groaned at the thought of teenage girls helping me go to the bathroom. It would be so embarrassing. At the same time, maybe one of them would be cute.

I was put in a wheelchair for my trip to the plaster casting room. I didn't know what else to call it. I asked and was told they referred to it as casting.

That caused a disconnect for a moment as I thought of movie casting.

It didn't take very long for the man to wrap my arm. First, he placed what he called a mesh stocking on my arm, and then wrapped it in soft cotton. After that Plaster of Paris was used to make the hard shell.

It didn't take long to set up. I was still told not to stress it for several days as it had to cure. Since the only thing I had to do for the next several days was to revise for my exams, it would be no problem.

Boy, was I wrong.

I did not realize the whole event was on film and shown shortly thereafter on TV. I just thought I was considered a hero before.

The first real inkling I had of that was when what I thought of as a Candy-Striper type started asking me questions. I hadn't paid her any notice when she came into the room.

When she opened her mouth, I realized she was not a fourteen-year-old girl but a thirty-something woman.

I pushed my call button. The nurse who answered it immediately saw the problem and had the disguised reporter escorted from the premises.

After this incident, the hospital administrator came to see me. He asked if I would do a press conference as there were a multitude of reporters trying to get in. The Candy Striper had got the furthest but there had been several other attempts.

I was considering it when my parents showed up. They had flown all night to get here. Once Mum had checked me out to see if the doctors had missed anything, we talked about the news people.

We finally all agreed that I would make a statement, answer a few questions, and claim I was tired. That wouldn't be a falsehood. I was tired from the events of the day already, short as it had been.

The press conference was set up in the hospital dining room. It was the only room that was large enough, and it was full.

A stage with a low podium and a microphone was set up. When I was wheeled in a side door pandemonium let loose. Questions were shouted left and right.

I had been this route before so let them keep at it for a while. When they showed signs of settling down, I read my statement, which was a bald recounting of the facts.

I also let them know, yes, I was scared; and yes, I knew that I might die but the children's lives were important. No, I wasn't a hero for jumping into the river, anyone would have done that.

Of course, they wouldn't report it that way, but I had to try. I then opened it up for questions. I answered five inane ones and then pled tiredness, which was true. I don't know where my energy had gone.

I was wheeled back to my room where I collapsed back into bed and promptly fell asleep.

When I woke, Dad was sitting there. He, Mum, and Grandmum were taking turns. He told me, congratulations. You made the Fox Movietone news and are being seen in theaters worldwide.

Just what I needed. It was early evening and I had unexpected visitors. The royal family had come to see me.

Charles and Ann wanted to sign my cast. I even got an ER. Philip went the whole hog, titles, and all. That broke the ice for the next couple of days, and everyone wanted to sign it.

The doctor had told me that it would take six to twelve weeks for both my shoulder and arm to heal. Then I would need some therapy to build the muscle tone back up. I was given a set of exercises that I had to perform.

I was only in the hospital for another day and was discharged.

Chapter 24

The doctor had told me that I would heal in about three to four months and that I was not to try to use my arm to lift anything for at least a month.

After that, my body would tell me what was too much. That held for both arm and shoulder.

The whole incident had thrown my plan to spend a couple of days revising for my exams. I now had to face them without doing any review.

I passed all of them. I wouldn't be graduating summa cum laude, but I passed everything. Since I wasn't even certain that I would end up with a degree it didn't matter.

I did have a Message hand-delivered from the palace. I say Message because it was more than a letter. The envelope had the wax royal stamp and gold ribbons.

I used a letter opener to cause as little damage as possible to this formal missive. I bet I would be keeping this for a long time.

It was an invitation to present myself at the palace for investiture as a Baron of the Realm. If I want to accept this honor, please reply with my new name.

I asked the equerry who had delivered the envelope if I had to answer right then. He told me that I had to have an answer by Saturday as that was when I would be at the palace.

It was traditional to use a place name associated with your life. I couldn't see Baron Bellefontaine, Baron California, Baron Ohio, Baron Greys, or Baron Essex for example. Neither Baron Jackson House nor Baron Meadows worked.

It left me in a quandary for several hours until I had an idea. I called Chief Redfoot in the US. He told me it wouldn't be a problem, just the reverse.

So that is how I became Baron Blackhoof.

Lord Richard Jackson, Baron Blackhoof, or better yet, Colonel Lord Jackson, KG, OBE, LOH. No ego here!

The equerry had told me the title was a "life peerage", not inheritable. It was for my rescue of those children.

I think I was getting numb to all the honors I had earned. They just weren't that big of a deal anymore. I still put my pants on, one leg at a time.

There was one sour note in all the proceedings. Pinewood studio executives made an appointment to come to The Meadows. It seems the delay caused by my injured arm and shoulder was too long. They had arranged financing which would run out.

Rather than take a huge loss on the two-movie package they were canceling them now. They would be made someday but not soon.

This irritated me as it had messed up my school schedule, but I understood their position, so we parted on good terms.

I did ask if Diana Rigg was being taken care of as she had turned down a TV show for the movies. It turned out the show was delayed getting into production, so she was back in. It was called the *Revengers* or something like that.

While I attended classes or rammed around The Meadows bored out of my mind, Dad got back to me on my proposed park outside of the Roman ruins.

The theme park people would be delighted to work with us. Their proposal went way beyond what I had envisioned but it sounded like fun.

I had thought of reproductions of the various buildings with walkways between. They also added guides in Roman gear, shops with food, and souvenirs. There would be staged events like chariot races and gladiator fights.

In other words, like a Disneyland in ancient Rome. It sounded like fun to me. It was lucky the estate next to ours was for sale. Dad had already set it in motion to buy the two thousand acres.

Everything would be built away from The Meadows towards the new property.

I about had a fit when I learned there would be gladiator fights between Julius Caesar and Spartacus. Then there would be the Cleopatra Tunnel of Love with Nile barges. To top it all there would be flume rides down a Roman Aqueduct ending in a Roman bath.

After some serious long-distance phone calls, it was agreed that a duplicate of the ruins would be a precise copy with paths. There would be costumed docents to answer questions. There would be no charge for children up to the university level. There would be a nominal fee for adults.

The park portion would be separate and built on the newly purchased grounds. They would rent these from Mum who owned The Meadows. They would be free to commercialize it as they wanted.

They had plans for several rides but none that would require an "E" ticket like at Disneyland, at least yet.

The stores on the ruins side would only sell minor souvenirs and food. The theme park would go full-blown commercial.

Even with this, they didn't see it as an enormous moneymaker. Its main benefit would enable them to keep their design and construction crew together for some big project they were considering for somewhere in the southern United States.

My portion of the ruins would be a tax write off. It made me feel good to be able to further the education of British children in their heritage.

Maybe this was what my future would be like. I still liked the idea of helping get mankind into space but didn't know how to go about it. I had missed a chance offered by President Eisenhower to meet with Werner Von Braun.

As far as I knew, NASA had all efforts in space locked down. It would be nice if commercial ventures could try their hand at it.

All of this was going on while I was still in some pain in my arm and shoulder. It was hard to concentrate when in pain, but I managed through my exams.

Worse than the exams were the phone calls with the theme park crew. All the sweetness and light while wishing on a star were put aside when they got down to business. The KGB was easier to deal with. At least I could kill them if things got out of hand.

While all this was going on, I had an airplane being converted to a flying office and hotel.

In the meantime, I had a trip to the palace to formally become a Baron. I was informed that I needed to visit the London tailor Ede & Ravenscroft. They had been in business since 1689 and were the principal supplier of the robes worn.

The robe is a full-length garment of scarlet wool with a collar of white miniver fur. It is closed at the front with black silk satin ribbon ties. The robe is cut long to have a train, but it is usually hooked up inside the garment.

On the right-hand side of the robe are two miniver bars edged with gold oak-leaf lace. This is the symbol of a baron. A viscountess like Mum would have two and a half bars, earls would have three, and a duke four.

I was gathering quite a wardrobe of fancy dresses. Ede & Ravenscroft would store them for me when I was not appearing officially at the palace or the House of Lords. It made me wonder which outfit would take precedence, the Order of the Garter, or baron. I guessed it would depend on the function.

One thing I knew was my little sister would be honked off. She was addressed in writing as "The Honorable", but not verbally. Either Mum would have to get a promotion for Mary to become a lady or she would have to earn it on her own. I wouldn't bet against it.

One thing that was becoming more obvious all the time was the shift the family was undergoing. We were now emphasizing our

British heritage. I hoped I would never be forced to choose between the two.

My fan mail was reviewed for the attitude of the fans. A summary was then generated by their overall attitude. First of all, they still loved me; many wanted more movies and some more songs. (Some fans are insane).

None of them appeared to have a problem with my dual nationality and thought my being a baron was a neat thing. Of course, these were my fans. I wondered what the United States government thought.

After thinking about it for a while, I decided to ask. Now I could dial the president directly but thought that would be a little presumptuous. I could call Ike, but that would still be a little too close to the seat of power.

In the end, I called another ex-president. Herbert Hoover. The main reason I picked him was I knew where he lived and had his phone number.

I was lucky as he was in and took my call. We spent a little time with him wanting to know all about the Roman ruins. He liked the idea of a duplicate model for the public but was doubtful about the theme park.

He congratulated me on the rescue and being raised to the British peerage. This gave me the perfect opportunity to share my concerns. He laughed and told me that the Kennedys would have no problem as old Joe Kennedy would have given his eyeteeth to be in my position.

The official US position would be to not recognize my honors. Since they wouldn't recognize them, they could take no action based on them.

Chapter 25

My parents were still in England, so they attended the brief ceremony at Buckingham Palace. We arrived separately so I didn't see Mum until we were presented to the queen.

She wore her robes for the occasion. I must say she looked more natural in them than I did. Something was different about her robes, but I couldn't put my finger on it.

Then it hit me, she had three solid bars on her robe, not the two-and-a-half of a viscountess. She had the insignia of an earl or a countess as she was a female.

We both advanced to the queen who read the reason for the peerages. Mine was for extreme heroism, saving lives at the risk of my own.

I had been ordered to wear my Coldstream Colonel's uniform. I was to receive a second Meritorious Service Medal. Dad pinned it on me.

Then I was just about bowled over as the queen announced that I would be inducted into the Royal Victorian Order at the level of Knight Commander. This now makes me Colonel Lord Jackson, KG, OBE, KCVO, LOH.

I had to wonder why this was happening. As soon as I could ask, first my parents, then Mr. Norman, and if they didn't know I would go to the queen.

Mum's new rank was for unspecified acts of bravery during World War II in North Africa. I had to find out what she had been up to!

Well, if nothing else Mary was now Lady Mary. The boys were now Honorable. We had tea and crumpets after the ceremony. How British!

Elizabeth told me she had seen many moments of heroism and had read of many acts of valor. My cold-blooded jumping into that raging stream was one of the more memorable. Most heroes did what they had to do in the heat of the moment.

I tried to ask what Mum had done but the conversation kept being rerouted. Dad seemed as puzzled as I was. I would like to hear the conversation that would occur later.

I just knew it had to involve dead bodies and probably sex. Eww! My Mum would never have sex. Yeah, yeah, I know, I wasn't found under a cabbage.

We all posed for the obligatory pictures. I was reminded that I couldn't be "seated" as a lord until I was twenty-one. From what I knew about the bunch of old fogies in the House of Lords, it would be much older if ever.

A man from the tailors was waiting for us as we left the queen. He took our robes so they wouldn't get messed up. With care, legend had it, one set of robes had lasted a family for over three hundred years.

I was told this by the tailor; I have no idea if it was true. That would make them older than the United States. Would the fabric even hold up? I think it would rot.

I quizzed him on this, the main body of the robe had been replaced twice, it had been restitched four times as the thread had rotted, and the fur four times.

Now I got it, it was like my camping hatchet. It had belonged to my dad's dad. The handle had been replaced three times and the head twice, but the hatchet was over eighty years old.

The way my family lived, I had better budget a new set of robes for next year.

The tailor asked me if they should go ahead with my KCVO robes since they had my measurements. I gave my permission.

Of course, the press was waiting in the palace press room. My mother, the ratfink, removed her robes before going into the room so her new title was not the subject of questions. Mine was.

The first question to me was whether I going to surrender my US citizenship. I gave a simple "No" in reply.

Then it was, "Are you going to join the smart set of young title holders."

I probably shouldn't have said that the smart set of young titleholders was an oxymoron.

One of the reporters, a younger one, asked me what an oxymoron was. I was on a roll, I told him to look in a mirror.

The majority of reporters broke up at that. He would never live this one down.

About that time my Dad took me by the arm and escorted me off the stage while telling the reporters the interview was over. I don't know why he did that. I was having fun and just warming up.

I only whined a little about the fun I was missing. Dad wasn't amused; he used a saying about nobody liking a smart ass.

Quickly changing the subject, I asked why I was getting all these honors. I understood the medal that was within the army regulations. Why the KCVO?

"Rick, the royal family is in the publicity business. They represent the British people and must look good at all times. Right now, you are viewed very favorably worldwide, so the queen wants you to be identified with the royals. Your good standing will reflect on them as a whole.

"That is the royal view; the British government wants to bind you to England because of your money. Going forward your tax bill will be enormous. They would rather you be an English ratepayer than an American one.

"Then back to the queen, she views us as part of her extended family and wants to do well by us."

"Would it have anything to do with Mum and North Africa?"

"It may, but she won't talk about it. I bet it has a lot to do with dead bodies."

At least Dad left out the sex part.

We went to my suite at the Plaza. There we all changed into casual clothing. After ordering lunch, we went down to the lobby where our limo was supposed to be at the curb. It was.

There also was a huge mob of well-wishers, reporters, and Cambridge pie throwers. They missed me and Dad. Mum took one square in the face.

She was not amused. Stepping forward she head-butted her assailant. Blood spurted from his nose. She then kneed him in a most delicate place. As he withered on the ground, she glared at the crowd and yelled, "Next!"

As the police grabbed the guy rolling on the ground the rest melted away. An alert doorman presented her with a towel.

We entered our limo and left London. That was the last of the pie assaults. Every paper in the country agreed that it was beyond the pale to attack Countess Jackson. Besides being beyond the pale, it was utterly stupid as the pie thrower found out.

Later I found that he was sent down from Cambridge for his actions.

Mum fumed a bit on the ride back to Oxford. Her fuming included Composition C and the Cambridge clock tower. Dad and I tried to convince her it was an overreaction.

She agreed and moved on to fires in their libraries. She was confident the fire brigades could save some of the books. Did I ever mention my Mum was the bloodthirsty sort?

She finally settled down. She did tell us the pie tasted good and that we should find out who baked them. I had already found out and shared the name.

She told me she was disappointed in me; a simple firebomb would have cut off the source of pies. It would never occur to a Cambridge student to go to another baker.

Did I ever mention Mum was the bloodthirsty sort? To her, the war was not a game.

When we arrived at home there were reporters at the gates. Since we now had guards full time at The Meadows gates, they didn't bother us. The guards were brought on because of the Roman ruins.

In the early days of the find many people had knocked at the door with explanations of why they should be allowed into the ruins to explore, and of course, keep anything found.

By the time she had showered and changed clothes, she had cooled down. Most people were either hot or cold burners. She was both. She was over the hot stage. She now was planning her long-term revenge plan on the pie throwers.

Dad and I were able to convince her to let it play out in the court of public opinion. She should stand above the fray. Well, that might be difficult as she had entered and ended the fray. That guy would be walking funny for a while.

Later after the newspapers took her side, she agreed to let things go. Several years later I found out that she had acted behind the scene. She bought out the baker and closed the shop down. The baker moved to America and opened a company with Mum's backing. I forget its name, something about Smith's Pies.

Chapter 26

Before Mum bought out the pie company, something else happened. She had decided not to take revenge. I hadn't. I didn't want Mum to have to stoop to this fray. That didn't mean I wouldn't.

I recruited my friends to my plan. I had read in the Oxford paper about an event at Cambridge. It involved the bigwigs. They would be giving a public speech on the court. Since the police would be there and on the lookout for anyone bringing a pie, I came up with another solution.

We would use the new super soaker squirt guns with dye in them. Not the wimpy food coloring but fabric dye. This would teach those Cambridge tabs.

I knew we would probably get caught and I pledged to pay all fines. I couldn't see it being considered anything but a misdemeanor or whatever the British courts call a small crime.

We showed up at the correct time and place. There were plenty of people on the small stage. We had to elbow our way to the front. Per my direction, we pulled our weapons from under our coats and let them fly.

I had one of those frozen moments in time as I pulled the trigger. My target made direct eye contact with me. You could tell he recognized me. His mouth opened to shout "No," but it was too late. I pulled the trigger and dyed the chancellor of Oxford University a brilliant blue.

It was too late to retract my enormous error, so I did the only logical thing. I turned to run. Unfortunately, some misguided Cambridge people didn't want me to leave. I was pulled down and sat upon until the bobbies arrived.

My partners in crime all made it safely away. At least that would save me some money. I was put in a panda car and taken to the local lockup. I was told I was to be remanded to appear before a magistrate in the morning.

They had a separate wing for youthful offenders. It seems that Cambridge students acted up as much as Oxford ones.

I had to go through the picture-taking taking, fingerprinting routine. I suspected my mug shot would be in all the dailies. As Mr. Monroe always said, "Any publicity is good publicity." It would help my bad boy image that was for certain.

I was allowed a phone call. I called The Meadows and asked for Dad. Mum should only know of this after the fact. A jailbreak would be too dramatic.

Dad just laughed at me and told me to spend the night in the pokey. He would pick me up in the morning.

It must have been a party night in Cambridge as I had a lot of company. Drunk, loud, and stinky company.

Between no sleep, no clean clothes, unshaven, and bad breath I was not an impressive sight at the magistrates' hearing.

He must have been in a hurry as he had to go through all the students. When my crime was announced he asked if it was my first offense. When told it was my first, he announced a fine of twenty pounds and hammered his gavel down.

Well worth it!

After retrieving my belongings which had been kept in a plastic bin, I paid my fine and was released.

Dad was out front waiting for me. He had a camera to get some pictures for himself. Mum had decided to stay home, which was probably for the best. Someone had let the press know so they were waiting for me.

Flashbulbs went off and questions were shouted. I held my head high and didn't respond as I walked to the car. None of this hiding under my coat and running for me. I had got revenge for Mum.

When I got home, Mum told me I was a silly berk for not having a getaway plan. I told her I had no intention of getting away.

I knew it would be a minor fine and that I wanted the public to know that Cambridge wouldn't be allowed to attack my mum without repercussions.

Then the other shoe dropped. Mr. Hamilton let me know that a messenger was at the door asking for me. There was a letter that had to be signed as received.

Wondering what this could be about, I took delivery after signing and opened the official letter from Oxford University. It was a summons to appear before a university disciplinary committee.

I hadn't given the school's reaction any thought. This could be bad. I suspected that they would take a dim view of my dying the chancellor a bright blue.

Not that the color mattered. I doubt I could plead anything down because I hadn't used puce.

The school wasn't messing around. I had to appear the following morning. The letter contained the rules of appearance. I was to come alone, no barristers allowed!

So dressed in a suit and tie to put my best foot forward, I went to the appointed time and place. Why did that sound like execution was a possibility?

When I entered the room there were four men and one woman sitting bchind a tablc. I had to stand in front of them. No chair was provided for me. This committee was making a point to those who appeared before it.

First, I was asked to confirm my identity. I announced myself as Sir Richard Jackson, Baron Blackhoof. I had to use every name I had.

It didn't appear to cut any ice. I later learned that the student before me was heir to a dukedom. They had no truck with the privilege of nobles. We had no privileges with them at all.

Once they confirmed I was the person they were looking for, they asked me if I had sprayed the chancellor of Oxford with a purple dye.

I could simply deny the charge since I had sprayed the chancellor with *blue* dye, but there was no point in trying to evade it in general, as there were too many witnesses, and I was still proud of what I had done.

Upon further questioning, I let it be known that the chancellor was not my target. It was an unfortunate event that I squirted him before I recognized him. I had intended to color the Cambridge officials for not cracking down on the pie throwers.

This public service I was trying to provide didn't seem to impress them at all.

They openly discussed my good points. A hero who had just been rewarded by the queen, a fine student, and a strong financial supporter of the school.

As such they would show me leniency.

I heaved a sigh of relief, another twenty-pound fine coming my way. That didn't last long as I learned that I was only being sent down for the rest of the school year.

Oops! That seemed over the top. I asked if there was any way to appeal this sentence. The head of the committee told me there was. I was to provide a written argument to the chancellor as to why my punishment was too severe.

He looked to his right as he said this. This was when I realized there was a spectator over to the side. From his blue-enhanced glare, I realized that I would be wasting my time to appeal. The chancellor did not look happy.

I thought briefly about appealing to the Crown but realized that would be a chump move. I did the crime, now I had to do the time.

I drove slowly home as I tried to think of ways to present it to my parents as a positive. I could have driven to Skarfskerry and back without coming up with a good reason.

I bit the bullet and told them outright what had happened. They didn't react poorly at all. I thought I would have a peal rung over me, instead, it was, "Well you deserve it, what are you going to do with your time?"

That was a good question; what *was* I going to do with my time? I knew that treating it as a vacation wasn't acceptable.

"I have to give it some thought. My business trip starts next week. I would like to spend some time with Nina. Beyond that, I'll have to think about it."

"Rick this is not a big deal. This is the first trouble that you have gotten yourself into. At the same time, you do have a public image to maintain. You need to be seen spending your time productively. You don't want to be seen as an idler."

Now, that I had never been nor will I be.

"I hear you; I will try to find some good works to do. Maybe I could feed some puppies for Mary."

"She is Lady Mary now; forget that at your peril."

I could hear my little sister now. I bet her friend and enemy Patty was gnashing her teeth. Maybe I didn't want to get involved with any of that.

"I have had second thoughts about feeding puppies; maybe I could do a telethon or something.

"Whatever, you need to counterbalance this with something positive."

And so ended the Great Pie War. Nobody wanted to have to face the music for extending it.

Chapter 27

The tabloids had a field day over me being expelled for the rest of the school year. Good boy gone bad was the theme. Then some led with, "Bad boy lives up to expectations."

My fan clubs sent letters by the tens of thousands. I didn't even try to read them. A team at the office sampled them and found that I still had my base's support.

A few even sent pictures where they had dyed their faces blue. I hoped it was food coloring. I had been told the chancellor wouldn't be making any public appearances for over a month.

I felt a little bad about the whole deal. He didn't deserve to be dyed a bright blue. It would be okay if he were a fan of Everton F.C.

I felt even worse about not hitting the Cambridge chancellor. Now he deserved to be dyed blue; he hadn't reined in his pie-throwing thugs.

I had been told that I should show remorse for my actions. The only remorse I felt was for hitting the wrong guy.

I had an appointment at the aircraft leasing firm. They had my jet configured for my business trip. I needed to do a walkthrough and give an okay on the final design.

This was to be my eighteenth birthday present to myself. I had greeting cards from friends and family and a few gag gifts—what could you get someone who had the money to buy almost anything they wanted?

Since I was in England and the family was in the States, it was the lowest-key birthday I ever had. Thinking of the States, I would have to sign up for the draft the next time I went home.

I tried to imagine the scene if they tried to draft a colonel of the British army. I couldn't do it. If I went back to Ohio, I could drink 3.2 beer. Ugh, think I will pass. I now found American beers to be like dishwater, and 3.2 beer must be terrible.

These musings helped my drive to the leasing firm.

I checked in at their front desk. The receptionist gave a little squeak when I announced myself. This could have nothing to do with my picture on the front page of the tabloid she was reading.

At least the managing director didn't have one in his office. I wouldn't have made a bet on the contents of his private loo.

We walked out to the airfield to the plane while he extolled the virtues of what I was about to see.

The first thing that jumped out was the fact that my plane was painted in British Racing Green with black trim and my coat of arms on the tail above the tail number.

It looked sharp.

"I thought you were going to lease this out to other people when I'm not using it."

"We figured it would take a while for this idea to catch on, and the paint job wasn't that much in the whole scheme of things. Besides, we think you are going to love it so much that you will want it reserved for your exclusive use."

"I would like to tour it by myself to form an opinion."

"No problem, Sir Richard. Let me know if you have any questions."

At the top of the jet stairs, I looked into the first compartment. In the front of the cabin opposite each other were two aisles' loos. They appeared to be larger than those found on normal commercial aircraft. I liked that as I had a hard time using those at my size.

I took the opportunity to look at the flight deck. It was different from those I had seen previously. It was an extended version with curtained bunk beds on one side and a crew lounge on the other.

I inquired as to why and was told on extended trips such as the Pacific there would be two flight crews in rotation. This was a safety measure that commercial airlines felt like they couldn't afford.

That made sense to me, and I certainly could afford it.

Back to the main cabin, there were eight rows of first-class seats, four across so I could have up to thirty-two people accompany the trip. The seats were my colors, the adopted British racing green with thin black trim. It was well done. Another feature was my coat of arms worked into the fabric. It was in a slightly darker green, almost black, and small, but it was there.

The last row had a wide space behind it so that a jog to the right could be accommodated. On the right side of the cabin was a hallway running the rest of the length of the cabin.

On the left side of the wide space was a small service kitchen for a stewardess to serve the main cabin. Nosing in the kitchen, I found real china and glassware.

Again, my colors and coat of arms were used in the china pattern. I could see that we had to have some giveaways or people would pinch the plates.

The silverware was real, real silver that is. The design on the handle was once again my coat of arms.

I could sense a pattern here and also a grandmother and Queen Mum at work. They were the only two I knew that would go over the top like this. Not that I minded; it was really neat.

There were doors, all open along the hallway. The first door directly after the main cabin was a conference room that could seat ten people comfortably. It even had a TV at one end and whiteboards along the far wall. There weren't any windows. Once again, the racing green and coat of arms motif were worked in very discreetly.

The next room was an office support room with a telex, radio, a copy machine, and an open cabinet with office supplies. They had even stocked my favorite yellow legal pads for notetaking. This room was bland in comparison to the others.

It also had a small service area for coffee, tea, and snacks. I liked the way they thought, never far from food, my type of airplane!

After that, there was an office set up for me. It had bookshelves lined with the books and class notes from the classes that I should have been taking this Michaelmas, my next term.

Oh well, I could get a jump on next year.

Next was a small private sitting room for my use. It had a sofa, a coffee table, and a lounger. There was even a lamp on an end table for reading. It looked very cozy. It would be easy to while away the hours of a long flight. The design motif continued.

There was no doubt as to whom this airplane belonged. I also made up my mind on the spot to purchase the aircraft. It was mine!

Then there was the full-size bedroom. The bed was a queen size. These along with king size were now all the rage. I had visions of a club I had heard of but knew that Nina would never go for it. I don't even have to describe the bedcovers and their design.

The last room on the plane was the bathroom. It had a full-size walk-in shower. I had been told that a bathtub would be problematic, and if the aircraft had to maneuver quickly it could be disastrous.

After my walk-through, I returned to the office and told the managing director I approved. I also told him I would like to immediately reserve the aircraft for my personal use and that I would like a purchase price worked up.

You could see him swell with pride at their work.

"Thank you. I will get on it at once. You do know that other people have learned of your compartment idea and have commissioned us to build them."

Yeah, I thought, after you called them and told them of the possibilities. Since I hadn't entered this with the idea of making money, I let it go.

"Glad to hear it, I hope you remember when it is time for maintenance and upkeep on the interior and give me some priority."

"If you would allow us permission to give tours, we would give you two years of free upkeep."

"That sounds good. Have your people draw up an agreement for my people to review."

This was a long way from Ohio.

I was staying overnight in London so returned to my hotel suite. I immediately called Grandmum and told her someone had pinched china and silver from my aircraft.

From her reaction, I had found one of the guilty parties. I couldn't keep it up, at least not with my grandmum, now if it had been Mum or Mary.

She admitted that she and Queen Elizabeth had learned of my project and approached the company. I realized that there was no way that the company would refuse the Queen Mum.

I also found out that Grandmum had paid for all the upgrades. I thanked her for the effort and asked her to relay my thanks to Queen Elizabeth. They had done a wonderful job.

After that, I called Nina and told her about my new flying setup. As I suspected she was intrigued by the mile-high club but wasn't about to join it anytime soon.

We chatted for a while about her school days and modeling work. She told me that being a Queen Bee in the school social scene was becoming boring. When she was on the outside looking in, it looked like the place to be.

Now she was on the inside it felt like too many demands were being made to make it worthwhile. The scheming the girls would go through to become models was incredible.

I did like the story she told me about the girl who was an inch too short to be considered for model work hanging with weights on her legs.

Poor girl. Why didn't someone tell her that Mary's fashion line had all age groups so that she could pose as being younger, and of course shorter?

Chapter 28

Nina asked me what clothes I was taking on my trip. That was when I realized that I had made no allowances for clothing. Not even a closet!

After hanging up with Nina I called the managing director of the conversion company and confessed my oversight. He started laughing at me. Your grandmum wins the bet.

She bet the Queen Mum Nina would trigger you to your error. The Queen Mum didn't think you would realize it until you were airborne.

"Do you have any idea of the bet?"

"It was a shilling, so the queen won't have to raise our taxes too much to pay for it."

"The queen sets the tax rate?"

"No, but the prime minister leads the House of Commons, she has some influence with him. Off with his head type of the influence."

I knew she didn't have that sort of power, but on second thought I wasn't going to test it out.

"So, what can be done?"

"Well, you could come back and look in the cargo hold. The ladies have your complete wardrobe there. I must say you have a lot of clothes."

"A lot? What did they do, load my entire wardrobe on board?"

"They had duplicates made of everything."

"That means I have three copies now, one in England, one in America, and one onboard the aircraft. I wonder who keeps it all straight."

"I was told your valet took care of it."

"I have a valet? Will he travel with me?"

"That is what I was told."

"Where will they be on the aircraft?"

"They will share the stewardesses area in the cargo hold. We have set up Pullman- Coach-type rooms with bunks. He has a work area for tailoring, but laundry and dry cleaning will have to be done ground side."

"How do they get back and forth inflight?"

"You didn't notice the small elevator in the main galley? There is one on most 707s now for extra food storage, etc."

I thanked him and hung up.

I no sooner rang off than the phone rang. It was the managing director.

"You didn't give me a chance to pass on some other information."

"Such as?"

"The ladies also had a complete set of your gear, swords, bows, and such placed on board. Since the cargo hold on a 707 is so large, they also put a car in the hold. We had to enlarge the doors to double size so the car would fit. It will take a heavy-duty forklift at each airport to unload it."

"What car?"

"I haven't seen it, but I was told it is a Bentley S2 Continental Convertible. They tried for an Aston Martin like you already have but none were available."

"That was thoughtful of them. I wonder who is paying for all of this."

"Why, you have, Sir Richard. The purchases were made through us and we have billed and been paid. We appreciate the timeliness."

The only access my grandmum had to my accounts was The Meadows household accounts. I could see the monthly bill now: five pounds of sugar, five shillings; one pound of butter, five pence; one Bentley, seventy thousand pounds.

Thinking of it that way, I had to laugh. The anger I had been starting to feel melted away.

Next, I called Grandmum and thanked her for taking care of the clothing issues. I also asked her about this valet I now had in my employ.

It seems he is the son of Prince Philips's valet, and this was his first independent job. He trained under his father as an apprentice so there was no question about his knowledge.

Now to see if we could get along. From my reading, I knew that a man's valet knows more about him than his mum. Now that was a scary thought.

I tried an act of small revenge on Grandmum when I told her that I had just bought a car to take with me.

I just thought I had revenge; she never missed a beat.

"That's nice, Richard; I will use the convertible here at The Meadows."

I had to backtrack quickly.

"Age and treachery beat youth every time."

I couldn't argue with that.

"Besides, I talked it over with your mum and she said it was okay. I put everything on the household accounts."

That did it. I managed to choke out goodbye and hang up I was laughing so hard.

After I settled down, I called Nina back to update her on my latest aircraft finds. She thought the clothes and car were a nice touch. Also, a valet could help my image.

I didn't know how to take that. Did I have a bad image because of the way I dressed? I was also smart enough to leave the comment alone. Some conversations could turn awkward, and this was one of them.

It ranked right up there with, "Does this dress make me look fat?"

We talked about trips we could take after I purchased the plane and completed my business trip around the world.

I would need to check on my estate in Spain one of these days. I did receive regular reports and things seemed to be going well.

Nina's trips revolved around the fashion world. This would mean trips to Rome, Paris, and New York. She was also interested in learning if there was a fashion center in India. This could be a huge untapped market.

I asked her how she felt about China.

"Do they have fashion in China? All I have seen are those horrid suits worn by Mao Tse-tung. Also, since they are closed to the West, we couldn't do business anyway."

"I wouldn't be too sure about that. I think they may be ready to open to the West. If they are, we will have an inside track."

"How is that, Rick?"

I guess I had never mentioned my trading deals with China involving rubber in exchange for my cargo handling system. Also, there was the fact I was shipping wheat to China to stave off a famine.

To say she was impressed was an understatement.

"Rick, you are one of the most important people in the world!"

"Hardly, though I might make the top one thousand."

"And how many people do that?"

"Uh, one thousand?"

"Rick! You know what I mean. Things that you are doing affect a lot of people. Why haven't I heard this on the news?"

"China has to save face; if these events became public, they would rather let their population starve."

"Surely you exaggerate."

"That is what my Chinese contact told me, and I have no reason to disbelieve them. They look at the world differently than we do. They have six hundred and sixty million people, so what if a few million starve."

"Oh, what a horrid thought."

"I'm trying to prevent that, so please don't tell anyone about what I just shared."

"I won't, my silent hero."

Now, I don't know if she was taking the piss or not, but it was time to get out of this conversation.

We ended the phone call with the normal pleasantries, but she added, "I think I am in love with you."

"I think the same, but we are still too young, aren't we?

"I'm rethinking that almost every day."

I got off the line and went, "Whew!" I felt like I was in love with Nina. She was everything I could ask for in a wife. She is smart, pretty, same American value system as me, and did I mention pretty?"

The only problem was that I wasn't ready to get married. Kids our age were doing it all the time; I felt that I had to grow some more before committing to marriage.

There was no other girl on the horizon, but I didn't want to rush into a lifelong marriage. I knew divorces were becoming more common but that wasn't my style.

Married is married, so like a carpenter, I was going to measure twice before cutting once. Hmm, somehow that sounds dirty in this context.

I went downstairs to dinner. A stranger was sitting at the table. As I surmised, he was my valet. Grandmum introduced us. I liked Harold Green at our first meeting. Time would tell how we would wear on each other.

He was about five-ten and one hundred and fifty pounds. His handshake was firm, and he had a ready smile. His hair and eyes were brown, and he had a typical English pale complexion.

I knew I would like him when he told me he should probably be paid more since my sleeves and legs were so long that ironing would take forever.

Since I had no idea what I was paying him I told him no, he should be paid less as the ironing would go quicker as there would be an economy of scale.

He chuckled at that, and we started a long-term relationship that ended as true friends.

How could you not like a guy who laughed at your bad jokes?

Chapter 29

The next morning, I had to face something I had been putting off. The stops for my worldwide check-up on my businesses had to be finalized.

The idea was to first talk to the leaders of the major divisions and after that a select group of their direct reports. I needed to make certain that what I was hearing were the facts of the matter, not what someone wanted me to hear.

This would give subordinates a chance to give me the word on any problems directly. I hope that there will be none, but unless I checked I wouldn't know.

The groups under Jackson Enterprises that I would visit and give the subordinates a chance to talk to me started with Transportation, led by Todd Goodson.

Under him were the Scottish Lines, directed by John Churchill. This was based in Liverpool. How did it get the name Scottish Lines?

Then there is Howell Freight led by Robert Wilson. This had started as a joint venture between Jackson Enterprise and the Howell family. The Howells came to us with an offer to sell it to us.

They only had so many family members and they wanted to concentrate on their oil business and farms.

I wondered why a farm could take so much time and effort, a judgment based on my large spread in Spain. On inquiry, I learned that my operation, if placed in the Argentine, would be considered a hobby farm. Their ranches and farms were huge!

Freight's production operation that produced the actual cargo containers had a new VP named Harold Finnigan. He reported to Todd Goodson and was the person I was most interested in talking to. He had been on board for a year now, and I hadn't met him yet.

It would be most interesting what he would say when given the opportunity.

After Transportation, I wanted an update on Personal Products to see how Don Pearson and his team were doing. Even though the real money was in Transportation, this group along with Home Products under Mark Downing was most dear to my heart.

Jackson Entertainment wasn't a huge concern as there were no new movies or songs. They just were keeping track of residuals at this point. It was a nice chunk of change but was mostly a bookkeeping operation at this time.

I had no new movie offers at this point and wasn't certain if I wanted to make the time. As far as songs go, the twelfth of never would be too soon.

The bookkeeping aspect applied to the Brokerage operation. We had grown this by buying up firms in many countries. Each firm was still being treated as an individual and operating under many of the same leaders using their original policies and methods.

This was more like an alliance rather than a single business. It was making a lot of money so maybe it was a case of if it ain't broke, don't fix it. Ah heck, I knew that I would fix it when time allowed. I wanted a unified presence in the business world.

Also, who knew what policies were in place in countries like the Federation of Rhodesia and Nyasaland?

It was time for me to visit my Spanish operation.

Then there was the question of what port operations to visit. After dithering for several hours, I selected Hong Kong, Tokyo, Long Beach, Savannah, Hamburg, and Valencia.

Ideally, I would start at the nearest operation, Liverpool, and work my way around the world ending up back in England.

To achieve my objective, I had to visit Jackson Enterprises headquarters in LA first, then Pittsburgh, followed by a trip to Liverpool for the Scottish Lines, then on to Howell Freight in Buenos Aires.

After that would be port operations: Hamburg, then Valencia, then head to Hong Kong, then Tokyo. Then in a weird hop, Savannah, and finally back to Long Beach. Might as well visit the *estancia* in Spain while there.

I know this itinerary would add time and many extra miles, but I also know I could handle only so many projects at a time. I would start at the top of the enterprise and get updates on all the business.

I'd work my way down the chain to individual port operations. This was inefficient as all get out.

While inefficient, the itinerary would let me concentrate on each business segment separately. This would avoid confusion. Besides, I had been booted out of Oxford, so why not travel for a while.

I would never share this with anyone, but I was embarrassed by the entire episode and wanted a change of scenery. Getting caught with that desk in high school had been the single most embarrassing thing that I had done up to this point.

At least it didn't make worldwide headlines in the entertainment section. I guess the front page would have been worse.

I had been told many times that any publicity was good publicity. I don't see how being seen as stupid on the world stage could be considered good.

I typed up my proposed trip along with the rationale for each stop. My first impulse was to call my dad and see what he thought of my plan.

As I was picking up the phone, I had second thoughts. He wanted me to be more involved in running my businesses and know what was going on. I had to figure these things out without running to him for everything.

I thought it through as to who I really should be contacting. It boiled down to Jim Williamson and Todd Goodson.

They had the complicated parts of this plan. Everyone else was on a business visit. I thought about how I could handle the logistics with one in Pittsburgh and the other in LA while I was in London.

Silly me, here I had a 707 and flight crews sitting idle.

I placed calls to Todd and then Jim. They were both available on Wednesday. This was Monday. I would fly to Pittsburgh tomorrow; Jim would fly to Pittsburgh, and we would jointly go over my plan.

I used the copy machine to make extra copies. After that, I called the flight center to arrange my plane for tomorrow. It was short notice, but they were able to do it.

Next, I found Harold watching a cricket match with Grandmum and let him know we had a meeting in Pittsburgh on Wednesday morning. We would spend Tuesday flying. His response was a nod while he watched the match.

Grandmum asked why I was going to Pittsburgh of all places. She thought they still had red Indians roaming that part of the world. I tried to tell her otherwise, but I don't think she believed me.

Anyway, I gave a brief explanation of why I was going. She told me to be careful in the Argentine, as she had heard stories about the wild women there. If she only knew.

Tuesday morning Mr. Hamilton drove Harold and me out to the Oxford flight center. He was having fun with the world as he wore a grey chauffeur's uniform and accompanying hat.

He was able to drive onto the airfield and take us to the steps to the aircraft. He jumped out to open my door. Since I had nothing but my Hartman briefcase, it was an easy transition.

I did look around and saw that quite a few people had stopped to stare. How disappointed they would be if they knew it was only me and not some important person.

Then I remembered Nina's reaction to my current activities. Nah, I'm still not that important.

The flight itself was uneventful in that there were no inflight concerns. It was fun exploring all the facilities on the aircraft. I even used the elevator down into the cargo hold.

Since it was only me and Harold as passengers, the stewardesses didn't have much to do. When I went downstairs, as I thought of it, they were sitting around with their high heels off relaxing with a glass of what I thought was white wine.

I ignored this as I didn't think they were supposed to be drinking while on duty. I was disabused of this thought when one of the hostesses picked up a can of Seven-Up and refilled her glass.

Well, she started to; she caught a nail on the pull tab. I learned a new expression which I shan't repeat.

She and the other women agreed that it was some dumbass male who designed this pull-tab. They were convenient if working on a commercial flight, but they had all caught and lost a nail to them.

I decided that I had urgent work in my office.

I also started giving it some thought as to how to improve the design so this wouldn't happen.

That was all the excitement we had in the back of the plane. I thought I would go up front and see how the flight deck was going.

Chapter 30

The flight deck was a normal flight deck for a 707. As this was a long flight over the water there was a flight engineer along with the pilot and copilot. What were the different three guys sitting in seats behind the flight deck? They were the relief crew for long flights.

One was reading and the other two playing chess. I didn't know that much about chess, but looking at their game, I could tell they weren't Borgovs.

I talked to all the crew for a little while. They wanted to know how it was to land a 707 single-handed.

My reply was a simple, "Scary."

"It might have been scary, but you did it. What do you attribute the success to?"

"A good emergency checklist and professional guidance from the ground. From my training, I mostly knew what to do, but not when to do it, or how much to do it. The checklist told me what to do in what order; ground control told me how and when to do it. Plus, the head stewardess assisted me with communications."

"The point is you didn't freeze up."

"I didn't allow myself to think about the consequences if I failed. I just listened and followed the instructions like a robot."

"Rick, I heard the cockpit recording. You sounded like you had ice water in your veins."

"That is from my training. Mr. McGarry drilled me into sounding calm no matter what I felt inside."

"I read about your training from Bill McGarry. It must have been something to be taught how to fly by a hardened combat pilot."

"It was. If you need an airfield strafed, I'm your man."

"I think we will leave that to the Air Force."

"I was in the RAF for a while."

That led to a conversation about my military career and how I ended up as a colonel in the Coldstream Guards.

"What is the queen like?"

"She is a lot like my Mum, gracious, warm, loving, intelligent, and compassionate until you attack one of hers, and then the game is over, no mercy."

"Your mum, Countess Jackson, has had quite a career in her own right."

"Yes, she has."

"How does your pater handle being married to someone so strong and famous?"

"Very well actually. They met in the war before the fame. They knew famous people but weren't wealthy or famous in their own right."

"There is speculation about your family's wealth. From nowhere to extremely wealthy in a very short time."

"I had a few lucky ideas and we built on that. It may not have taken long, but we worked hard for it."

At this, I took my leave from the flight deck. The conversation was starting to go to places I didn't want to go.

I decided to take a nap so went back to my very own bedroom on the plane. What a surprise I had. There in my bed was one of the stewardesses. She was sitting up in the bed.

She might have been completely nude. At least she had nothing on top. Quite an eyeful.

"Join me for some afternoon fun?"

In a panic, I turned and ran to the elevator to the cargo hold. What had the flight crew said about me being cool under pressure? They wouldn't think so if they could see me now.

On the bottom deck, I went to the lady who had introduced herself as the head hostess, Debbie Thomson. Looking around I could see everyone I had met except one.

"Which stewardess is not here?"

Looking around. she replied, "Joan."

"Joan is nude in my bed; get her out of here and off my plane as soon as we land. If you don't want to wait, that is fine with me."

She took off like her tail was on fire. She was followed by all the other stewardesses. I never saw Joan again after that. I don't know where they had her and didn't care.

Other women had tried to entrap me in the last several years, but that was the most blatant attempt yet.

One of the hostesses came down and let me know my room was now clear and clean sheets had been put on the bed.

Debbie came back all apologetic.

"Our company does not condone such behavior, and she has been suspended from all duties until our HR department can handle the matter, and no, I didn't pitch her out the door."

"Probably for the best, yet we might have gotten away with it in International airspace."

"I was tempted. Please don't hold one bad apple against us."

"I don't. Had she worked for you long?"

"This was her first and last trip."

"As you can imagine, I have to watch out for this type of action all the time. Let your bosses know they get a free pass this time, but if it happens again, they lose the business."

"Yes, Sir Richard."

I was surprised at the sudden formality then realized that I had come across pretty strongly. Maybe I was channeling Mum.

It couldn't have been Dad because I hadn't decked anyone. Dad was a hot burner, Mum cold. Dad would hit you and forget about it. Not that he ever did more than tap us on the butt.

Mum would wait and strike when least expected. Kids would get slapped upside the head; the older we were the harder the hit. She probably would use a cricket bat on me now if I warranted a hit.

I knew that really bad guys died.

The chief pilot was told what had happened. He came to me and asked the same thing as the lead hostess. I assured him the acts of one individual didn't reflect on the company, but they had to make certain their employees understood this behavior wouldn't be tolerated.

This held for both men and women. He looked at me funny and I just nodded my head yes. Being rich and famous had its advantages but also some drawbacks.

That is one of the reasons I was content to date only Nina. Besides, she was intelligent; I got along with her, and she was hot!

Events had gotten me worked up, so a nap was the last thing on my mind now. I went into my private sitting room and got with one of my extra reading books from school.

You know I was desperate when I was reading about the elasticity of the money supply, though I must say it gave me a lot of food for thought. My dealings with the Chinese while on a commodity basis transferred as credits.

These credits were pouring into several different countries' economies without their central bank's awareness. This could ruin some forecasts and plans based on them.

The rest of the flight was uneventful. We landed in New York at LaGuardia airport to refuel and deal with Customs, who paid little attention to us beyond a passport review. I looked out the window to see a young woman being escorted off the plane. This was a harsh lesson for her, but I wasn't going to keep someone like that near me.

From there we had a short flight over to Pittsburgh International. At least it seemed short. It was now late afternoon here. I waited while they unloaded my car.

I know this wasn't needed as it was a short trip, but I wanted to drive my right-handed steering wheel on an American road.

Harold with my luggage took an airport limo to our hotel.

The car drove like a dream as I turned out of the airport. I wasn't a quarter mile down the road when there was a flashing red light in my rearview mirror.

I wondered what I had done; I hadn't even stepped on the gas. I had to chuckle when the state trooper went up to the American driver's side window.

He looked in and did a double take, then came around to my side.

After the normal driver's license and registration requests, He asked if I knew why he had stopped me. I told him I had no idea.

"I didn't see a driver behind the wheel. I didn't figure it out till I looked in on the left side and saw you sitting over here. How did you get this auto here?"

"I just flew in from London with the car in the cargo hold."

He gave me a look like, pull the other one. He then took a second look at my license.

"I see. Are you the actor?"

"Yes, I am."

I thought they didn't do titles in America, but he asked me, "Sir Richard," if I would give him an autograph for his daughter, a huge fan.

I had some of the ever-present publicity photos in the glove box so gave a personal inscription to his daughter Jane.

Chapter 31

My policy was to play it straight with the police; they carried guns and had to put up with a lot of people.

"Then you also are the owner of Jackson Enterprises."

"Yes, I'm surprised you know of us."

"You, Sir Richard, are getting to be one of the largest employers in Pittsburgh. The area has been declining, and your company has done a lot to save the area."

"I'm glad to hear it."

We then proceeded to talk about my Bentley, which he admired greatly. As he was getting ready to leave, he left me with a parting word.

"You know I will have to report this courtesy stop to my captain. He will bump it up to his boss, and then the governor and the Pittsburgh mayor will want to welcome you to the area."

"Then they better be quick about it, as this is only a short meeting. I will be back in the air by lunchtime tomorrow."

"I'm curious. How much do they charge to carry a car in the cargo hold?"

"No idea. It is my plane, a 707."

"Oh."

That was a showstopper. The friendly policeman gave me a wave as he left. While we were talking, as usual, traffic slowed down. Since it was the major road into Pittsburgh, it came to a stop.

This made it a hassle getting back on the road. While doing this, I smugly thought that when the interstate system started by Ike was completed, these would be a thing of the past.

I reluctantly let the valet at the Penn-Sheraton take my car. Harold was waiting for me at the check-in desk. He had taken care of that.

"Spot of bother on the way in, sir?"

"Not really. The cop didn't realize until he had me stopped that it was built to drive in England. He thought the driver was in trouble."

"I see. That would be a little unnerving."

"Then there were the autographs, etc. Which reminds me," I said, turning to the front desk clerk who had been listening to our conversation.

"I'm only taking calls from family or Jackson Enterprise employees."

"Yes sir. Let me make a note of that for our switchboard."

This turned out to be a mistake.

Harold and I had a pleasant dinner in the Terrace Dining Room at the hotel. I thought the mural, *The Taking of Fort Pitt*, was a bit much for dinner but since my back was turned to it, I managed.

I had no trouble sleeping in my suite. I used to think it a waste to have a suite for a night's stay, but I was now used to it. This certainly wasn't the Fountain Lodge!

I woke to knocks on the door. I found a robe that Harold had staged for me and stumbled into the living room to answer the knocking which had now become almost thunderous.

Harold came out of his room at the same time. While opening the door I sniggered at him, he was wearing bunny slippers.

When I opened the door there was a man dressed in a suit and tie.

"Sir Richard Jackson?"

"Yes."

"I'm from the mayor's office; he wants a meeting with you at eight o'clock to plan your day. You will have to hurry as it is almost seven."

I didn't reply. I just gently closed the door.

Going to the phone, I dialed the front desk and asked for the manager. He must have been waiting for my call.

"Why is someone from the mayor's office hammering at my door? I didn't think it was policy to give out room numbers?"

"I'm so sorry, Sir Richard. You must understand this is Allegheny County and that we have to do business here. If I hadn't given out your room number, we would have lost our liquor license by lunchtime.

"Our switchboard wouldn't put a call through as per your instructions, but I decided to give out your number."

"I do understand. They have you by the throat. No worries from me, it was just a rude awakening. Have room service deliver breakfast, English style. After that have someone available to show me a back way out and have my car there ready to go."

Harold and I ate; I tasked him with his bunny slippers.

"They were a birthday gift from Prince Phillip, and you can make all the fun you want. I love what they represent."

Talk about taking the wind out of your sails!

"I just wanted to tell you that pink is the perfect color for those slippers. My sister has a pair just like them."

Not the best recovery but one does what one can. After eating, I took the map and written directions Harold had for me and called for someone to get me out of here.

I was quickly led to a service elevator, and everything was tickety-boo as I made a clean getaway. The directions were simple, so I had no problem finding the Jackson Transportation Headquarters building.

The front gate and reception desk had been informed of my imminent arrival and Todd Goodson stood waiting at the front desk.

We greeted each other and proceeded to his office. He didn't sit behind his desk but led me to a corner where there were a couch and several chairs. It made the conversation much more informal.

It also avoided the problem of who got to sit behind the boss's desk, not that I would do that to him.

He started with, "Jim Williamson is due here momentarily. While we wait, you have the mayor's office in a bit of a lather. Why didn't you attend your meeting?"

"It wasn't my meeting; someone from the mayor's office pounded on my door at 6:30 and informed me I was due at the mayor's office at 8 a.m. to plan my day. You can tell how I feel about that."

"They gave me poor information; how did they even know that you are in town?"

I told him about my traffic stop, which brought a smile to his face. About that time Jim Williamson was escorted in, and Todd received a phone call.

While Jim and I greeted each other, you could hear Todd getting agitated on the telephone. He turned to me as he hung up.

"That was the mayor's office; they informed me they have told the control tower at Pittsburgh International your aircraft is not to be given clearance to take off until they give the word."

I felt a familiar cold enter my body.

"May I use your phone?"

"Certainly."

I first had the operator call the British Embassy in Washington. I was able to get through to the ambassador; this title was good for something.

"This is Baron Blackhoof. I'm having a bit of bother in Pittsburgh, PA. I thought I would let you know that I will be exercising my diplomatic privileges and taking off from the local airfield as Queen's Flight Three."

The ambassador suggested I inform the White House.

"Yes, sir. That will be my next call."

The Jackson Enterprise operator was very professional as she connected me to the White House.

When connected, I asked for President Kennedy knowing full well I wouldn't be speaking to him. I did get through to his chief of staff. I informed him of my situation and that I would be using diplomatic privilege to leave.

"We can call the mayor and get this all cleared up."

"Don't. He tried a power play; I want to return the courtesy. You might give the FAA a heads up that the locals are trying to usurp federal control."

I knew that would throw the cat amongst the pigeons.

"I believe the mayor is a member of your party so let me be the bad guy."

"Thank you. We will take care of it behind the scenes while you stomp all over that jumped-up son of a bitch."

I wondered what this was going to cost the mayor in his next election. I found out that it cost him nothing, as he was a real powerhouse in the Democratic party. Not that I cared.

After that little fracas, Jim, Todd, and I went over my proposed trip plan. I was very upfront with them in explaining that I felt a need to know how key people felt about their leaders.

Todd thought this a wise move, and he had been going through the same exercise ever since gaining his position.

Jim, being almost as new to this high-level game as I was, quickly saw the merit of knowing how things were being run, instead of just taking a subordinate's word.

There were a few changes to the timing of each visit but no changes to the overall itinerary. Todd told me that he had wondered about the fancy jet I had purchased, but he now understood the need.

I asked him and Jim if they wanted to go out to the airport with me for a tour of my new toy. They both jumped at the chance.

Chapter 32

After we had it clear who would notify whom on this trip, we left for the airport; Todd and me in my car and Harold and Jim in a company limo.

Taking an ounce of precaution, Todd had me leave by a side gate. The limo went out the main gate. As we drove by the main gate, we saw they had barely cleared the gate and had been pulled over by Pittsburgh Police.

I stepped on it a bit and tried to get to the airport before getting pulled over. It was a close call. They would have had me if I hadn't been able to drive onto the airfield in the private aviation sector and run up the steps to my plane.

As it was, one of the flight crew had the sense to close the 707's door in the cop's face. I had no desire to be taken into local custody. What a brouhaha that would turn out to be.

When the door was opened to let in Jim and Harold, the policeman tried to enter but was refused as he didn't have a warrant.

From the relieved look on his face, you could tell his heart wasn't in this.

The tour took the better part of an hour. There were good questions and maybe an underlying tone of jealousy. That probably was my imagination at work. They said nothing to lead me to my conclusion.

I probably just wanted them to be jealous of my new toy. That brought up an interesting thought; when had it stopped being a tool for my job and become a new toy?

Oh well, tool or toy, it is cool, and I'm proud to own it.

After the tour and reconfirmation of the upcoming trip and what each of us would do to make it happen, we went our separate ways.

Jim to catch a flight, first-class, back to LA, Todd back to his office, and I was going to be taking off for London shortly.

The flight captain, what do you call the head pilot of an aircraft with multiple crews on board, approached me in my office.

"We received a message for you from the British Embassy."

It was short and clear.

"Do not use the call sign Queen's Flight Three. You are officially Queen's Messenger One. Use this for any non-commercial (military or civilian) aircraft you fly on. It has full diplomatic immunity for the aircraft, contents, and passengers.

"Brilliant!"

That was my comment and thought. This took care of the immediate issue and any others in the future.

The chief pilot had of course read the message, but we discussed it to make sure we both understood. Any flight that had Colonel Lord Blackhoof onboard was to be known as Queen's Messenger One.

Now that will cause some heartburn in Pittsburgh. I wanted to be on the flight deck to hear the conversation with the tower.

It wasn't as dramatic as I thought it might be. The FAA control tower people kept to business and cleared us immediately, to the point of giving us priority on the runway.

I could hear some shouting in the background, something about the mayor's office. Well, the mayor had started the chest-beating contest. I had just shown him who could beat the loudest.

The takeoff and flight back to London were very peaceful. It was about four in the afternoon when we took off. I went to bed around ten, and we landed at Oxford at about seven o'clock in the morning. Immigration and Customs came on board the plane to look at our documents. My diplomatic passport got me an immediate wave-off.

I could learn to travel like this. Even Harold got a cursory examination. One of the lead inspectors recognized him as traveling with Prince Phillip and his dad.

The inspector asked Harold if he still tried to play football in the aircraft aisles. Harold blushed. There was a story there that I had to get one of these days.

While they unloaded my car, I called the palace to speak to Mr. Norman about my new designation as Queen's Messenger One.

"Our American ambassador let us know of your situation in Pittsburgh. Her Majesty advised not using Queen's Flight Three due to your past association with the RAF. That, after all, is their bailiwick.

"It was suggested to her that we use Queen's Messenger One. Since you are the first pilot messenger, we thought it appropriate. Besides, several senior messengers need their noses tweaked a bit."

Ah, palace intrigue, I would have to hire a taste tester if I attended any messenger dinners. Did we have messenger dinners? I even asked Mr. Norman if we had any get-togethers.

"What on earth for?"

That answered that. I dropped the subject and rang off. I wondered if I should have discreet lettering on the plane calling it Queen's Messenger One. Probably not. Some bean counter would want to take the plane into Her Majesty's Service.

Next, I started to call my dad at home in LA. Thankfully I remembered the time difference before the call went through. I would call him after lunchtime here.

In the meantime, I was at loose ends. No school, and business has been taken care of for now; what should I do?

Even Nina would be in school.

I decided to get a round of golf in before lunchtime. My layoff had been long, and I had probably lost my edge. It was early in the day and the weather, while not the best, wasn't horrid. There was no rain, though it might later from the looks of it.

When my car was available, I drove to the golf course and checked with the pro to see if there was a tee time available. It turns out there will always be a tee time available for US Open Champion Colonel Lord Blackhoof.

This name, rank, and title thing was strange at first, then a little ego-building, but now it was just a lot of words to roll off the tongue.

I was put in with three strangers. They turned out to be a group of doctors. Why is it always doctors? Don't they have people to practice on?

They didn't know me from Adam, and I liked it that way, especially as my long layoff from golf showed.

It showed to me, if not them. I beat all of them handily. My arm had healed enough that I could swing a club with no problems.

They bet amongst themselves. On the first hole, the bet was ten pounds closest to the hole on their second shot was the winner. One of them apologized to me for not including me, but they realized I was a poor student who couldn't afford such high stakes.

They thought I was a student as I was wearing an Oxford pullover. I regretted their mistake as I ended up closest to the pin. I was on the green and none of them were.

After that, nothing was said about me and betting. They continued among themselves as it appeared to be a tradition. I would have won seventeen out of eighteen holes.

When we broke for a snack at the ninth hole, one of them asked a question about the starter. It was about me, so the game was up. I was thanked for not hustling them, and no insult about relative wealth was intended.

As middle-aged men, they were interested in my movie appearances with John Wayne and singing with Frank Sinatra. They had met Arnold Palmer and all agreed that he was a true gentleman. Not all professional golfers have that reputation.

The one person they didn't ask about and I was certain they would ask was the queen. She was held in such high respect there would be no mere gossip about her.

After the round, which was mildly disappointing to me and made me determined to get out more often, I returned to The Meadows.

From my office, I called Dad in LA. I managed to catch him before his day started so he had time to talk. I shared what I had set up and asked him if he saw any holes in my plan.

He didn't and was most complimentary of my taking charge of the situation. He brought me up to date on what he was involved in. He was part of a group purchasing the Irvine Ranch. They intended to develop it, but not to sell any of the property. It would be let out on ninety-nine-year leases.

If this worked out, the other investors and our family would be rich forever.

After I hung up, I realized I was tired. This being a member of the jet-set was very tiring. A nap was just what the doctor ordered. Well, my imaginary doctor. The doctors I had played with earlier recommended more practice if I were to play seriously in the coming year.

The nerve of them. I had a seventy while they were all in the nineties.

Chapter 33

After playing golf I went back to The Meadows. I was really at loose ends. I called Nina but she wasn't home from school yet. It wasn't her real home; it was an apartment she shared with two other girls.

One of them answered the phone and took a message. I then went out to the Roman villa project. Watching an archaeological dig is like watching paint dry. Only a couple of students were working so I moved on to the theme park.

Here, at least, earthmovers were being used. Did you know that one bucketload of dirt looks like the previous load?

I thought about driving down to Pinewood Studios to see what was happening there, but it was too late in the day.

I hate being bored. I returned to my room and tried to read a novel but couldn't even get into that. Setting that aside, I randomly picked a suggested reading book from the library.

These were books that were referenced in my class textbooks. Usually, they were more interesting than the textbook itself. This book made paint drying look exciting.

A phone call from Nina saved me. She had returned to her apartment and got my message. I asked her how things were going. We hadn't talked in almost a week.

All was fine, though she was a little upset about a lost modeling opportunity. It was for this Saturday in New York City. She had missed enough class time for work that she couldn't take any more days off.

Short of chartering a jet, she couldn't get there and back. Hmm, what are rich boyfriends who own their own jet for?

I inquired if it was too late to accept the work. It wasn't, but she had to make the phone call today. I told her to make it; I would get her there and back.

She knew about my business jet, but not that it was now in service. A very excited Nina told me she would call me back.

I took the opportunity to call my flight crew company, Hastings Aviation, to have the jet ready to fly to New York City on Thursday evening after picking up Nina in Zurich. The Hastings people were on top of things and told me they would have it good to go.

Hastings Aviation was one of the oldest flight service companies in the world. The grandfather of the current Duke of Hastings was an early aviator who didn't like to miss a meal while flying.

He founded a food service company for commercial airlines, expanding into fueling and providing aircraft and flight crews. It was a full-service organization.

I had met the current duke at a reception at the palace. There we talked for a while. He showed me a picture on the wall of one of the halls. It was one of his multi-great-grandfathers.

I think he did it for the shock value. His many greats were black, I mean black as a coal bin. The original duke had gained his title for saving a British town in Africa with his native troops.

As the current duke explained, in Regency England the only color they cared about was the color of your money. A title helped. Many marriages down the line and the family was white as they come.

That is Hastings Aviation Services. Nina had given me one very disturbing piece of information. Her mother would be accompanying us.

I had never met her mum so didn't know what to expect. I knew and got on well with her ex-husband. She had left him, and he was a good guy, so did that make her bad?

Having no experience in these matters, I set the thought aside. I will find out this weekend.

When I told Harold the news you would think I was moving a regiment to new quarters. I told him to get used to it. This was not the royal household where things were planned days, weeks, months, and even years ahead.

I was still in my teens and impulsive. I said that! He collected himself and told me all would be ready.

I hated to be that hard on him, but it was training. He was to be trained as to my ways, not the other way around.

I updated the family on my plans for the weekend. Mum liked to know what continent I would be on. She didn't even care about which country anymore.

Mary was even more pragmatic. When asked where I was, she told everyone I was flying to London. It seemed like I was always doing it, so it was a safe answer.

Dad, Denny, and Eddie, when asked the same question, would just shrug.

My flight, as announced to the control tower, Queen's Messenger One, left on time. That means it left when I was on board and buckled in. Have I mentioned it is nice owning your jet airplane?

The flight to Switzerland was quick. It seemed like we were in a landing pattern as soon as we took off. We weren't but it seemed like it.

We landed and taxied to the private aviation terminal. I descended the stairs to meet Nina, but she wasn't in sight. Her mother and a gentleman I assumed was her stepfather were at the gate with their bags beside them.

I didn't know anything about the stepfather. Nina only mentioned once that her mother had remarried. I had the impression she didn't care for him.

I approached the couple and welcomed them to the flight. I didn't give my name which was probably a mistake.

The man's only response was, "Boy, carry our bags."

I picked them up without saying anything. I don't think I cared for Nina's stepfather either. About that time the young lady herself came walking up.

She gave me a funny look as I was walking behind the couple carrying their bags. I don't know what was in them, but they were heavy. The couple proceeded up the steps without looking back at me.

When we got to the steps, one of the flight crew reached for the bags. I shook my head no; I wanted to see how this would play out.

When I reached the top of the steps, the man told me to place them in a closet. For grins, I held out my hand as though I expected a tip. The cheap so-and-so did tip me, about twenty-five cents American.

I took the money and thanked him and called him sir. That proved to be an error as he corrected me that he was Count Victor Lustig of Austria. I murmured, "So sorry, Count."

He said, "I shall be reporting your poor behavior to Lord Blackhoof." Saying that, he turned to his wife and asked, "What sort of title is Lord Blackhoof? I understand he is an American. I suppose one can't expect any better of them."

Nina was standing there, and she couldn't stand it anymore.

"Mother, I would like to introduce you to my boyfriend, Richard Jackson, a Colonel in the Coldstream Guards and Baron Blackhoof.

At least her mother blushed. The stepfather just turned up his nose.

"My family has been titled since the 1500s, so we don't bow to any upstarts."

I pulled out my biggest royalty gun.

"My family, the Jacksons is collateral of the Habsburgs and trace back to 780 AD. Yes, our most recent titles have been earned along with our fortune."

I was pissed.

He didn't respond. Maybe it was because he was too busy ogling one of the stewardesses.

Later I was to find out that the Count was in extreme financial difficulties and was hoping that I would bail him out.

Fat chance of that.

I told Nina I had to speak to her in private and turned the care of her parents over to a hostess. Nina and I moved back to my office. After a hug and a kiss, we sat down.

"I don't think I like your stepfather."

"I despise him, I think Mother has finally seen through him and is using this trip to New York to get away. She has been almost a prisoner in their house. On this trip, she is going to accompany me on a photoshoot and then disappear."

"Does she have plans?"

"Not really."

"Does she have money?"

"Only the few hundred I have saved."

"You only have a few hundred saved? I thought modeling paid better than that."

"I didn't put that well; most of my money is in longer-term investments. I keep little cash on hand."

"That makes sense; I will help your mother get away from that creep. Do you know where she wants to go?"

"She has a sister in Northern California. She and her husband own a vineyard. They have told her she is welcome as long as she wants."

"Tell her to leave her bags packed in their hotel room and we will get them to the airport."

Chapter 34

"After we get my mom free, what can we do with Lustig?"

"I have put in a call to Mr. Norman at the palace from our in-flight radio. He is checking to see if there are any Interpol warrants out on Lustig. If there are, our problems are solved.

"New York's finest will meet the plane and take him into custody. If we are so lucky your mum won't have to sneak around at all."

"Do you think we could get into his briefcase? He has Mom's checkbook, controlling it all like it was his. I would like to get back what is left."

"That's easy. It is sitting in the onboard closet right now. Let me retrieve it."

I walked to the front. Lustig was in his seat sound asleep. I collected the briefcase and took it to my office. It had a good lock, but he hadn't even bothered to lock it.

Nina's mom's checkbook was there along with half a dozen passports. Out of curiosity, I looked at the checkbook register. The amount was far higher than I thought it would be.

Lustig must have been using her checking account to hide his funds. This theory was supported by the fact he had a checkbook in his name which only had a couple of thousand in it.

I left his checkbook in the briefcase and returned it to the closet. I went back to the office where Nina was waiting. Without comment, I handed the checkbook to her.

She opened it to the register. Her explanation was, "This can't be! There are over seven hundred thousand dollars here. There is no way my mother could have that much money."

"Well, she does now; it looks like Lustig was hiding his money in her account."

"But Mother told me he complained about money problems and that he was going to try to borrow some from you.

"Won't she have to give the money back?"

"Not if they don't know about it. The cops will take him and his possessions with them. I left his checkbook in his case. I doubt that he will complain that your mother's checkbook is missing."

"Keeping that in mind, it probably would be for the best if your mother proceeded quietly to her sister's and filed for divorce. Since the house in France is in her name from what you told me, she should be set for life. Not a bad payment for the misery he put her through."

"I wonder how he got his money. I would hate to think that innocent people lost their life savings to him."

"If there are Interpol warrants, we can figure that out."

I went up front to the flight deck and asked if there were any messages for me. There was one from Mr. Norman. It was simple and direct.

"Lustig wanted for art theft. Police will be waiting."

I let Nina know what would be happening. We decided not to tell her mother until after we landed. We would be nervous wrecks by then, so why put her through that?

When we landed, things went exactly as planned. Lustig cursed me as he was taken from the aircraft in handcuffs.

Since we were now on the ground, I made a quick trip to flight services and called Mr. Norman. He told me that the art thefts had been several years ago and that insurance had been paid out on them.

I thought about telling that to Nina and her mother but decided not to. I don't pretend to be a saint and didn't see any reason to return the money to an insurance company that had written off their losses on taxes.

I had killed people. What was a little tax evasion? I try to be a good guy, but only to a point. I said nothing when I rejoined the two ladies. Nina's mother was crying, and she rushed to hug me.

"Thank you. Thank you. Thank you," she said over and over.

"I have been living a nightmare."

Nina and I rode over to the commercial aviation side of LaGuardia with her. They have a nice shuttle service between the two sides.

There was only a two-hour wait for her TWA flight to Los Angeles. We spent it in the Ambassador Lounge.

It seems mother and daughter had a lot of catching up to do as they talked almost the entire time. Nina took the opportunity to present her mother's checkbook to her.

She explained that this large amount of money had no way of being traced as to its source. Since her legal husband had put it into their joint account it was hers as much as his.

It would be best if she moved the funds to another account in her name and closed this one out. The sooner the better.

Her mother agreed after she got over the shock of having so much money. Lustig had kept her on a very small household budget. You could see the worry lifting from her shoulders as we talked.

We saw her off at the gate for her trip. I had booked her first class and paid for the tickets.

She could afford them now, but I wanted to butter up the lady who might be my future mother-in-law.

On our ride back to my plane, Nina thanked me for returning her mother to her. I didn't think I played that big of a part in it but took her kisses graciously.

Since this was going to be a short trip, I hadn't brought the Aston Martin. We took a limo into the Waldorf Astoria. On the way, I told Nina about track 61 and its history.

She wanted to see it. I told her I would try to get us down there.

We checked in with no fanfare. Harold had charge of our luggage. I had one suitcase while Nina had seven.

A three-bedroom suite had been rented; I think Harold had taken care of that. I had just expressed a need in his general direction, and it happened. I thought he was working beyond his brief, and I should up his pay.

I asked him about that. I was surprised when he told me all he had done was relay the need to my London office. There was a staffer who took care of those arrangements for me. Live and learn.

We all had separate bedrooms. I respected Nina too much to try to crawl into her bed. She must not have respected me completely because she knocked on my door right after we retired.

We made out for a bit then she returned to her room. I had to take a cold shower. What a witch, I thought, or is it what a wench? Maybe it is which wench?

She knew how to keep me interested!

The next morning Harold ordered room service for us while we talked about our day. Nina was being picked up for her photoshoot in an hour.

Harold wanted to go shopping on 5th Avenue. It seems he and I were lacking in some necessities. He didn't tell me what they were, and I didn't ask.

That left me at loose ends for the day.

After they left, I thought about the trip over and what had transpired. I was uncomfortable on one issue. Who was I to decide that Nina's mum could keep that money, and was I that bad of a person?

The more I thought the more I realized I had made a terrible decision. I had to make it right. Since I had convinced Nina and her mother that it was her mum's money legally, I was going to have to bear the loss.

Mr. Norman had given me the insurance company's name. Their head office was there in New York City. I called them, identifying myself. This got me up the food chain quickly.

I explained to the vice president in charge of loss recovery about Victor Lustig. He was aware that Lustig was in custody. He was locked up as he didn't have enough money to cover his bail.

I told the VP I had a lead on where he stashed his cash. I was told in no uncertain terms they had no interest in the money ever coming to light.

The tax benefits to their loss far outweighed the almost million dollars. If that money were returned, they would have to give up the tax benefits.

I thanked him and assured him it was now a dead issue. I let out a sigh of relief, I had done the right thing and it ended up costing me nothing. Life should always be so kind.

Still at loose ends, I called the front desk and after identifying myself asked to be connected to President Hoover. They transferred me and his man asked the president if he would take my call. He would.

I told the president I was in town for this one day and had nothing to do. I then had to explain how this happened. He got a chuckle out of me flying my girlfriend across the Atlantic on a whim.

I was invited to his suite for some coffee and conversation. I of course accepted as this is what I had been angling for.

Chapter 35

I went directly to the president's suite. It seemed odd to call a man by that title who had left office long before I was born, but that was the etiquette.

Knocking gently on the door, I was let in and taken by his guard or secretary of whatever function it was called, to President Hoover.

He welcomed me warmly.

"It is nice to talk to someone who doesn't want something or cries about what could have been. Good to see you Rick, or is it Lord Blackhoof now?

"Rick will do, sir."

"Can I offer you a refreshment?"

"Do you have any Coca-Cola?"

"I believe we might have some."

His factotum, love that word, delivered a bottle with a glass of ice in short order. We settled into our chairs. Mine was the softest leather I had ever touched. I hoped I could keep awake.

I should have known better than to think that I would drift off while having a conversation with President Hoover. He was an educated man, an engineer by degree, and had a world of experience.

He started by telling me that he had a good laugh about my pie-throwing escapade and subsequent expulsion.

"College gives a good background but doesn't assure success. I was a mediocre student at best and did well for myself."

"I have found that many who teach have their theories and will never let them go no matter what the facts prove to be. Unlike high school, they go at their own pace instead of that of the slowest student. In many cases, their pace isn't conducive to anyone learning. Add to that the fact that some of them are so boring you can't stay awake. It is a wonder any learning can occur."

I had to nod my head yes at that, I had seen it in action at Oxford. I also had met enough people to realize that self-made people used this to justify their lack of a degree. I resemble that remark.

After that teardown of higher education, we moved on to world affairs. It was pretty mellow right now; there were some conflicts but nothing like a war.

President Hoover thought that someday Europe would unite. It would achieve that by first developing a common market. From there the international differences would be eroded until it would seem natural to use a common name.

I wasn't too certain about that, as nationalism was pretty ingrained. When the subject got to China, he surprised me.

"You will be the Chinese Armand Hammer."

I knew a little about Dr. Hammer and that he was considered a friend of the Soviet Union while at the same time a good American.

Mr. Hoover told me about Dr. Hammer's career and how it started with him selling medical supplies to the newly created Soviet Union. Since then, he has been the go-between for Soviet leaders and the US president.

I could see how my business relations with China could be construed that way, but I wasn't an unofficial ambassador by any stretch of the imagination.

I stated that, but he begged to differ from me.

"China will be undergoing great changes in the coming years. There will be a struggle for power after Mao dies. Then the new leadership will have to face the reality that TV and radio communications will prevent them from keeping their people in the dark.

"This will lead to them having to open China for trade to raise their standard of living. The first group in power may not understand that, but there will be revolutions until the new leaders get it.

"You're providing them modern port facilities is one thing, feeding their people is another."

"I'm doing that to make a profit. Sure, I don't want people to starve but the object is to make money."

"The Chinese wouldn't respect you if you didn't want to make a profit. They are very pragmatic people. They play the long game. Mark my words, it won't be in my lifetime and maybe not in yours, but they will have the largest economy in the world someday."

That was a lot to take in. He wanted the details of my rescuing those children. I told the story and he winced about my broken arm. It had healed enough that I no longer wore a sling.

He had a different take on my being raised to a peerage as a reward.

"Queen Elizabeth is going to be recognized as one of the great leaders of our time. She can see that you are headed to greater things, and she wants you to be associated with the Crown. Any good that you do will reflect on her and the Crown."

I was about to get on my high horse when I stopped and thought. If Mum had made that statement, I would have agreed wholeheartedly.

Why wouldn't the queen want to have a success attached to the Crown? Not that I saw myself as that sort of success. I had done some things that were viewed as heroic and made a lot of money, but so what, many people had done that.

Well, maybe not as much.

We turned the conversation to sports, which I didn't follow very much. It turned out that President Hoover didn't follow them either.

We both had a good laugh when we both turned to his Secret Service agent for confirmation on which team was doing what. The agent was his factotum.

It must be nice having an armed guard. That is when I remembered that I had a .38 in my shoulder holster. I wore it so much I didn't give it a second thought anymore.

That also reminded me that I needed to spend some range time, as I needed the practice. It would wait until I got back to England. As an active member of the military and Queen's Messenger, I could go armed at my discretion.

My discretion told me always to be armed. They were out to get me.

It was a pleasant two hours, and Mr. Hoover must have felt the same way as he invited me to drop in whenever I was in town.

Entering the elevator, I met General McArthur coming out. He nodded at me. I nodded back while restraining a smile as I remembered him retreating into this very elevator from a crowd of teenage girls.

It was still early enough that I decided to take a walk outside. The Fifth Avenue shops weren't that far so I could do some window shopping.

FAO Schwarz had an interesting display. The main window had toy puppies; stuffed and mechanical. What was interesting was that they were dressed in "Save the Puppies" shirts.

I suspected my avaricious sister was making a few coins from this. Of course, most of it would go towards saving puppies, so it was all good.

Strolling further on down the street I saw Harold coming my way with his arms full of bags. I waved to him and hurried up intending to help him.

We were almost together when a man came running out of a jewelry store. I knew he was up to no good because he had a gun in hand. A guard came running out after him also armed.

The robber had the advantage as his weapon was up and pointing at the guard. Before the guard could raise his gun, he was shot. He went down hard.

During the seconds this was occurring, I drew my .38 and shouted, "Stop. Police!" I am a US Marshal after all. In response, the man turned and fired at me.

Almost as a reflexive action, I fired at him. I hit him center mass, and he fell. As I was taking the half dozen steps towards him, he raised the gun and aimed again.

I had kept my weapon aimed at him and pulled the trigger before he could bring his completely up. This time he stayed down.

Stopping at him only long enough to kick his weapon beyond his reach, though from the hole in his forehead, I was certain he was beyond anyone's reach.

I moved over to the guard. He had been hit in the leg and was bleeding profusely. It wasn't a gusher like a femoral artery would be, but serious.

I used my belt as a tourniquet to slow the bleeding. Events kept moving around me. A policeman who had been on the corner came running over.

He had his weapon drawn and understandably aimed at me as I was now the only one who was armed. I set my pistol down and raised my hands.

Chapter 36

As he came up to me, I said, "US Marshal, my shield is on the inside of my jacket."

He reached down and moved the lapel side open and saw my badge.

"What happened here?"

"This guy must have just robbed the jewelry store. I saw him running out, gun in hand. The guard came out behind him. He shot the guard.

"I shot the thief, and he got a shot off at me. He went down but came back up, so I shot him again. I kicked his gun away and then put a tourniquet on the guard. I hope an ambulance is on its way."

His partner had arrived.

"One is, I stopped at the call box and asked for help. Since shots were fired, they will send an ambulance along."

"Good. The guard needs help quickly; we can't leave this tourniquet on, or he will lose his leg."

"That, and we better see how bad your wound is."

"My wound?"

The cop pointed at my left side. My shirt was all bloody. I had been hit and didn't even know it until just now.

As soon as I realized that, I came over all dizzy and my side felt like it was on fire. Harold was now standing there, so I told him to let everyone know that I had been wounded but was alright.

He nodded and took off before the cops realized a material witness was leaving the scene. As was typical of New York, people were walking past us as though nothing had happened.

The store manager confirmed that they had been robbed, and the dead guy was the one who did it.

I was now sitting on the sidewalk and the world was not feeling any better. Despite all my adventures and being shot before, it hurt. It is no fun; I can tell you that.

While we waited for the ambulance, the one policeman explained what had happened to the precinct sergeant who had shown up along with three other cars.

My original policeman and I talked while the crime scene was roped off. He was bothered by the fact that we both carried .38s, and it took two shots for me to take the thief down.

We agreed we needed something with more stopping power like a Colt 1911 A1 .45. They were developed to take a man down no matter where he was hit. It had such force it would cause hydrostatic shock. That is, it hit so hard that the liquids in the body were compressed, and it was all over.

I had read in *Gun Digest* this theory was being questioned as the body is made up of many different materials, and they reacted differently.

It was all academic. Hit a person with a big enough bullet traveling fast enough, and they would go down. No sense in giving someone a second chance to kill you.

The police had figured out who I was by this time. My diplomatic passport along with my federal ID probably gave it away. I was treated like a rock star.

That is until the ambulance team showed up. They treated me like an idiot who got himself shot in a gunfight. They briskly cut my shirt away and determined that the wound was a through and through in the fat on my side. Not that I have a lot of fat.

By this time, the news people had shown up and cameras were flashing. I was glad to be put on a gurney and driven away.

At the hospital, my GSW, a gunshot wound, was treated as no big deal. They saw much worse several times a day.

I was patched up and given a shot that numbed the pain and my mind. I was awake but didn't care about anything.

A police officer stayed with me the entire time. The hospital staff wanted to know if I was under arrest. If I weren't, the cops would have dumped me here.

He told them I was a US Marshal, and he was to stay with me until someone from the marshal's office showed up. After several hours one did.

I think I listened to what the marshal and the New York City cop talked about but to this day I have no idea what was said. I did see my credential holder being waved about.

I fell asleep.

When I next woke it was to the sound of Nina sobbing. She was in a chair next to my bed and crying her eyes out.

I managed a croak for water. She heard this, and instead of giving me water, hugged me.

"Oh Rick, I was so scared you would die, and it would be all my fault because I had you bring me here."

"Water."

At that, she pulled herself together enough to pour a glass full from the pitcher sitting on the table next to my bed.

A small sip allowed me to talk.

"Nonsense, first of all, it is not a life-threatening wound, and second, there is no way you could have foreseen this happening."

"I know, but I feel so bad."

"How did you get here?"

"Harold called around and found out what hospital you were in. Then he called your parents and the palace, and when I got back to the hotel, we came right here."

"Where is he?"

"He is sitting outside; they would only let in one visitor at a time."

"Okay, we know how my day went. How did yours?"

"Other than my boyfriend getting himself shot, it went fine. They are even talking about me doing more work for them."

I noted how it went from her fault to mine. Flexibility in thinking is a good thing, but only a woman could be this flexible.

She continued, "Your parents are on the way."

My first thought was why; this wasn't that big of a deal. Then again, maybe a son didn't get shot every day. I had thought about shooting my brothers....

Nina and I talked for a while. We discussed the remainder of the trip. She would work tomorrow and then board the 707 for her overnight trip home.

This would get her into Zurich on Monday morning in time for her first class. She would sleep in my bed on the plane. I had been hoping to get her in my bed for a long time, just not this way.

She asked if the plane could stay there long enough for her to bring her friends out for a tour of the aircraft. I told her yes.

The aircraft probably needed some basic servicing and refueling. It wouldn't hurt the crew to have some downtime. Most of all, I didn't want to say no to my girlfriend, and it would let me brag about my plane without saying a word.

I would be staying here in the hospital for at least another week until the wound had closed up enough that I could move around without tearing it open.

That plus the fact I was content to stay here where I could get the pain meds. This sucker hurt!

Harold came in after Nina left. We discussed the arrangements he had made. He had revised the hotel reservation for the next week. He and my parents would stay there.

After taking Nina back to Switzerland, the plane would return here to be available when I could travel.

I asked him to contact Todd Goodson and Jim Williamson to let them know I had to put the trip off. At the end of this week, we will revisit the issue to see when I could reschedule. What had seemed like an easy-to-do business trip was getting more complicated all the time.

I asked Harold if he knew how the guard who had been shot in the leg was doing. He didn't know but went to the nurse's station to ask. They told him they couldn't comment on his condition but that his wife had been in and walked out smiling.

Next in line after Harold left was a New York City detective. I hadn't been officially interviewed. It was pretty much cut and dried as there had been four other eyewitnesses who told the same story I did.

He told me that there was some confusion at first about me being a US Marshal, the deputy marshal who came to the hospital had never heard about my appointment, and I wasn't listed as an active officer.

They got it straightened out before he placed me under arrest for impersonating a marshal. My passport convinced the New York police, but he thought it could be counterfeit.

At least he made a phone call before he acted on his jumped conclusion.

The detective told me that the police on the scene recognized me and knew my history, so they believed I was who my documents said I was. It wouldn't have looked good for NYPD to let a VIP be arrested falsely.

I protested that I wasn't a real VIP; people read too much into it. I don't know why I even bothered as past President Hoover walked into the room about then.

The cop just looked at me, shook his head, and said, "Sure you're not."

He gave a respectful, "Mr. President," as he left.

bags packed in their hotel room, and we will get them to the airport."

Chapter 37

President Hoover just stood there and looked at me.

"It is hard to believe that anyone could get into as much trouble as you can, Rick. It is even more surprising that you can survive it. How are you doing, son?"

"Fine, other than the pain. They tell me I will have it for a few more days, and then it will tone down."

"Did they tell you about the guy you killed?"

"No."

"He had a rap sheet a mile long. He had been in and out of Sing Sing most of his life. He had beaten two murder charges. He had been put away for armed robbery three times. He was just bad news.

"What I'm trying to say is, don't feel guilty about shooting him."

"I don't."

"Then you are most unusual."

"It's not the first time I have shot someone."

"I wasn't aware."

I told him about the bank robbers in Colorado. Those were the only ones I related. My problems with the KGB would be best left alone.

"I'm glad for you, Rick. Most people suffer mentally when they have done the right thing. It is the rare person who can separate the evil they had to do from themselves.

"Yes, killing is evil, but it is not wrong to kill true evil. Our minds have a hard time separating the two. That is why so many soldiers end up shell-shocked."

I'm not certain how I felt about that. It was good that I could do the right things without feeling false remorse. At the same time, it made it easier to kill. It shouldn't be easy.

I shook aside that self-destructive line of thinking and asked him, "Do you know how I could get a decent cheeseburger around here? I'm hungry."

He sputtered a little and said, "Son, I have no idea how to do that. I'm only an ex-president. You would need Mandrake the Magician to summon good food in a hospital.

He told me he would stop in later in the week to see how I was doing. Also, he would like to meet my parents. He assumed they would be coming here.

I told him he was correct and that they would be staying at my suite at the Waldorf. That gave me a thought. The next time Harold came to see me, I would ask him to see if I could obtain a permanent suite there.

That was the end of my visitors for the day. A nurse informed me reporters were trying to get in to see me, but they had fended them off. One had even tried it dressed as a nurse. I asked how they had recognized her as a fraud.

"It was easy; we don't have any male nurses."

We both got a good laugh out of that. I did ask her to have a hospital administrator stop by when they could. The only way to stop the reporters was to give them something.

"I will, but the administrator will be coming up here anyway. They want to know how they will be paid."

"Will they take a check?"

"Yes, once they are certain it is good."

I thought maybe I should just buy the darn place.

"I'm pretty sure it will clear."

"You will be surprised how much this is going to cost. It will be in the hundreds."

I chuckled at that thought.

"I may have enough in my wallet."

She looked at me like I had two heads. I asked her to hand me my wallet which was in a bin with my other few belongings like my watch and signet ring.

She did and I counted out seven one-hundred-dollar bills.

"Do you think this will be enough?"

"Are you married? If not, I could divorce my husband and go with you."

I laughed at that; she couldn't be serious, could she? From the look on my face, she knew she had me. She smiled and said, "Gotcha."

That was good. The last thing I needed was a fifty-some-year-old lady as my wife. Now I grant you, she was a good-looking fifty but come on!

By this time I was exhausted. I slept all night; that is, I would have if they hadn't woken me every two hours to give me a pill, a shot, take my blood pressure, or rewrap my wound. I got grumpy when one asked for my autograph.

I signed her nurse's cap; it was one of those funny-looking ones they all wore.

The next morning my parents came in. I had to go through the whole incident with them. Mum told me I needed more time on the shooting range and a weapon with more stopping power. She suggested a .357 magnum, but one of those wouldn't fit right in my suit coats.

There was no excuse for not taking him down on the first shot. My mum is so tender and loving. Well, at least with me. Bad guys not so much.

My doctor came in and went over my condition with my parents. The prognosis was good. I just had to take it easy and not tear the wound open.

As soon as he left a hospital administrator came in. He had a stack of forms to be signed. They were releases and payment forms. He asked Dad to sign them.

He got an ornery look.

"Rick is emancipated. He is on his own legally. Have him sign them and pay you."

The administrator, a short mousey- looking guy, looked alarmed.

I asked how much the first bill would be.

"Six hundred and fifty-eight dollars to date. Before you are released, it will probably be another couple of hundred."

"Oh, is that all?"

I knew I had seven hundred dollars on me so grabbed my wallet, handed them to him, and asked for a receipt.

I know, petty of me, but I couldn't resist it.

To give him due credit he didn't bat an eyelash.

"I will be right back."

While he was gone, I asked Dad if he would get a check cashed for me. He would, so I wrote one for a thousand.

Dad smiled when he saw it.

"We are a long way from Bellefontaine. That reminds me; the high school shipped your bull riding and golf championship trophies to Jackson House."

"They kept the ones you won as part of the golf team. They needed the room. Where do you want them?"

"I don't know; just stick them in my bedroom for now."

Mum wasn't for that.

"I will have a display case built to show them off in the library. Between you and Mary there is quite a collection."

"What are Mary's for?"

"Save the Puppies and her other charity work."

"What other charities work?"

"Saving the kittens of course. Now she is looking at horse rescues, especially ponies."

I wonder what her slogans would be.

My parents said all the loving, worried words one would expect and told me to be careful. Like I could get in trouble in a hospital bed.

The hospital administrator came back, grumbling as he came in the door with my receipt in hand.

"These reporters won't give up. They keep trying to sneak in."

I asked, "Would it help if I had a press conference here?"

"It can't hurt. If it made even half of them move on it would be worth it."

"Do you have a room we could use?"

"Since this is a teaching hospital, we have an auditorium which will seat a hundred."

"That should work. Ask my doctor if it would be okay and what we need to do."

'I will take care of everything; anything to get these damn people out of here."

"The sooner the better."

"Then I had better get going and thank you for doing this, it has disrupted our patient care, and I don't like that."

Who would have thought the mousey-looking administrator cared about the hospital and patients and would go to war if needed? It must be true that you can't judge a book by its cover.

I almost did get in trouble because of my next visit. It was the owner of the jewelry store that had been robbed. I thought he had stopped in to see how I was doing and to thank me.

After introductions, I asked him if he knew how the guard was doing.

"I don't know. The stock shouldn't have chased him and got shot. If he thinks I owe him anything, he has another think coming."

This attitude took me aback, but I didn't respond.

"I stopped in because I'm thinking about suing you for disrupting my business. Your shooting that guy caused me to close my doors for almost half a day. You owe me at least a thousand bucks for that."

"Go ahead and sue."

"You will regret this. I know people."

"Okay, so do I."

"Yeah, you're a big shot actor, I know the guys on the docks."

Better call Popeye.

Chapter 38

I told the jewelry store owner, "When you talk to the guys on the docks, ask them to check with Popeye or Mr. Lucky first, and be sure to use my name."

The guy looked uncertain as he left.

At my request, they had hooked up a telephone in my room. I called Harold at the hotel. He was sitting with my parents. I asked him to check on who owned the building the jewelry store was in.

I was interested in buying it, at a premium price if needed. The phone was loud enough that Dad could hear me. He took the phone from Harold and asked what was going on.

I explained the situation. He told me he would take care of it. As far as the building went, he would buy it. He had been thinking about real estate in New York City so this might be a good start. It was in the right location.

Mum then took the phone.

"We weren't gone half an hour and you were in trouble in that hospital bed. Now Richard Edward Jackson, keep out of trouble!"

She then softened it with, "At least for the rest of the day. Love you, son."

About that time the administrator came back.

"I've arranged the press conference for six o'clock, an hour and a half from now. Your doctor has approved it if you stay in a wheelchair the whole time."

No standing and putting pressure on the stitches. I began to wonder how strong his stitches were; maybe he used the wrong thread?

Mum and Dad returned from the hotel and kept me company while the nurses got me ready for the conference. The nurses had planned to have me in a hospital gown. I wouldn't stand for that.

Mum and Dad saved the day. They had brought a suit and a complete change of clothes for when I got discharged. After some back and forth, my doctor was the final judge. He told the ladies it was okay for me to wear real clothes.

Then it became an argument between two of the younger nurses as to who would dress me. The head nurse, or at least senior by age, took over and told them she would help me.

Mum looked happy with this arrangement. Dad mouthed a "sorry."

Between one thing and another, I was on the stage for the interview at the right time.

The room was full. Later I found that only half were reporters. The rest were staff on break or who had snuck away from their jobs.

As soon as I went on stage the shouted questions started. I had learned how to handle this a long time ago. I just sat there in my chair.

The shouting finally died down. Since this was a teaching auditorium it had a full sound system with microphones for students to ask questions, and of course, for the teacher to answer.

When it was finally quiet, I pointed to a gentleman I had met before and who hadn't been shouting.

"The gentleman from the *New York Times*, your question, sir."

"Jason Blair, *New York Times*. The police reports state that you identified yourself as a US Marshal and had the badge and credentials to prove it."

"Is that a question?"

"Are you a US Marshal?"

"No comment. The gentleman in the second row on the end with a blue tie."

"Drew Pearson, the *Washington Post*. Are you in the habit of going armed?"

"No comment, the gentleman two rows back with the pork pie hat. I thought pork pie hats went out with Mickey Rooney."

"Ed Norton, the *LA Times*. First of all, Mickey Rooney is still alive and well; second of all, why won't you comment on the questions?"

"No comment, the lady in the last row."

"Hedda Hopper syndicated columnist. Are you having an affair with Elizabeth Taylor?"

"Most definitely not; her latest husband would shoot me, and I don't need any more bullet holes. I don't want to think what Nina Monroe my girlfriend would say and do."

"That's it. No more questions."

I signaled my accompanying nurse to wheel me off. I liked this type of news conference. Mum and Dad were waiting off-stage.

I told them with a large smile, "I think that went well?"

Dad started to say something twice but stopped each time. Mum just shook her head. We could still hear the reporters yelling like stuck pigs.

The hospital administrator was standing there. He had a smile on his face.

"I have dreaded press conferences my whole tenure in this job. You have given me a lesson on how to handle the beasts. Thank you, oh great one."

I was wheeled back to my room. Once there, I was returned to bed. When my suit coat was removed my white shirt was bloody. The stitches had pulled out.

The doctor was summoned, and he sewed me up once again. I think he skimped on the numbing agent. Also, I accused him of using 100-weight quilting thread the first time.

He didn't see the humor in it. I think that is why I didn't get much Novocain.

Mum and Dad didn't seem too sympathetic or even appreciate my sense of humor. Dad leaned over and slipped a small package under my pillow.

I waited until they had left, and the nurses went back to their station. I was correct in my guess of what the package contained. It was a semi-automatic pistol. A Walther P .38.

The police had retained my .38 as part of their investigation. This was normal in any shooting. They needed to be certain that the bullets in the bad guy were fired from my gun.

I pulled out the clip and it was full, working the slide showed one had been in the spout. I reloaded the pistol. My parents cared.

There was no guard on my door. If I had committed a crime, I would have had police there. I wasn't going to be a witness since the only one involved was dead, so they didn't think I needed protection from anyone.

In that sense they were correct. They didn't include reporters in their concerns. I knew that my "press conference," hadn't ended their questions.

I had just put it on record that it wouldn't be easy to get their questions answered about being a US Marshal.

President Eisenhower had made me a special marshal. I didn't know if President Kennedy knew or would continue it if he found out.

This was a no-win for me. If I came out and told the story, then the cat would be out of the bag. By refusing to answer I had at least a chance of it not becoming known.

As I shortly found out, there was no chance of keeping it a secret. The Deputy US Marshal who had questioned my authenticity at the crime scene knocked on my door frame and walked in.

He was here for one of two reasons, to collect my badge and credentials or to tell me I was still a marshal.

"For a reason which I wasn't told and which I disagree with, you remain a special Deputy US Marshal."

"I'm not at liberty to tell you the complete story, but no one said I couldn't tell why I am a marshal. For reasons that must remain undisclosed, the KGB has made multiple attempts on my life because of services rendered to the United States government.

"President Eisenhower made me a marshal, and apparently, President Kennedy is continuing this."

"Thank you for sharing that. At least I now know there is a good reason. May I tell anyone else?"

"I don't see why not; the Soviets certainly know. Just try to keep it within the marshal service."

"Thanks again."

After he left, I slept. It was a good thing because I needed to try to sleep twenty hours a day to get eight hours in, as the nurses were relentless in their rounds.

After sleep, food was high on my list. The food was not bad, it was just bland. The next time I get shot I think I will demand the ambulance stop for Tabasco sauce on the way to the hospital.

Better yet, have some smuggled in like Dad did the pistol.

Nina came into my room late in the afternoon. She had finished her photoshoot and was on her way back to school. After a hug and kisses, she let me know that her mother was safe with her sister.

I told her about my conversation with the insurance company. The money was her mother's, free and clear.

She asked if it would be okay if she could take her friends on a tour of the aircraft. I told her that was no problem. I wrote out a quick note for her to give to the flight crew.

I thought we had talked this over before. It wouldn't hurt for the crew to have it in writing. We exchanged more kisses, and I may have tried to grope a little. If I did, I was rebuffed.

"Down big boy. I will come to visit you when you get back to England.

"TTFN."

Chapter 39

After Nina left and I had my bland dinner, I tried to go to sleep. I had slept enough during the day that I couldn't relax.

I tried just lying there with my eyes closed and relaxing each part of my body. Ever try to relax in a busy hospital? There is always some noise in the background.

I had lain there for what I thought was half an hour but could have been ten minutes or an hour for all I knew when I heard a noise. Someone was in the room with me.

I was facing the direction of the noise, and my hand was under my pillow, so it was easy to grasp my pistol and slip the safety off. Maybe I was being paranoid, but the nurses always made a noise to see if I was awake.

The noise I heard was a scuffle as though someone was trying to slide their feet to move silently.

I cracked an eye open and could see a man dressed as a janitor going through the items in my basket.

I said, "May I help you?" as I sat up and drew down on him.

Startled, he dropped my US Marshal's credentials.

"I'm just making certain the room is clean."

"It looks like you are either a thief or a reporter. Care to elaborate?"

I wriggled my weapon slightly to remind him that I held the upper hand.

'I'm not a thief."

"Then what organization do you work for."

"None, I'm a freelancer."

"You made it further than anyone else. Now go home."

"You aren't going to call the cops?"

"Nah, it's not worth the loss of sleep, and besides, I admire people with gumption."

He had been edging to the door as we talked.

"Wait a second."

He stopped.

"It would be interesting to read about the guy who almost got the story. It would be a story within itself."

He paused in thought.

"Yes, it would; however, it would be taken as a work of fiction if I didn't have something to back it up."

"Simple, write that I now carry a Walther P 38."

"I thought it was a German luger."

"These were made as a replacement. I will show this to someone tomorrow morning so get your story out tonight."

"Thanks, I will get right on it."

"Whose byline should I look for?"

"Jack Nelson."

"Good luck, Jack."

"Thank you, Lord Blackhoof."

I thought Americans didn't do titles.

After that, the nightly nurse's parade started and lasted for an hour by the time they checked my blood pressure, and took my temperature. Next, they made certain I took my antibiotic pills. Then cleaned and rewrapped my wound.

I must be getting old; this wasn't the first time I had been shot. There was that guy in East Germany. The only reason I remember that is because I didn't have antibiotics there and almost went out of my mind with the infection and fever.

The next morning when Harold showed up, I had him contact the local police precinct and offer double time for two men twenty-four hours at my door.

Within the hour I had two cops in uniform at my door. They would be there for four hours and then replaced by another two.

I explained that reporters kept trying to sneak in. As far as I knew no one else was after me. To prove my point, a reporter walked up as I was talking to the two policemen.

He had a press badge and all, so I looked at him and said, "No comment."

I took the opportunity to pull the Walther P .38 from under my pillow. I didn't threaten the reporter at all. I just very clearly gave the pistol type and told the cops this was the replacement for my .38 which had been kept as evidence.

The reporter took the hint and retreated. The policemen and I had a good laugh after I told them about what had happened last night.

I asked them to round up the newspapers from downstairs to see if Nelson's story had appeared in the paper.

It had run in the *New York Daily Mirror* under his byline. If Jack kept this up, he would end up with a Pulitzer Prize.

The cops had experience doing this as they soon had chairs to sit in, and a small table for their coffee cups while reading the newspapers I had brought.

I had no problem with this. It wasn't as though the Stasi was going to make a try at me. As soon as I had that thought I looked for wood to knock on.

The wonderful thing about hospitals is that they're where you go to get well. The horrible thing about hospitals is they're where you go to get well. They are boring!

Two days later I was told I could leave if I wanted to but had to have someone available to change my dressings for the next week. By then it should be healed enough that the wound didn't need to be covered.

I couldn't wait for that; I needed a real shower. My doctor told me I could have a nurse journey with me. I thought about that but decided I didn't want another female in my life.

Nothing against a nurse I didn't even know; it was finding a stewardess in my bed that made me gun shy.

I told the doctor the story very briefly. He responded.

"Normally I say you shouldn't look gift horses in the mouth, but I admit that filly did sound like trouble."

He told me that he had a young intern who could use a week's break. The doctor's name was George Chamberlain. I met him on one of his breaks. He seemed nice enough, so I made an offer.

He grabbed it. I didn't realize interns got paid so little. He would earn more in a week than he would have in two months. Also, he would get a trip to England out of it.

I called Nina and she told me that it was okay for my plane to fly back and pick me up in two days. Just whose plane is it anyway?

She told me that her flight back to school was delightful. She slept in my nice big bed for most of the trip. It was so cool to arrive back in Zurich in time to attend her first class all refreshed.

The tours of my plane went over well with her classmates. The teachers made it a field trip day as they wanted to see it too. The boys' school which stood next to theirs got in on the fun.

After the joint tour, a dance was held that night, and it was keen. Somehow, I wasn't thrilled with all of this but kept my mouth shut. At least she was letting me use my plane.

She made me feel better when she told me that she wished I had been there. She missed me already. The girls in her class were so jealous! I had raised the bar on defining a great boyfriend.

The trip back to England was ho-hum. I had crossed the Atlantic so many times it wasn't an adventure anymore. The airplane was nice, but when you got down to it, it was an airplane. Of course, my airplane was more comfortable than commercial jets.

One of the flight crew had picked up the latest issue of *Aviation Today*. It had a pictorial tour of my airliner. I had to give the builders credit that they got their advertising out quickly.

They claimed this was the future of air travel for the well-to-do. A Pullman car in the sky.

It also explained the note I had received from the White House chief of staff about having some of their people look at my plane.

When I landed in Oxford, I had a message from my aircraft builder. Well, they didn't build the plane, but what should I call them? My interior decorators?

They had requests from seven heads of state and sixteen well-to-do people about tours of my aircraft. I thought about selling tickets for the tours but decided that might be considered tacky.

The only condition I put was the plane was to be clean and available when I needed it. They assured me it would be.

Grandmum had a limo waiting for me. Harold, George, and I were more than glad to get to The Meadows. After George changed my dressing, Mr. Hamilton showed him to his room.

We did nothing for the rest of the day. Dinner was casual, meaning no coat and tie. Several of the neighbors were there. Two daughters of my age were brought along.

Let's say I have been to dog shows with better-looking entries. Not that I let on. One behaved poorly, and I wanted no part of her, as she tried to feel my leg under the table.

The other was pleasant company but just not my type. She would do well in the marriage market if they had her buck teeth fixed. Maybe a nose job and chin reduction would help. Not good-looking but a very nice person.

Chapter 40

There followed several days of short walks in the morning, studying until lunch, and sessions with Dr. Chamberlain rubbing my wound to lessen scar tissue and redressing. Also, I tried on clothes for Harold as he insisted on updating my wardrobe.

The formal clothes were all fine, but it seemed my casual clothes needed replacing every season. It wouldn't do for me to be seen in the same outfits.

At least he arranged for tailors and clothiers to bring their wares to the house. I would first say if I would wear an item, then try it on for size, after which it would be sent back for adjustments.

I had learned to keep the decision about what I wore in my hands. I wasn't ready for Carnaby Street fashions which were getting more *outré* all the time.

Some afternoons I would check out the Roman dig. I wanted to go horseback riding, but that was kyboshed by Dr. Chamberlain. It would pull at my stitches. I understood but needed some activity.

Archery, swordsmanship, and target shooting were all ruled out. I didn't even bother to ask about boxing and unarmed combat.

Dr. Chamberlain proved to be a nice guy, but I always felt he was acting in the role of a doctor rather than being one. He was almost too good to be true if you understand what I'm trying to say.

I wasn't even allowed to go to the pub with my friends.

Dinner was always with a different crowd of local dignitaries and their eligible daughters. I asked Grandmum why she was doing this to me.

"Richard, I know these gals mean nothing to you. It does help your stature in the area that you are willing to break bread with these people.

"They will be able to drop your name with their friends. You know like, 'Lord Blackhoof said, or Lord Blackhoof was most taken with our daughter at dinner'.

"It's a social game with you being the greatest prize. By being able to dangle you as bait I become the arbiter of fashion in the area."

So Grandmum was using me to increase her standing. Now I understood the game, I was all in. I mean if you can't help your Grandmum, who can you help?

Not that I would go so far as to date any of these girls. I was pretty stuck on Nina, and none of them held a candle to her.

Once I understood the game being played, I made certain that I complimented each girl at the table on some item they had. I was careful not to talk about appearances. That could be misconstrued.

Saying how you admired the hat or blouse they wore was just that, admiration of an item, not the person. They could brag about that to their friends without sending any false messages.

Bored out of my gourd, I tried to straighten up my room. Fibber McGee had nothing on my closet. I gave up, jammed everything back in, and took off. Maybe Harold would find the mess and take care of it.

I went to Oxford. Even though I was kicked out of class I wasn't banned from the campus. I spent some time with my military friends in the hall. I didn't receive much sympathy for getting sent down.

You were supposed to respect authority even when they were wrong. I'm not sure that I like that part of the military mindset. I even expressed that thought and got corrected.

"Rick, you don't have to respect authority when they are wrong, but at the same time, you follow the chain of command when expressing displeasure."

"I report to the queen. You mean if I disagree with her, I can't throw a pie in her face?"

From the stunned expressions at this *lèse-majesté*, I gathered not. Not that I would but I wanted to make a point.

This led to a discussion based on, "I was just following orders." We all agreed it was best not to allow such a situation to come up because it could have no good ending. Sort of kill me now or kill me later.

Someone mentioned they were off to one of the parks on campus. There was a street festival going on. Festivals at Oxford were more interesting than your average street fair, so I decided to take a look.

It wasn't a long walk so I left the Aston Martin parked at the Hall as I knew it would be safe. To get to the festival you had to walk through the Alley. The Alley was a long walk in the park between the most gorgeous trees on both sides.

They were probably four hundred years old and were of tremendous size. I think they were chestnuts.

If they were chestnuts, it was appropriate because lining the walk were a bunch of chess nuts. Pun intended. It didn't seem organized as there were games with clocks, speed chess, and without clocks.

Patzers were commenting on the games. Even I knew the game better than some of them. Not that I had ever played seriously. I wouldn't fall for the Scholar's Mate, but a Queen's Gambit Declined would do me in.

Even a Queen's Gambit accepted would do me in. To tell the truth, I knew the terms but not the openings. For all I knew, white should play a French Defense.

There was one row of boards that caught my eye. One player was taking on ten players at once and beating them. It was a slaughter. I saw her fork two queens, exchange a knight for a queen, checkmate two, and two resignations on the same turn.

The little redhead was quiet and polite with everyone as she shook their hands after she won. She had a soft Kentucky accent.

I wondered how she ended up playing chess at her age in Oxford, England.

The lady who I thought was her mother was spending more time flirting with one of the dons than time with her. Mum also appeared to be tipsy.

One never knows what one will see at Oxford.

Next was a carnival row. Tent after tent with things like coconut shies. I wanted to throw at the coconuts but didn't take the chance of pulling a stitch.

Besides if I won, what would I do with the coconut?

There was a fortune teller's tent. She advertised palm reading. I must have been desperate for something to do as I went in.

I was glad I had. The palm reader was too old for me, but she was gorgeous. I crossed her palm with silver. It was a five-pound note.

She had no list of prices, but I thought I would get some change back. Silly me, I was dealing with a real live gypsy.

She took my hand in hers and studied my palm. She told me my lifeline was long so I would live to a ripe old age. It also indicated that I was a rock in other people's lives that put them first. My actions would make me a role model for many others.

Mine was so long that it predicted I would be a hero over and over.

My headline was also long. It indicated I was an analyzer and would come up with many good solutions. It also indicated that I could change as needed almost to the point of being an actor.

My heartline indicated that I was a rational analytical thinker. This worked with my headline. I would become an inventor.

I was blown away as she told me these things. I didn't realize palm reading could be so in-depth and correct. I had to look into it some more.

I thanked her and turned down her offer of a private reading. I wasn't ready to go that far yet. Besides, I had heard tales about the gypsies and didn't want a husband with a long knife after me.

As I was walking out of the tent she said, "Come back and see me some other time, Sir Richard. I love reading about your adventures in the tabloids."

Maybe there isn't as much to palm reading as I had thought.

Leaving the park, I noticed a theater was playing a revival of Sir Richard Jackson's movies. I gave it a pass. Several Street performers were singing my songs wearing outfits similar to what I would have worn. I tossed coins in their hats but didn't linger.

One guy was so bad I just stood there and shook my head. He saw me and got upset, "If you think you could do any better, get up here."

Sometimes a man does what a man's gotta do. I turned tail and got out of there quickly to the laughter all around.

I slunk back to the Hall and my car. Looking back the only cool thing all day was that young serious-looking girl playing chess. I hope she does well in the future.

Chapter 41

George removed my stitches. I was healing very well. I no longer needed the wounds covered. The scars were puckered both front and back He told me that it looked like I had extra butt holes, except they were in my side.

I wonder how girls would take to that.

He told me to still take it easy and avoid my more strenuous activities, but I was free to move ahead on my trip. He was planning on a couple of days in London before flying home.

I knew he had met a boy who lived in London, and he would be staying with him. Each to his own.

First, I met with my chief pilot. We had decided on that title. We went over the itinerary to ensure that the plane would be refueled and restocked as needed along the way.

I was getting excited about the trip and so was the crew. This job was an unusual one for them. There would be multiple passengers at different times but nothing like commercial flights.

Also, they only had one person who had to be pleased, me. While I was in meetings, they would be free. My stays would be longer than they normally had so it was like a mini vacation for them.

The stewardesses were chattering like magpies, but it was fun to hear the excitement in the office where we held our meeting.

After that meeting once we all agreed on what needed to be done, I called Mr. Norman at the palace to see if anything was going on there that I needed to know about.

There was, and he didn't want to talk about it on the phone. My meeting with the flight crew had been in their company's office in the Oxford Aviation Center, so I had my Cessna wheeled out and flew down to London.

A black cab to Buck House and a quick trip through security had me in front of Mr. Norman within two hours.

"Mr. Norman, what's up?"

We had been on an informal basis ever since I got him some autographed Sinatra albums.

"We had the most curious message for you."

"Oh?"

"Your dry cleaning is ready."

"Did they say where to pick it up?"

"Here is an address in London in the south near the Brixton tube station. Under no circumstances are you to go near the station."

"Did they say that?"

"No, I did. It is getting to be one of the most dangerous areas of London. Gangs have moved in. We will have a car with a security team to take you there. You pick up your 'dry cleaning' and get back in the car, nothing else."

"Sounds easy enough."

He replied, "For most people. How are your wounds healing? Is your broken arm back up to snuff?"

I think he was trying to make a point.

"When do I go?"

"Now would be a good time. No time was specified so I would like it to be in the early afternoon—less trouble at this time."

"Okay, let's do it."

"It isn't us; I'm too old for this type of jaunt. Now back in the war...."

I didn't pick up on that line. I had heard too many of the old days' stories. What I did hear was machine-gun bullets smacking against a landing craft door. I didn't need their stories, but I would give my respect.

I was loaded into a large four-door auto. It was a Humber Super Snipe and ugly as sin. Along with me were a driver and three others. All were in civilian clothes, but I suspect they were Coldstream Guards as they currently had palace duty.

We arrived at the dry cleaner with no issues. My bodyguards got out first, and I ducked into the dry cleaner.

I told them I was here to pick up my dry cleaning but had lost my ticket. The woman behind the counter glanced down. I could see my picture taped to her desk.

"Wait here."

I should have known as my favorite Chinese dry cleaning lady from Los Angeles came out from the backroom.

"Thank goodness you got here so quickly. It's so hot back there."

"Why am I here?"

"I need to give you a warning about your trip. Since you have helped my country so much, you will be asked to visit Beijing so they may thank and honor you."

"That doesn't sound bad."

"China is approaching a bad time. Chairman Mao is declining, no matter how many rivers you may see him swim. There are competing groups to take power.

"Those who are following his wife want to run the country like warlords. They are willing to cut China off from the rest of the world. This would stop the port projects and the food shipments.

"They would rather millions starve to death than surrender power. The other group wants to modernize and move away from communism.

"They would rather live the life of rich capitalists. They feel China could become the strongest economy in the world in fifty years.

"Mao's wife's people will try to capture you and give you to the KGB. That way you are gone, and the Soviets will be blamed."

"So, I just won't go to China when asked."

"You have to go to keep the programs going. If you don't, the warlord group will use it as an excuse to shut them down."

"If I go, how will my safety be ensured?"

"You will be surrounded by bodyguards your whole stay. They have already been vetted."

"Not to sound paranoid—you can vet all you want, and the most loyal guard will turn when their families are held as hostages."

"We aren't *shù lín lǐ de bǎo bèi*. You would say babes in the woods. These guards are from a special group who haven't any families. They are alone in the world."

"I'm still skeptical."

"If you don't take this chance, you will be condemning a million people to death by starvation."

Talk about your guilt trip.

"I will probably do it."

At that, I turned and left. My bodyguards were adjusting their clothes as if they had been in a scuffle. No one else was in sight.

We went back to the palace where I relayed my conversation to Mr. Norman. He called another office. MI6, I assumed.

A gentleman showed up quickly. His office must have been almost next door to the Queen's Messenger's office.

I told my story while he took notes. He made no comment when I finished. He just left.

I told Mr. Norman I was returning to The Meadows and I would call my parents from there. He asked that I stay overnight in London as there might be more questions later.

I agreed and left for the Plaza. The thoughts kept running around in my head. Go to almost certain death or live and let millions die. I knew I couldn't have those deaths on my conscience, so my decision was made.

At the Plaza, I called my parents. They were in an upbeat mood until I told them about China. They had no instant answers. We agreed we would let the situation develop for a few days and see what MI6 had to say.

Dad wondered aloud if we should call the CIA, but I answered his question with the name Robertson. If MI6 wanted to pass it on, let them do so. From what we had seen the CIA wasn't competent. That may be unfair, but the proof of the pudding is in the tasting.

Rather than end our conversation on a gloomy note, I was updated on family events.

Denny had been made a full partner in the photography studio. He now had a girlfriend and was lobbying for a driver's license. He wasn't sixteen but he made the case that I had one at fifteen.

Eddie had made Star Scout, well on his way to Eagle. He still thought girls stank, all except Mary, and she had girl cooties.

Mary was acting more mature each day, at least business-wise. She still liked to play with dolls and ride her pony. That and dabble in the stock market. What every first grader was doing.

Dad's business was going like gangbusters. He now was buying newspapers, radio, and TV stations all over the world. He wanted to have a presence in every major capital in the world.

He wanted to keep the politicians of the world as honest as he could and try to prevent wars. Just then he had a paper in France that was exposing those politicians and businesspeople who were trying to keep fighting the Vietnamese.

He thought if that war went on, we would be dragged into it, and everyone knew that a war on the Asia mainland was unwinnable, everyone but the politicians.

Mum continued her charity work. She had started in the LA area with small groups and then expanded to larger groups covering California. She was considering a request to be on their board from the American Red Cross. Her only hold-up was the fact the nonprofit paid such high internal salaries.

On the other hand, if they were worth what they were being paid in terms of results for the organization, there was no reason to deprive the professional staff of competitive pay. Figuring out whether they were worth it was the hard part.

I bet she would end up with the Salvation Army or some such that passed the money on. She did say she thought she could change the organization from the inside.

From what I was learning of the world, I doubted it.

Chapter 42

Monday of the first week in October we finally took off for Los Angeles on my business survey. I settled on calling it a survey as I was surveying the state of my businesses. Taking care of business, one could say.

Mr. Hamilton drove Harold and me to the Oxford Aviation Center. We had made enough trips in the aircraft that it now seemed like an old hat. When we boarded, I did look around to see if there were any damages from all of Nina's friends traipsing through.

If there had been any damages, everything was set to rights now. I mentioned that to the head stewardess. She told me that the groups had been very respectful and other than the odd candy wrapper and chips bags, they left the plane clean.

The flight crew kept track of how many people had gone through. Nina told me she had a few friends over on several tours. Did you know that Nina had one hundred and thirty-six friends?

Her Queen Bee rating must be sky-high now.

Good for her.

Anyway, we took the polar route to LA and arrived without incident. The flight didn't seem that long as I put in a regular type day, having real sit-down meals and doing schoolwork in my office. I even worked in a nap after lunch.

In LA once past immigration and customs, it was smooth sailing. Since we had landed and parked in the private aviation area the officers came to us.

Immigration stamped my US passport. No sense in raising questions about my citizenship. They had an extra person with them in plain clothes. His look screamed spy!

Even though I used my US passport, we were announced as Queen's Messenger One. Immigration ignored this.

The extra person dressed the part, for goodness's sake; a trench coat and sunglasses? He showed me an ID that was from the State Department. As if. He asked if we could talk in private.

I took him to my office. The way he gawked you would think he had never been on a plane before.

"Sir Richard, we understand that you have been asked to visit China."

"That is not entirely correct. I have been told that I will officially be asked to visit China."

"Do you intend to do so?"

"Under the circumstances, I have little choice in the matter."

"What are those circumstances?"

"If your masters have not told you, then it is not my place to do so. If they had told you, then you already know."

"Now that is not a very cooperative attitude."

"The CIA has never cooperated with me before."

"I'm with the State Department."

"And the green fairy does not lead to hallucinations."

From his puzzled look, I don't think he knew the story behind absinthe. Hysteria had caused the spirit to be banned in most of Europe and the Americas. It was still banned in the US even though you could order a Sazerac in New Orleans.

I regretted the statement, as it would take too long to tell the story and would sidetrack the conversation, though that might not be a bad idea.

"I will tell you this, I have no desire to see millions of people starve to death."

"That confirms what we had heard. The US government won't be able to help you on this trip, but we wish you well."

"Thank you. I must say I have concerns about my safety, but I must go."

"If the time and opportunity are correct, you can mention that the US would like to normalize relations."

"To which faction would you like to normalize?"

"Ah, that is the question, isn't it— the winning side of course."

"With instructions like that, I'm glad I don't work for your group."

"At times I wonder also."

At that, we returned to the front of the aircraft where customs were waiting. You would think my nothing to declare would have gotten us on our way.

Instead, customs had a hard time believing that I had no baggage, only my briefcase. They insisted on checking the aircraft to see if I had anything that should be declared.

The customs agent wondered if I had any exotic furs that were banned or would have duty required.

Harold took him to my wardrobe in the belly of the aircraft. The agent came back shaking his head. He told the immigration people who waited for him that he had never seen the like.

Harold had explained that I had identical wardrobes at The Meadows in England and Jackson House here.

"I just thought I knew what rich was. This aircraft is rich, the wardrobe is insanely rich."

Seeing the writing on the wall, I asked if we could be on our way, and would they like a tour of the aircraft.

They would.

From the dirty look the head stewardess gave me, I owed her one. I didn't feel too guilty, as they would be staying in Beverly Hills within walking distance of Rodeo Drive.

Dad met Harold and me in a limo. I could tell it was the one Mary usually used from the hand-drawn pictures taped to the rear-facing seats. I didn't even ask.

"Your mum has the other one. She is finishing up at an event and will meet us at home. Welcome home, Rick."

"I thought it must be something like that. Turning to Harold, I explained about this being my sister's regular ride to school. He didn't bat an eye. From his dad's job, he was used to such things.

Once home and settled in, I sat down with Mum and Dad and had a long conversation. Most of it was about China and how I was to be careful. The rest was about my meetings tomorrow on the status of Jackson Enterprises.

Dad told me Jim Williamson had worked his crew into a frenzy, and I should calm them all down. They had rumors flying like crazy, everything from selling the company to my stepping down.

They knew the financial condition of the company, so bankruptcy has never been mentioned, though one theory was that I had been to Monte Carlo and gambled the place away.

Well, I had been to Monte Carlo.

Dinner was a pleasant affair. I hadn't sat down for a meal with the whole family for a long time. Even Mrs. Hernandez was there. It seemed it was a rare occasion for her to eat at home anymore.

She had become the official representative to the Hispanic community for the Jacksons. She had the family authority and checkbook behind her. Mary spoke up and told us that she had seen Mrs. Hernandez being picked up by another guy.

Mrs. Hernandez had many different gentleman friends and wasn't about to be tied down to any one of them. Go, Mrs. Hernandez!

Her presence had us use Spanish for the entire meal. Even my parents had broken down and taken immersion classes. I used my British accent to liven things up.

Being home was great. Denny, Eddie, and Mary all brought me up to date on the things my parents had told me, but I acted as if it was all new to me.

Though there was one big change since my last family phone conversation. Mary and Patty were friends again!

Who would have thought? I could see fifty years in the future where two very rich ladies would be at each other's throats when they weren't pushing their grandkids' strollers together.

The next morning, I went to my office. Dad went to his. This was my show. I collected a cup of coffee and asked the staff to come to the conference room.

I started down the hall to that room when Jim redirected me.

"That is now the executive conference room. We have had to expand and have a much larger room to meet in."

I wondered what else had changed without me knowing.

We walked down what was once a short hallway. Now the dead-end wall opened into the next set of offices in the building. There was a large open area with many of the new cubicle-type work areas.

I don't know if I would like to work in one of those. Off to one side was a large cafeteria that served full meals.

I remember when we had snacks in our small kitchen after I insisted we give the coffee away instead of putting money in the jar.

We entered a theater-type conference room which could be subdivided into smaller meeting or training areas. Today it was one large common area that could seat a hundred or so people. All seats were taken, and some people were left standing.

I asked Jim if we needed to expand the offices again. He said negotiations were in hand. We were trying to take over another floor. The landlord was being difficult about the rent.

"I thought Dad owned the building."

"That's the problem. He knows you can afford the exorbitant rent he is asking."

"If he wants to play hardball, we could buy another building, or better yet, I could whine to Mum."

"That might work, the head of a multi-million-dollar company whining to his mother works every time."

Chapter 43

I went to the front of the conference room, stood on the small, raised podium, and put the rumors to rest. This was nothing more than a survey of my business. My stop here was to check into the overall status of the company.

After my announcements I took questions. From their tone, I don't think we had any real problems, at least in LA.

Moving to the smaller conference room we had the divisional meetings. The agenda allowed an hour each for Jackson Personal Products, Jackson Home Products, and the Entertainment Division. Jackson Transportation was in the afternoon.

First up was a review of Personal Products. The meeting room was set up with a sideboard with the usual coffee, tea, orange juice, bagels, and donuts.

I had juice, coffee, a bagel with cream cheese, and a crème filled donut. I had skipped breakfast at home and was hungry.

The new markets which opened in Brazil, Argentina, Peru, Columbia, and Chile had brought in five million so far this year. Ahead of projections, it looked solid. It looked solid overall in Africa, but hairdryer sales were not doing as well as projected in South Africa. Some market penetration had started in Egypt and Southern Rhodesia. We still couldn't get a foothold in Liberia.

Don had talked to the managing director of the Firestone Plantation. Mr. Dawson was helpful, but everything was held up by the corruption in the Liberian government. We were refusing to pay the bribes requested. These weren't things like a round of golf. They were large cash payments. I supported our position.

Australia and the New Zealand markets had taken off well above projections. Europe was still spotty. The Mediterranean countries were still slow adopters while the Scandinavians couldn't buy enough dryers and curling irons.

The R&D department had just been opened with the first personnel brought on board. I was reminded that I had committed to being available for a ribbon cutting on the new building sometime in October. I would have to work it in. I suggested that we do it before I flew to Pittsburgh.

The bottom line of the division was that it was going to earn over fifteen million dollars in profit this year, well over the ten million projected.

Mark and Sharon Downing were in town, so they were present for my review. It was good to see them. Sharon was expecting. I made all the usual "happy for your noises" and made a mental note about a gift, maybe a fully endowed college fund.

They had bought out a competitor that had been approved at the last board meeting. The production facility and its infrastructure were exactly as needed. Ninety percent of the old workforce was kept on. We lost ten percent due to retirements.

The profit pace had been projected at four million. Instead, it would be four and a half. Mark's sister's wails could be heard all over the world.

Last before lunch, we reviewed the numbers of the Jackson Entertainment Division. The accounting group gave us dry numbers from movies and music.

This again included money due from the failed surfer movie and estimated revenues from *Over the Ohio*. OTO was doing fantastically. It had set US box office records and had done the same when released overseas.

On the movie front, it now looked like sixty million dollars. The music from all songs had been projected at $500,000 but was now at $400,000. Maybe people's ears weren't as bad as I thought!

As a side note, I was told Susan Wallace was doing very well. Mr. Spiller had set me up as a silent partner in her talent agency and was kept informed. Even so, I kept my hands off and would continue to do so unless she called for help. By keeping informed I could step in if her pride stood in the way of asking for help.

After lunch was Jackson Transportation, the largest review. It included the production of shipping containers, the Scottish Line, and Narrow Freight.

The additional financing approved at the last board meeting allowed them to grow. I could hardly believe the numbers involved.

Freight Forwarding now had been spun off as a new and separate part of Jackson Enterprises. I still liked the FreightEx name for Freight Express but yielded to the rest of the board.

The Scottish Line had added four more ocean-going freighters at fifty million. We had only talked of one, but the business required more ships. The prices were less than I thought. Maybe someone had a buy-one-get-one-free sale.

The book value of the company was now over one billion dollars. This year's profits had been estimated to be two hundred and twenty-five million dollars, but instead, they were three hundred and ten million.

Putting it all together I would make almost four hundred million dollars this year.

Jim Williamson gave me the numbers his overseas accounting teams had recaptured for us. There was no grand theft in under-reporting of royalties on the beer can pull tabs, but the nickels and dimes added up. The group more than paid for itself.

I liked it because it showed that we paid attention to the small details. This would prevent large thefts.

Sam Wingate, our corporate attorney, had a tax accountant update me on my earnings and tax position.

I was still in the ninety-one percent marginal tax bracket and the only way I would ever get out of it was for the government to change the tax rates.

My three-million-dollar salary, oops, five million (so easy to forget what I make), wasn't the real money. It was the company's profits. On those, I would owe over eighty million dollars. Of course, I would keep two hundred and thirty million. Not bad for an eighteen-year-old.

I made a mental note to think about spreading my money around a bit. The US stock market was great but there were other markets around the world. Then there was land, maybe Australia.

At the end of the day, numbers were spinning in my head. It is a good thing I took a lot of notes and had copies of the presentations.

As I was leaving the building Alice Thompson approached me. She was an old girlfriend's aunt. After greeting me she let me know that my old flame Emily was no longer going with that Roman guy and would like me to stop by if I had time.

I told her it was good to see her, which it was, and that if I had time I might stop by Emily's. So, I lied. It wouldn't have been polite to say what I felt about that.

After thinking for a moment, I realized that I had no feelings for Emily, positive or negative.

Mum, Dad, and I went to dinner at the Brown Derby. They had suggested it, and I thought they might have a specific topic in mind. I kept waiting for the other shoe to drop but it never did. They just wanted to have dinner with their eldest son.

We reminisced about the old days, two years ago in Bellefontaine. We had come so far and changed so much. Each of us had grown into our new environment.

I thought Dad had grown the most, from the railroad extra board to a media empire. Not bad for a child of the great depression.

I think Mum had always been titled. Maybe not by birth but by the way she carried herself in her life.

Frank Sinatra and Dean Martin were there having dinner. We stopped and chatted for a few minutes on the way out. Frank asked if I was ready for another song. Dean protested it was his turn.

I gave neither one an answer. The next day a reporter who had partially overheard us wrote that the three of us were going to sing together. What I liked was that he even knew that we would be singing about all the girls we loved. My verse would be very short, the other two not so much.

They had to scramble out in Cucamonga, but we were able to do the grand opening of the Personal Products R&D center the next day.

By having such a short timeline, we managed to avoid most of the politicians who would have invited themselves. We did have one surprise guest.

The man who put Cucamonga on the map showed up. Dad thought it would be neat to have Mr. Benny there. It was. It took a lot of pressure off me to have a real star present.

The center had been up and running for two months so it was staffed and had projects underway. I thought several ideas looked promising but didn't think they could make a handheld calculator.

I ate at home with the kids that night. We had a pizza party. The pizza was good but not as good as Shively's in Bellefontaine.

The next morning my traveling circus gathered at the airport, and we took off for Pittsburgh. Harold updated me on my LA wardrobe. It was a good thing I was able to order, repair, and replace some items, Milord, or it would have been a *soigné* disaster.

I thanked him for his diligence. What is *soigné* anyway?

Chapter 44

I looked up *soigné* and found out it was the same as well dressed. Why didn't he say so?

The flight to Pittsburgh was like most flights, uneventful. We left early in the morning. We lost three hours due to time zones but gained one due to tailwinds.

We landed in Pittsburgh, boarded a limo, and went to our hotel to check-in. Todd met us in the hotel dining room for dinner. I still didn't like the mural.

We discussed the agenda for tomorrow. I had been open with my staff, letting them know that I would be talking to some of their direct reports. I wouldn't be asking any leading questions but if the employee wanted to bring something up, I would listen.

I was going to do a tour of all the operations. I had never done this before. I was most interested in how iron ore turned into steel.

I expressed that and was told I would see it all.

In the morning I was taken over to the main office and outfitted with steel-toed safety shoes, earplugs, a hard hat, a bright orange vest, a pair of leather gloves with steel wire in the lining to make them cut-resistant, and safety glasses.

Todd had his custom-made gear. If I did this very often, I would have to do the same. I was made to sit through a safety demonstration and sign that I had done so.

"Don't touch anything without asking first. Keep within the yellow lines when walking. Look upwards for overhead transfer lines. It wouldn't do to have a crucible of molten iron dropped on your head."

When I was all geared up, I felt like a knight of the roundtable or in this case knight of the steel mill.

It was fascinating. The ore along with lime and coke were put in a blast furnace. The ore came from the Mesabi iron range in

Minnesota. I asked why the ore wasn't smelted there. It was cheaper to ship ore to Pittsburgh than coal to Minnesota.

Once the ore was fed into the furnace and everything but iron and some impurities like carbon were burned off, the molten iron would be poured into a crucible for moving to the Bessemer process.

Here the molten iron had recycled steel mixed in along with oxygen being forced through the mixture. This eliminated most of the carbon which would make the metal brittle. In a sense, it was like glass making using broken glass, cullet. If this weren't done the metal would have to be remelted several times to eliminate most of the carbon.

The molten mixture, now steel, was stirred to effectively homogenize it. The molten steel was poured into molds, in our case to make a slab of steel.

The slab then would be sent through a series of rollers to thin it down. This was called hot rolling because the slab wasn't allowed to cool. In some operations, cold rolling could be done.

The slab started as six inches high; it ended up as a sheet that was an eighth of an inch thick.

I probably misunderstood a few things on the way, but it was impressive. I was introduced to the men supervising the operation and some of the floor workers.

All seemed happy to meet me and gave no indications of wanting to say something. I was accompanied by Todd and several members of his staff, but they stayed in the floor office when I was talking to the floor people.

Todd was even smart enough to take a long restroom break while I had coffee with his staff. Again, there were no negative vibes. If anyone wanted to bad-mouth the boss, they had their chance. I did inquire if they were having trouble meeting production goals or were short of any needed equipment, manpower, or buildings.

It seemed the only problem brought up was that they all thought they should get a raise. It was said humorously, but it was kidding on the square.

From the steel-making operation, we moved on to fabrication. Here is where the steel sheets were prepared for assembly into a cargo container.

There had to be holes drilled for rivets and the metal painted. Once the metal was formed by a metal brake machine and holes drilled, it was ready to be assembled. The painting process was powder coating. The paint wasn't in a liquid form but a powder.

The metal was given an electrostatic charge, then the powder was sprayed on a grounded surface, in this case, the metal of the container to bond it to the metal. Heat in a hot-air-drying tunnel was then applied to cure the paint. This gave a better, as in harder, and more evenly applied coating.

Again, this is a very simplistic explanation of what I saw.

What was hard to wrap my head around was that I owned all of this, and the people were my employees. The tour lasted all day. I was worn out by the evening. That was with just a general overview of the big stuff, none of the fiddly bits.

There was no rest for the wicked. I had fled the mayor the last time I was in town. This time I had to pay my dues.

There was a reception for me being held in the ballroom of my hotel. At least I got to take a short nap before I had to clean up.

Todd and his wife Billy had dinner with me in my room. They were to be by my side. They would introduce me to people and bail me out if things got awkward.

This time the governor of Pennsylvania had enough advance notice to attend. Todd told me the two gentlemen would have a short agenda. One would be to get as large a political contribution from me as possible.

The other would be to talk about the benefits of unionizing my plants.

"What benefits are there?"

"None for us, a lot for them. Unions contribute to their campaigns and provide workers and your basic thug to disrupt their opponent's gatherings.

"For us, we have to deal with another layer between us and the worker, which does not have the worker's best interest at heart. When they were smaller, they cared about the workers; now they care about the union. The union cares about their politicians who care about their support. Round and round it goes."

On that cheerful note, we went down to the ballroom. The program was hors d'oeuvres with a string quartet in the background. The rest would be a meet and greet. I would be asked to say a few words. I planned to do that, say few words.

We were cornered as soon as we walked into the room. An aide had been detailed to watch for us. He approached Todd whom he recognized and told him that we were to follow him.

The mayor and governor were waiting in a side room. My first impulse was to not go. Who were they to tell me when and where I was to go? Fortunately, I had time for a second thought.

Todd and Billy had to live here; I didn't. My hesitation must have been noticeable because Todd thanked me when I turned to follow the aide.

When we entered the side room it was all hail and well met. That lasted for maybe two minutes, and then it was time to get down to business.

The first order of business was money, contribution money.

The mayor asked, "What political party do you back, Sir Richard?"

His use of "Sir" gave me the perfect opening.

"As Sir Richard Jackson, I'm a Monarchist."

From the stunned look on their faces, they expected almost any answer but that. The governor recovered first.

"When you aren't Sir Richard, just Rick Jackson, who do you support?"

"As you may know President Eisenhower is my godfather, but President Kennedy and I get along quite well. You might say I'm not tied to any party, but the person and the issue."

"Then it wouldn't be out of line for officials of the state where your income is produced to ask for a contribution."

"It would never be out of line to ask."

From the little twist of his mouth, I could see that I was getting to the governor.

I turned to Todd, "Do we have someone locally to take care of this?"

"Yes, we work through our legal department."

"What would be the standard donation in this situation?"

"Twenty thousand to the governor and ten to the mayor."

From their looks, the two men would be happy to get this.

"Make it thirty and twenty."

Now it was smiling all around.

The mayor now took his turn.

"Sir Richard, you must know Pittsburgh is a strong union town and it has done well for us."

"I'm sure it has done well for you. I'm not sure it will do well for my company. I will take it under consideration."

"That's all we can ask for."

Neither was going to push harder and endanger their contributions. I was certain another shoe would drop before the evening was over.

We made nice again as we bid each other farewell.

Chapter 45

As soon as we moved far enough away, I told Todd, "Donate through discreet sources twice as much to their opponents. Also, when we do our in-depth financial review, let me know how much we can do to beat the union rate while still having a profit."

"There will be no problems with these items. Billy here is the head of the local Republican Party women's club. She will take care of that. We have already run the other numbers as I was going to bring this up."

It's good when the boss and his team are on the same wavelength.

"Rick, I wondered how you would handle those guys. I thought you were an amateur at this sort of thing."

"I learned at the Court of St. James; that's the big leagues. Even the White House isn't that tough of an audience."

We went back to the main reception room. We were approached immediately by a big guy wearing a dark blue suit and red tie. The only reason I mention that is he looked like he had just got out of prison. Something about him shouted Bad Guy.

He didn't mess around. He came straight to his point.

"I'm from the Metal Workers Union, and we are going to organize your plant."

"I think the workers have a say in that."

"You're going to sign a contract with us. We don't need their vote."

"You talk pretty strongly; can you back it up?"

"Guys get kneecaps broke that don't do as we say."

I opened my jacket so he could see my shoulder holster.

"Somebody could end up dead."

"You don't scare me."

I turned to Todd, "Better call Popeye."

"What about Mr. Lucky?"

"Hold off on that. If things go bad, we will bring him in."

The thug stood there, his head going back and forth as we talked.

"You guys are supposed to be wimps. How do you know such heavy hitters?"

"Popeye is my uncle. Mr. Lucky used to date my mum."

The last wasn't true but he didn't have to know that. We moved on leaving the befuddled thug behind us. It was amazing the reputation Popeye had gotten in the last few years. I wonder how that occurred?

On second thought it was better that I didn't know.

The next day we spent all morning going through the financials in depth. Everything looked in order. At one point Jim looked up and nodded his head. It all looked good to him.

We spent time figuring out how much of a raise to give our workers. This was the perfect time to do so since the unions were negotiating their contracts right now. They were looking at six percent across the board but realistically would settle for four.

We could give eight percent and still make over two hundred million in the coming year. Since it was out of my pocket, I didn't need anyone's permission. What is the difference between me getting two hundred and fifty million or two hundred million?

I remember when I mowed lawns for a buck.

The raise would take away one of the union's strongest arguments, that our workers were piggybacking off the union's effort. Instead, they looked like they couldn't take care of their workers as well as we could. Why would anyone join their union to get less money?

Of course, most employers weren't like us. Most tried to shave the beard off Abe Lincoln before they paid a penny more than they were forced to, but we took a more forward-looking view.

Later that afternoon Harold, Jim Williamson, Todd, and I boarded my plane. We were flying to Liverpool overnight.

Todd had managed to call Popeye, who said he would take care of things.

After take-off, we sat in the conference room and rehashed the day. We agreed the union wouldn't be a problem and that the politicians would be happy with the money.

Eventually, the politicians would learn of the other donations, but I didn't care. It wasn't as though I had any speeding tickets to be fixed.

After dinner, I retired to my room and had a good night's sleep. The others slept in their first-class reclining seats. They were a new type that laid almost flat, so they weren't suffering that much.

The next morning, we got off the plane in Liverpool. I felt sharp after a good night's sleep and a large breakfast. Todd and Jim assured me they had a comfortable night.

After laying out my clothes for the day, a nice suit, Harold retired to his cubby hole in the cargo hold. He had a Pullman bunk there and I suspected that he was going back to bed.

His job is better than mine.

The Liverpool cargo facility was well underway. They had two of the six planned large cranes in operation. The port master told me they had already made a difference in their operational cost.

I asked him to tell me what the differences were. He and I adjourned to a small office with coffee while the others went on a tour of the yard. I declined the tour, pointing out that if you have seen one giant crane, then you've seen them all.

Jim and Todd knew what was going on so gave me no grief.

The thing that most excited the port master was the shortened turnaround time for the ships. Every day in port costs the shipping company a large part of their annual expense.

You would think the port master who derived income from the ships would want them there longer. His port traffic was up, offsetting the loss of revenue. In the long run, he estimated that it would increase profits by thirty percent.

Also, he was very happy with my company's performance, and especially the cooperation from my employees. No complaints whatsoever.

That told me everything I needed to know at this stop. It was clear that there were no problems not being reported to corporate.

From Liverpool, we were flying to Buenos Aires with a fueling stop in Senegal. When I boarded the plane, I was handed a message which had arrived from Whitehall. I was requested to call a US Army general, Brigadier Westmoreland. Whitehall asked that I cooperate if I could.

I called the general from the Aviation Center. He was aware of my itinerary and asked if I could reroute to Washington on my way to Buenos Aires.

I asked him why and he told me it was classified, and he couldn't talk about it on the phone.

Since Whitehall wanted me to cooperate, I told him the plane would be rerouted and I would see him tomorrow.

Again, we flew all night. The flight crew was getting hours in their logbooks. I had started the trip with the secret hope that I could get some more hours in on the big bird, but it wasn't to be. I couldn't stay up flying half the night and do my job the next day.

The next morning, we landed at Washington National Airport, on the private aviation side. General Westmoreland had a limo waiting to take me to the Pentagon.

Out of habit, I had worn my shoulder holster with my .38. I had yet to find a weapon with more stopping power that wouldn't ruin the hang of my suits. I was cheap enough that I didn't want to replace my fifteen suit coats times three with new ones.

It set off the alarms at security. They had one of the new metal detectors. You would think I was trying to invade the place.

When you saw how badly I was outgunned, it was ludicrous. It took my US Marshal credentials to calm them down.

After that, I was taken to a room somewhere in the Pentagon. That building is huge!

The general was waiting for me in his office. It was nice but not as nice as mine in LA or even at The Meadows. It did beat the one in the garage in Oxford. I know this was small-minded of me, but first impressions are first impressions.

The general was all business.

"We understand from Intelligence that you will be making a trip to China?"

Since it wasn't a secret to the Chinese I answered in the affirmative.

"We need you to check out the Chinese atomic bomb program at Haiyan. They call it 596 for some reason, and if possible, see how the construction of the test site is going at Lop Nor."

"There seems to be a mistake here, I'm not in espionage."

"You have done some work in that area with the KGB and the Stasi."

"Not by choice or training."

"Well, this is an order."

"Uh, I'm not in the US Army."

"I will contact your direct superior at Whitehall, and they will give you your orders."

"You would probably have better luck if you had the chairman of the Joint Chiefs contact the president, then have the president contact the prime minister, who in turn would call on the queen."

"Why would I do that?"

"Because I'm a colonel in the Coldstream Regiment but don't report to them in Whitehall. I'm an aide-de-camp to the queen and report directly to her."

From the look on his face, you could tell that I had trumped his ace.

Chapter 46

"We need this information."

"I don't doubt it, but your intelligence group hasn't given you the full story. While I'm there one of the political factions will try to assassinate me. I'm afraid I won't be able to sneak around and spy in any dark allies."

"I can see that I have this all wrong. My apologies."

About that time an aide knocked on the door and handed the general a note. He read it and handed it to me.

It was forwarded by the flight crew. It was from President Kennedy. He had been made aware of my arrival in Washington. He would like me to stop by if I had time.

The general had a very strained look on his face. It didn't take a rocket scientist to figure out why.

"No one needs to know all the details of this meeting. You asked me to be alert to any information on the Chinese atomic program. While not making any inquiries, I will pass on any information gained on my trip."

Westmoreland might get that second star someday.

I asked the general to have a call placed to the White House. He had me connected to the main switchboard.

As sheer luck would have it, I recognized the voice of the switchboard operator I knew. We had met briefly in the cafeteria on a previous visit. Her voice defined sultry.

"Ah Sophia, this is Sir Richard, I'm returning the president's call."

The icing on the cake, I was put right through.

"Mr. President, how may I help you today?

"I understand, I will ask if the Pentagon can have a car bring me over.

"No sir. General Westmoreland wanted to know if it would be possible for me to share any passive information I would acquire on my trip, especially if I end up in China.

"I thought his request was reasonable. I'll be there within the hour, traffic permitting. Okay, I will go to the helipad."

The General hadn't tried to pressure me, so I didn't drop him in it. He had to be impressed with my being so well-known at the White House. Sometimes you get lucky.

By the time I got to the helipad Marine One or one of its clones was waiting for me. A two-minute flight and I was out on the White House lawn.

I had to go through a security screening and surrender my weapon.

I was then escorted directly to the Oval Office where the president waited in his rocking chair. Brother Bobby lounged on a couch.

"Sir Richard, thank you for coming. Bobby and I need to talk to you."

I had been thinking this might be about China, but now it didn't feel like it.

"What about?"

"You have offended some powerful people in our party. We need you to make amends."

"I gather both the governor of Pennsylvania and the mayor of Pittsburgh aren't happy with me."

"You may say that they are livid. How could you think they wouldn't find out about your other donations immediately?

"But they aren't the ones who concern me. It's the union. They are ready to issue a contract on you."

"And that is because?"

"The salary increases you are giving. It could end up destroying them."

"Why should I care? They would only hurt my workforce and reduce the profits."

It must have been his brother's turn to play bad cop.

"Listen here, Jackson; we are ordering you to take back the pay increase. It is not in our best interests for it to go through."

"I understand that the union is a strong supporter and donor for both your party and your campaigns, but I have to do what is best for me and mine."

"You could be heading for more trouble than you can handle."

"Should I take that as a threat to me, my employees, and my company?"

"Take it any way you want. By the way, you left out your family."

At that, the president stepped in to calm things down. Bobby had shown the stick, now I was to see the carrot.

"Rick, we aren't going down that road, but you must understand that this is very serious to us. We can make up your loss of profits by special tax breaks."

I had to bite my tongue. This was the party representing the workers against the rapacious rich capitalist. This didn't surprise me at all. I had seen Ike and Dick Nixon pull similar stunts on previous visits.

This was the nature of the beast. Maybe I was a Monarchist at heart. You understand I would have to be the Monarch.

"I will back down to the point that my people will receive the same increase as the union."

"That will work. We will start the tax break through Congress."

"Thank you, Mr. President. Is there anything else? I need to depart to Buenos Aires."

"That will be all."

After retrieving my weapon, I was driven back to the airport. Once we were in the air, I explained my stop at the White House to them.

"Boy, they play hardball."

"Yes, they do. That is why I want to wait until after the industry contracts are signed and set up a better health care program, scholarships, and anything else you can think of to put the increase back in."

"Your name will be Mudd."

"They will get over it. Other things will have their attention. I also would like you to start a working group to study moving our Pittsburgh operations to England."

"What!"

"We aren't going to do it; the English taxes are much worse than here, the infrastructure not as good, and the workers are more often communist than not.

"I will get their attention. I can wave a stick also."

"What about a carrot?"

"The carrot will be not moving the operations."

"How old did you say you were?"

I didn't bother to answer that one.

We landed in Miami to refuel. We would have another stop in Rio for the same. Because of the time of day, we would spend five hours on the ground in Rio so we would arrive in Buenos Aires in the morning.

I spent most of the flight looking out a window and wondering if I had handled the whole Pittsburgh situation correctly. I was looking for problems in my operations. Maybe I was proving to be the problem.

After a while, I sighed and went looking for a snack. This introspection seemed to make me hungry. As I had some chips and dip along with a Coke, I came out of my little funk.

As we crossed the Caribbean there was a huge storm below us to one side. It wasn't a hurricane, but it did remind me of the last time I had been through here.

That time was in a ship, and I could still remember the screaming of the metal as we twisted and turned in the storm-racked seas. Man, I'm sounding poetic.

Poetic or not it had been the scariest thing of my life. Even being shot didn't compare. The shootings were quick. The storm went on for hours.

While remembering, I watched the lightning below me light up the sky in a magnificent show. All of nature's power was on display, and those of us looking out from the aircraft were the only ones who could see it from above.

Well, of course, there may have been other planes flying this route. I had to laugh at myself. My musing was all over the place. I think it was my mind trying to get comfortable with the fact that I had a clash with the president of the United States, the most powerful person in the world, and came out whole.

Time would tell about being whole, but I think it would be okay.

We landed on schedule in Rio. By the time we got over the South American mainland, the storm had died out so it was a smooth descent and landing.

We all deplaned once we landed. It was nice to get out and stretch our legs. Even the sedentary Harold walked with us.

The private aviation terminal was divided up so that we could go inside without technically being in Brazil. This way we avoided customs and immigration. With my British passport, I wouldn't need a visa, but with my American one, I would have had to have the stamp.

I was paged as Senhor Jackson, please come to the information desk. There was a message to call Dad no matter the hour.

With an operator's help, I was able to get through to him. I had all sorts of dire thoughts about my family. It was nothing of the sort.

"Rick, way to go. You have the president of the United States fuming."

"Why? I gave in to him on the wage deal; we aren't going to exceed the union package."

"He's mad about what you are planning later. He called me to get you to back off."

"How did he know?"

"When did you talk about this?"

"Not until we were on the plane with Jim and Todd and after we took off from DC."

"Did you land anywhere?"

"We refueled in Miami."

"Either Jim or Todd called the White House, or you have a spy on board."

Chapter 47

The first thing I did after hanging up from Dad was hunt up Jim and Todd. I asked them directly if they had talked to anyone about my trouble with the Kennedys.

Both said they hadn't and asked when they could have done so; they didn't get off the plane in Miami. Since the inflight radio would have taken the help of the flight crew, I realized it couldn't have been them.

We talked about who could have gotten off the plane in Miami and made a phone call. Of course, that person would have had to hear our conversation.

We hadn't seen anyone hanging around the office, but that didn't mean there wasn't someone hiding around the corner and eavesdropping.

I had the chief pilot come back. I asked him who all had gotten off the plane in Miami. From the question, he could tell something was up.

"Several of the crew and hostesses walked the runway but the only one who went inside the terminal was First Officer Raymond. He is acting as our purser on this trip. He went in to pay for the fuel."

"Would you please bring him back here?"

The chief pilot went up front to bring Raymond back. He came back alone.

"Raymond was seen going into the aviation terminal and going through immigration. He's not on board."

"Well, we know who our spy was and who he was working for."

Todd said, "Not necessarily, He may have been freelancing and called the Kennedys to sell it to them."

Thinking for a moment, "I don't think so. The president acted on the information immediately. That indicates a high degree of trust in the source."

"You're right, Rick, you should be a spy yourself."

"Lord Blackhoof here, Lord Richard Blackhoof."

That just didn't have the Bond ring to it.

"I wonder how many other spies we have on board."

"Why would the US have more than one?

"There's the Russians, the Chinese, and for all I know Luxembourg.

"Maybe not Luxembourg, but you get my drift."

Our meeting was interrupted by a man in a US Army uniform. He had been allowed on board by one of the hostesses. I wondered what new grief this would be.

His unit badges were from the Signal Corps. That seemed strange. He introduced himself as Captain Johnson. He was wondering if we could help him with a logistics problem.

He was escorting a lady to Buenos Aires to give a speech to a ladies' group. Their flight had been canceled and there weren't any others that would get them there on time. Could they hitch a ride?

Things couldn't get any weirder, so I said yes. He brought an elderly lady on board. She must have been seventy. He introduced her as Grace Banker. I told her I was glad to meet her and give her a lift.

She thanked me and took a seat up front and that was the last I saw of her. I wondered why the Signal Corps was escorting her around. I didn't care enough to ask, as I was thinking of spies.

Spying for information was one thing. My previous experience with spies was more serious, life and death serious.

The flight continued and we arrived on time in Buenos Aires. The Signal Corps captain and the lady he was escorting thanked me once more. As they moved away, I heard him asking her about General Pershing.

I wondered if she had ever been on track 61. Nasty thoughts Rick. Clear your mind!

The docks known as the Puerto Nuevo were in the Retire ward and run by the General Ports Administration. This meant a continual series of bribes, all low-level. More like a tip.

I had been warned about this so had a pocketful of one peso silver coins. Some things aren't worth fighting. Every official I was introduced to was an expert at palming these coins.

The port construction itself was going well. I had a conversation with the head of construction. He rated a gold peso.

I realized that as long as I kept handing out bribes, I would be told what I expected to hear. The only saving grace was that if someone else bribed them they would hear what they wanted, even if it contradicted what I had been told.

In other words, my trip here was a waste. I did manage to corner a couple of American engineers and ask them if things were to the blueprints. They told me they were, but it was running up costs by ten percent to keep everything that way. Those pesos added up.

I told them to keep the bribes rolling, the project safe, and on time. The cost overrun would just be part and parcel of the whole deal.

The irony was that the bribes being paid were being billed right back to the Argentine government, so they were paying for everything.

I wondered how long it would take for the wheels to fall off.

I had to go to a reception at the British Embassy that night. My welcome the last time was gracious as the son of Viscountess Jackson. Now as Lord Blackhoof, they couldn't do enough.

I was thinking about my last trip here when I saw them. They were standing with a group in the corner. I had to go say hello.

"Good evening, Colonel Frade, it has been a while."

"It has, Lord Blackhoof. I see you have done well for yourself. I may have been hasty in helping your departure."

"It had its moments—still worth a laugh now. I was shaking at the time. How is your daughter?"

"She is about to give birth to her first."

"Give her my best wishes."

I made a mental note to have a gift sent. After all the Frades were my partners in the Howell container operation.

I will never forget that glorious sight. It has dimmed with time, but the thrill is still there.

We chatted a bit. He was going to be present at Howell's in the morning, but I cut to the chase.

"Is there anything I should be aware of?"

"Minor issues, nothing that you need to be concerned about."

"That is good to hear. I realized today I will never get a straight answer on the docks."

"My people tell me things are going well there. It is in my best interest for the project to succeed, so I'm keeping an eye on it."

"Thank you, Colonel. If there is anything I can do for you, please let me know."

"There is. Next summer we are going to be in England. An introduction to the queen would be received very well by my wife."

"That can be arranged. While you are there you can use my suite at the Plaza on The Strand. Here is my card. Contact me when the event gets closer."

"I will, Lord Blackhoof."

We shook hands and parted. To think this was the man who sent me a shotgun shell and told me to get out and stay out of Argentina. I guess attitudes change when daughters are safely married.

Wait, is she married?

Going over the books at Howell the next day was boring. I already had what I came for. Later in the evening, we took our show on the road again. This time we were flying to Senegal for refueling.

It was a tiny airport and none of us chose to get off the plane. It didn't seem safe. I had heard so many unsavory things about the diamond trade here.

No one tried to sell me any of the bloody diamonds while we were there. I think we were all glad to get back into the air.

Arriving in Hamburg the next morning was a culture shock after dealing with South American and African officials.

The Germans were their usual efficient and oh-so-correct selves. It was like a breath of fresh air to know that I didn't have to reach into my pocket for a gift.

As they were leaving one of the customs officials asked if he could have my autograph as a gift for his daughter. I reached into my coat pocket for one of my publicity pictures.

He must still wonder what I was laughing about.

We went directly to the port for the obligatory tour of the new docks. I swear these cranes were looking bigger all the time.

I mentioned that to one of the dockworkers. He told me it was not as big as the League Island Crane in Philadelphia at the Navy Shipyards.

It must be huge. I stated that and he told me there were plans underway to build some with a million pounds lift capacity.

I spent a good half hour learning how modern ships were built. It was fascinating. I had no idea that ship compartments were built onshore, then lifted into place and welded together.

He joked that a compartmented ship could break in half and both halves float. Or worse yet one-half sink. It would be like the law of jelly side down. My half would be the one that sunk.

That was also the most interesting conversation I had in Germany. The books were correct, and all was well.

Chapter 48

There was one surprise on my trip. I was contacted by a representative of the German Federal Government. They asked me to come to Bonn to meet with the president. It seems they wanted to give me an award.

It would be the Cross of Merit 1st Class.

There was no reason not to go, though I wasn't certain that I had done anything in Germany to deserve the award. We flew there in the afternoon for a simple ceremony and a reception.

The award was for helping in the economic redevelopment of West Germany. The Germans had come a long way since the war, but having a major port updated was considered icing on the cake.

At the reception held at Hammerschmidt Villa, the official residence of the seat of the federal president, I was told of a second reason. Hamburg is a state of West Germany in its own right. There is a long-standing policy that their citizens will not accept any state or federal awards.

I couldn't understand, but the federal government liked to give these awards to people who made significant achievements in Hamburg as a stick in the eye. Politics! You gotta love it.

The president asked for Jim, Todd, and me to step into a library for a private conversation. As I suspected, he wanted to know if we were considering doing any production in Europe.

"If you are looking to place any operations in Europe, we in Germany would be most interested and would be willing to make significant concessions for a large factory that employed a thousand people."

"Sir, we haven't had that conversation internally, but I assure you if we decide to have production in Europe, Germany will be among those considered."

"That's all we can ask at this time."

At that, we rejoined the party.

I did get to spend some time talking to a pretty young actress named Hannelore Auer. There was no magnetism between us. It was a professional chat about show business.

I was a little surprised that she wasn't pushing to get into the US movies, but each to their own. I suspected she would have a good career here in Germany. She carried herself well. I could see her in the role of a princess.

We were staying the night at the Hotel Petersburg. When we got into our suite, we had a brief wrap-up meeting for the events of the day.

The president's question and offer were most interesting, but we decided to put off any discussion until we were back in the air. We were learning that walls do have ears.

After we were back on board the plane in the morning and were in the air on our way to Valencia, we met in the conference room with the door closed.

Todd and Jim told me they had been having discussions on the issue of European production. They wanted to work out the advantages and disadvantages before approaching me.

I asked if they had come to any conclusions.

"It would be very much to our advantage to have a production facility in Europe. It would have to be near one of the seas or oceans, but we are growing too fast for Pittsburgh to handle."

I contributed, "There is another plus to the situation. It would give some protection against US politicians. This time it is the Democrats; next it could be the Republicans. They all want a piece of us. Even if we would go to Germany those politicians would have their hands out."

Jim smiling said, "But you could play them against each other if they demanded too much."

On that pleasant note, I asked them to continue to take a serious look, even put together a team to cost the project out, including site selection.

This was to be done discreetly without letting any country know they were under consideration. I didn't need the pressure that would be generated.

I gave my newest decoration to Harold to put the ribbon on my bar. Inside the box were instructions on obtaining duplicates. He told me he would need at least a dozen for my uniforms. Even though it was a foreign decoration, I knew that I was authorized to wear a German one.

Well, at least one from West Germany. I didn't think the East Germans would be offering me awards any time soon. They would like to put something around my neck, more likely a noose.

I was getting quite a collection. Soon my Coldstream uniform would look like my Boy Scout one, in other words, a Christmas tree.

The flight to Valencia seemed like a hop, skip, and jump after our recent trips.

We started with a tour of the port which had been in operation since 1483. I suspect it is a little larger now.

There were no signs of the Spanish *mañana*. It was full speed ahead at all times. I almost got run over by a speeding forklift. It wasn't a small one like those used inside. This one had a forty-five-foot box trailer on its forks.

Walking around the one new crane, something looked different. It took a while to put it together. I asked Todd what he thought of the concrete foundation of the one crane that had been set up.

He looked at it and then kicked an edge with his steel-toed boots. The concrete flaked off. The head Spanish engineer told us not to worry about it. I didn't like this at all.

Looking around for the American project engineer, I didn't see him. I asked where he was.

"He asked for the day off."

"Do we have his phone number?"

It took some pushing, but we were finally taken to an office where I called the man's apartment. He answered the phone immediately.

I identified myself. His comment was, "Wow, the head office got through to you guys quickly."

"We've not heard from them; you say you have a call in for upper management?"

"Yes, I was forced to take the day off. They didn't want me on site when you showed up."

"Todd Goodson, Jim Williamson, and I are on-site right now. I wanted to ask about the concrete. Something doesn't look right."

"Good eye, boss, and there is more than that wrong."

"Meet us at the airport's private aviation terminal. Bring your passport."

Hanging up the phone, I told Jim and Todd to follow me. We walked out of the office to the car that had been put at our disposal for the day. The driver was not in sight.

"Get in," I said, as I got behind the wheel.

Without gunning it to alert anyone, I drove out of the port to the airport. It was a straight shot, so I remembered the way.

During the trip, Todd wanted to know what was going on. I told him what the engineer had told me.

"Then why didn't we face those guys down and fire them on the spot?"

"This is Franco's Spain. We might have ended up in jail; it depends if this is due to city, province, or national corruption."

We got to the airport where we met our engineer who had beaten us there. The flight crew was still on the plane or involved in restocking and refueling. I told them wheels up as quickly as possible.

Our chief pilot got the Master Pilot Star on his wings in Korea. He knew how to get wheels up. Air traffic control was sputtering behind him. He had followed all of their instructions to the letter. Just a lot faster than they thought should be done.

Once in the air, I had the flight plan revised to Rome. I didn't want to set foot on Spanish territory until this issue was taken care of, or at least out in the open and the rats identified.

Once on the ground in Rome, I worked the telephone. I was glad I spoke Spanish as I worked my way through the Spanish federal system.

I got through to the prosecutor's office that handled my *estancia* problem. They told me they would make inquiries. They didn't want to walk into a buzz saw any more than I did, so they would identify the powers involved before doing anything.

My next set of calls was to the *estancia*'s lawyers and told them they might have to represent Jackson Transportation in a lawsuit against the Port of Valencia.

To them this would be like a high school baseball team being told, you will be playing in the National League starting tomorrow. Scary as all get out, but wow!

While in transit to Rome the engineer Brad White shared the evidence, he had collected while on the job. The foundation wasn't deep enough, the concrete substandard, and only half the necessary rebar had been used.

The crane itself was solid but when it picked up a fully loaded container while at full extension there was a good chance it would fall over. I love doing business here; you can count on it being crooked every time.

Not mafia level crooked, nickel dime bribery crooked with each person only taking a small bit until failure occurs. I wondered if the culture would ever change.

Since we didn't dare go into Spain until we knew what sort of hornet's nest, we had opened we decided to go to our next stop, Hong Kong via India. I told the engineer to enjoy a week's vacation in Rome while we sorted things out.

Chapter 49

The flight to Bombay seemed to take forever. It seemed as if we had always been on this plane going somewhere and never arriving.

Like all good things, it came to an end. When we landed in Bombay, we found that the world had changed.

In China Mao Tse-tung was dead. The official word was a heart attack. The unofficial word was lead poisoning. Mao had always been considered to be in good health.

The *International Herald Tribune* reported that from his family health history, Mao would have been expected to live into his eighties. To die in his sixties was considered odd.

Deng Xiaoping led a faction that was now trying to take power. Fighting was reported in most areas of China. Deng had been an outspoken opponent of Mao over his Great Leap Forward which was causing starvation in China.

The article told how Deng and his people had bought grain in Canada and had it shipped to them to try to alleviate the situation. That was the last straw for Mao.

He would rather his people starve than admit any failure of his plan. He had ordered that Deng be arrested. It was speculated that Deng moved first.

One thing for sure was I wouldn't be going to China soon. Until the civil war was settled and new leadership in position, I wouldn't consider going. Even then it would be determined by who was in power.

Todd, Jim, and I had a serious discussion about even going to Hong Kong. A phone call to the palace led me to be put into contact with the governor of Hong Kong.

He told me that there were no signs of unrest and that it would help keep things stable if I proceeded. The Chinese workers who made the backbone of Hong Kong were now supporting the British government because of the jobs that had been created.

My presence would be considered a sign that job creation would continue. Based on those assurances, we as a group decided we should continue.

Todd and Jim seemed to consider it a bit of an adventure, but then, they had never been shot. I hadn't completely recovered from the last time. However, the Crown had asked me to step up. It reminded me of Tommy this, Tommy that.

We had no business to conduct in India. The customs and immigration people came on board even after we told the tower we were only refueling and leaving.

They made it clear we would not leave until we paid bribes. They even called it bribes; there was no shame. It seemed to be the official practice.

I wanted to throw them off the plane, but my chief pilot explained to me that we would never get clearance to take off unless we did. Not only wouldn't we get clearance we would also have to pay fees for the plane sitting on the ground.

Grumbling I told Jim to take care of it. I later found it cost two hundred dollars. Strangely enough, we were not charged an airport landing fee which was two hundred and fifty dollars.

Go figure.

Only when we were well on our way was I told that they had to bribe everyone they came into contact with, ground crew, fueling, and catering. An envelope was even sent to the control tower to facilitate our takeoff position in the queue.

By that time, I was ready to go to bed and didn't care anymore. One thing was for certain. I wouldn't try to do business in India for the foreseeable future.

We were met at the foot of the plane stairs by a representative of the Peninsula Hotel. He escorted us to a nearby Rolls-Royce

Phantom. I had read about their famous automobile fleet but wasn't surprised. Todd and Jim were awed.

I was too but didn't let it show. After all, I'm the world traveler of the group. Todd, who had never been out of the US before, made that observation when we were in Spain fleeing to Italy.

He was impressed that I spoke Spanish and knew the authorities there. I didn't disabuse him, letting him think I knew more than I did. I realized that it was an ego thing but hey, it's my ego.

At the hotel, they treated us like we were regular guests. At least I was. Todd, Jim, and Harold were treated well but as my functionaries. I better keep my ego in check. Having fun was one thing, believing it another.

I was discreetly asked if I would like a companion for my stay. I declined. What a temptation, but I managed.

Instead of going to the docks first thing, we met with Sir Robert Black, a Scotsman who was the current governor. He thanked us for coming. You could see he was uneasy dealing with a teenager, no matter my accomplishments.

Sensing this, Todd took the lead in discussing the port construction project. I was tired enough that I was glad to let him take the lead. I'm sure that Sir Robert would think I was a puppet, but so be it.

Sir Robert did lay a bomb on me as we were taking leave.

"Tell Lady Jackson that I asked of her and that I will always remember our adventures in Egypt."

I told him that she was fine and that I would relay his message.

This was the second time that Mum and Egypt were mentioned. When was she there, and what was she up to? I couldn't think of a way to get any information from Sir Robert so let it pass me by.

Jim asked me about Mum and Egypt. I told him it was on a need-to-know basis. I didn't tell him that it appeared that I didn't have a need to know, as Mum would change the subject when I brought it up.

The construction was first-rate and ahead of schedule. What amazed me was the scaffolding. In the US or UK, we used metal or heavy wood scaffolds that were bolted or nailed together. Here they used bamboo which by its nature looked flimsy and lashed it together with a manila cord.

It seemed a strong wind would take it down, but I was assured the scaffolds were very strong. I didn't volunteer to go up on any.

We spent many hours going over the project. It was late afternoon by the time we finished. We returned to our hotel to clean up and change for the reception being given at Government House by the governor.

On this occasion, Harold had laid out my colonel's uniform, mess dress variety. With that were all my medals and honors. Not the ribbons, the real medals.

When I looked in the mirror, it was amazing. I wore it well because of my size and physical condition. I could have played a prince in one of those corny romances—you know where the lovely girl falls for the guy and later finds out he is a prince. I doubted whether they would ever make very many of those movies.

My appearance in the sitting area took Jim and Todd aback. They knew of my rank, regiment, medals, and honors but had never seen me in full fig. Neither said anything but the sideways glances that I kept receiving told the story. Harold had let the front desk know that we would need a ride to Government House.

I expected one from the fleet of Rollers. When I appeared in the lobby in full uniform, it stopped foot traffic everywhere as people gawked at me. From my movie career, I was used to this and took it in stride.

My companions not so much; they shuffled and looked awkward with all the attention. I mean they weren't idiots like Don Knotts on

The Andy Griffith Show but you could see they weren't comfortable with the attention.

The hotel night manager came up to me, almost running, and then giving a small bow. "Lord Blackhoof, your car will be here momentarily."

That was strange. I could see a line of empty limos right outside.

Then my ride came into sight. It was the longest most ostentatious car I had ever seen. I found out that it was a Rolls-Royce 1934 Phantom II. It was beautiful; it was large, and did I say ostentatious?

From the huge headlights to the passenger cabin, it had every automotive excess known to man. I loved it.

By special arrangement whenever this vehicle was used, there were Hong Kong police cars as escorts, before and after. There were motorcycle police who would go ahead and shut down the intersections so we could drive straight through.

I thought this was incredible and wondered who paid for all this. I found out when Harold showed me my bill. Oh well, this excess was worth it. I now had an inkling of how the queen traveled every time she went out. One could get used to this.

The press had been forewarned of my arrival at Government House as they were there in full force. It was nice to have police form a barrier so we wouldn't get jostled by the commoners. I better stop being an ass!

Chapter 50

Once inside Government House, I was drafted into the receiving line to be introduced. That part was not so much fun. Guys would try to break my hand. Some stank of alcohol and tobacco, others just stank. I'm not talking of just men.

Then there were the mothers who were certain I needed to meet their daughters. As an aside to the governor, I asked him if he enjoyed doing this for a living.

He told me some days he would rather be back in a Japanese prison camp. Harsh!

As we stood there greeting people as they came in, I recognized a familiar face in the line. I didn't know what to call her. Maybe she was here to tell me my dry cleaning was ready?

She reached Sir Robert first.

"Lady Ping! You do us great honor in attending our reception for Sir Richard."

"I have a message for Sir Richard."

Turning to me she told me, "Do not come to China under any circumstances. Both sides would like to use you as a bargaining chip. At the same time, be prepared to increase grain shipments. We will be paying with gold."

Sir Robert asked, "From that, can I assume that Deng Xiaoping is winning?"

"For the moment he has the upper hand. I think he will take all power very soon."

This meant he would be the highest official in both the government and the Communist party.

"The Great Leap Forward is done, now we must save the people. That is what I'm here to ask Sir Richard to do."

"How will we handle the details?"

"Sir Richard if you do not mind, I and several others will attend you in your hotel tomorrow morning."

Thinking quickly, I asked, "How will I know that those accompanying you are not using you to get to me?"

"I will tell you that it is a beautiful day in Hong Kong."

"So, if I hear the 'words beautiful day in Hong Kong,' you aren't under any duress?"

"Yes."

"May I have a representative of the Crown there?"

"Sir Robert, you are welcome to attend."

He nodded, and she moved on into the room. She must have immediately left as I didn't see her again.

"Sir Robert, I have dealt with Lady Ping many times, in many places. Who exactly is she?

"She is the only descendent of Puyi the last emperor. If the Qing dynasty were still in power, she would be empress. As it is, she has worked all her life for the people of China. She will deal with anyone who makes it better for the people."

"Do you think she can ever regain power?"

"No, and I don't think she would want it. She has never married and has no children, at least that we know of, so there would be no successor."

There was an interesting mix of people at the reception. To my surprise an old friend was present.

"Hey, Pilgrim. Fancy meeting you here! That's quite a getup you are wearing. You should be on a set somewhere."

I started to draw the dress sword at my side. He faked fear. We had a good laugh. People watching us, and there were plenty of them, must have thought we were crazy.

"John, it is good to see you, I'm here on business. What are you up to?"

"Scouting a location; I think we will make an action movie here. Are you up to another movie? Not this one but a Western."

"When will shooting start?"

"I'm planning for the first quarter of next year. I hear you got kicked out of school so you should have the time."

"What studio are you working with?"

"Monroe's."

"Let's talk further. Could you have a script sent to me in England?"

"I have an extra one with me. I will bring it to your room later tonight."

"That would be cool."

We chatted about mutual friends for a while. Others had gathered around us waiting to talk to one of us. It turned out Mr. Wayne was more popular than me. Who would have thought?

There were a couple of cute English girls whose parents worked at Government House who were interested in flirting with me.

It was fun but meant nothing. While cute, neither one had two brain cells to rub together.

Back at the hotel with Jim and Todd, we discussed the evening. While I had official duty standing in line, and later, talks with every businessman who thought they could make a quick buck off me, they had enjoyed themselves mingling with the crowd.

There was a knock at the door, and John Wayne joined us. The men were having a whiskey, so he joined them. I had my usual Coke.

John started telling stories about me on the set. You would think I was a rabble-rouser and troublemaker the way he told them.

As he kept them spellbound with my supposed antics, I leafed through the script. It seemed to be one I could work with. Was I getting typecast as a cowboy?

I half-listened to his storytelling but had to object when he started telling the story of me in the stampede.

"I didn't ride any bulls through the herd!"

I gave up and went to bed at two in the morning. They were still at it. After a short night, I had room service provide breakfast. My two companions managed to get up and have coffee before going to the shower.

I took mercy on them and ordered a new breakfast set up after they were dressed.

Todd told me, "I learned a lot I didn't know about you, Rick. I know there was some exaggeration, but you have had an interesting time of it."

"Some exaggeration, yes. I killed a coyote; no, I didn't skin it on the set. I didn't skin it at all."

"But you did stand up to a charging rabid coyote?"

"Well, yeah, but it wasn't that big of a deal."

"Sure."

His "sure" was drug out and sounded almost like he didn't believe me.

We finished up breakfast and were joined by Sir Robert, Lady Ping, and two other Chinese gentlemen, and after introductions around, the business began. She told me it was a beautiful day in Hong Kong. Looking out the window at the sunshine, I agreed.

It started with a review of what grain shipments had been made and what was still on order. They wanted to triple their order.

"We have seized the treasury, so we can pay in gold if that is acceptable."

"It is, but I need to be paid in Canada or better yet in England as it is illegal to own gold or have it in contracts in the United States."

"We can do that—now, a sensitive question. It will take time to have the gold moved to you. Will you extend a line of credit so shipments can start immediately?"

I turned to Jim.

"How much credit can we extend without damaging any of our positions?"

He thought for a moment, "One hundred million with no problems; beyond that I would have to do an in-depth review."

I asked, "Will that be enough?"

"For the grain yes," stated Lady Ping. "There is the next matter: weapons, and ammunition."

Sir Robert stepped in, "Rick, I think this is an issue for Her Majesty's government."

Turning to Lady Ping, the governor said, "We would be delighted to sell you the materials you need to bring peace to China."

Then chuckling he added, "Especially when it gives us a chance to get some of Sir Richard's money."

I protested, "It is only a line of credit extended, not a gift."

"I know, but it is your money. You are becoming a Rothschild."

"I can't afford a canal as they did."

"Well, maybe not this year."

From the puzzled looks on Lady Ping's companions, I had to explain. "Lord Rothschild of the banking family loaned the money to England to buy shares in the recently completed Suez Canal. It was done on a handshake, no contracts."

At that, I held out my hand to Lady Ping. We shook hands and I had just put one hundred million dollars on the line. She wasn't even an official of the new struggling government.

The way I looked at it, if China didn't want to repay me, they wouldn't; and there wasn't anything I could do about it.

By making this *beau geste* I would either come up smelling like roses or be dead broke, well down to my last half a billion dollars or so. Having money can be fun.

Besides who can say they loaned money to an empress?

It was agreed that Jim would appoint someone from the London office to oversee the projects. Contact information was exchanged and they made their goodbyes. I got a hug from Lady Ping.

"You will always be known as a friend of China."

After they left Todd and Jim were both blown away by events. I had agreed to put up a huge sum of money to save starving people and provide weapons for a government to fight a civil war.

Jim asked, "Who exactly is Lady Ping?"

When I told them, it was the frosting on the cake. Todd exclaimed, "Now I know why fighting with the Kennedys doesn't bother you. You are power on the world stage in your own right."

I hadn't looked at it that way, but he wasn't far wrong.

Chapter 51

The next day we went over the local books with the accountants. Everything was under strict control, and we didn't even see anything questionable. This was the tightest run operation of any we had visited.

Maybe it was because they would cane for minor offenses and hang for major. Not just for crimes of violence but what we called white-collar crime.

No resort prisons for high-level offenders, I had not seen them but was told the prisons were terrible by American standards.

They even had local politicians locked up. It seems like the rest of the world should follow suit. I based that thought on how well this project was being run with high quality, on time, and under budget.

No one had ever told them that you can have any of the two above but not all three.

From Hong Kong, it was an easy flight to Tokyo. The Japanese appeared to be in a contest with Hong Kong as to who could do it best.

There seemed to be an international contest going on to see who could award me honors. I was invited to a reception in my honor, but I was wrong thinking I would be presented with another award.

It was being held in the main hall of the Diet, which is what the Japanese call their parliament, as the prime minister's residence was too small for such a function.

The bad part of this is that both chambers of the Japanese government would be there as it was their building. I would be introduced to most of them. I just hoped that all seven hundred-plus members wouldn't be present.

We were taken to our quarters to freshen up before the reception. Instead of the usual hotel suite, we were staying at a guest house rented by my company.

I had been told it was well-staffed and could cater to all our needs. I wondered if this meant hot and cold running Geisha Girls.

Upon arriving we were welcomed by the housekeeper. She said her name, but I missed it as I didn't get the pronunciation. After a shower, I changed into the suit Harold had selected for me.

I went downstairs and was directed to a living room that looked like it was out of a 1930s movie set. It reminded me of a set I had been on at Warner Brothers.

I was on that set because Dick Wyman had me there for a fight scene. I got engrossed in the plush seats and watched a complete dining room scene play out. It was based on eighteenth-century British manners but with an Oriental twist. It was probably nothing like the real Japan, but fascinating, nonetheless.

The housekeeper whose name I never did get asked if I would like anything. I told her a Coke would be wonderful.

Jim and Todd came into the room as my Coke was being served. It is a good thing I had been on that movie set. The young lady who served me came in, and with a smooth motion went to her knees while holding a tray.

She poured my Coke into an ice-filled glass and looking down, handed it to me. I took the glass; she rose in a flowing motion, bowed, and left the room.

Between my acting and having watched the little ceremony play out on the movie set, I was able to act like this was the way things were done.

Jim and Todd's mouths were agape.

As I read once, fake it until you make it. Boy, was I faking? To think this was real.

We were loaded into a limo for our trip to the National Diet. After the limos in Hong Kong this car, a Cadillac, was boring.

To my relief, I wasn't introduced to seven hundred people. There were only about one hundred present, and most weren't interested in meeting me. I had thought it would be the representatives and councilors.

Instead, it was members of industry, their suppliers, consultants, bankers, and others involved in rebuilding the Japanese economy. At this time Japanese products were considered a joke.

There was a rumor that Japan had renamed a town USA so it could claim products were made in the USA. I wanted to ask our host if there was any truth to this but realized it would be highly insulting.

Jim got caught up talking to some financial types. Todd and I wandered around. We saw a tall obvious American standing at an open bar. He had an attractive Japanese girl on his arm.

I looked at him too long and caught his eye. He came over to me. He introduced himself, W. Edwards Deming. He was there looking for work. He was a quality consultant who had a heavy statistical background.

I made the mistake of asking him how statistics could help in manufacturing. He explained, and then he explained some more. At first, I wanted to run away, but by the time he explained the difference between common cause and special cause I was hooked.

We needed this sort of expertise in our operation in Pittsburgh. Todd and I exchanged glances, and Todd took over saying we would be interested in his looking at our operations in Pittsburgh to see if he could help.

He was heading back stateside in two weeks and would be glad to visit Todd. He didn't pay much attention to me. I think since Todd was older, Deming assumed he was the boss. That was fine with me.

There were no awards for me at this event which was fine. There comes a point when it becomes a bit much. I was introduced to the prime minister, and he thanked me through his interpreter for my helping his country modernize.

The next morning, we were up for our tour. The tour went well, but I was getting to feel if you have seen one container port, you have seen them all.

There was one interesting conversation. Through an interpreter, I was asking how things were going. The only word that I recognized was Popeye. Did I hear right?

The translator told us that things were now fine on the dock since Popeye had straightened out the Yakuza. I asked if it was my Popeye, well I described him, and the dockworker nodded yes.

I asked the translator to ask if there was a body count. The answer was no body count, no bodies were ever found. They just went away.

The worker through the translator asked if I knew Popeye. My response that he was my uncle was accepted with wide eyes. The worker suddenly bowed to me three times and hurried away.

For the rest of the tour, I felt many eyes on me. Not because my company was building this, but because Popeye was my uncle. That made some of his fame rub off on me. What a weird feeling that was.

The tour only lasted half a day, so we spent the rest of the afternoon being updated on the project and its finances. Jim had a lot of good questions. Todd looked like he was learning a lot. I managed not to yawn.

At the end of the day, we boarded our plane for an overnight flight to Anchorage where we would refuel. We would then fly to Chicago, refueling once more, then on to Savannah.

I slept crossing the Pacific, so I missed seeing the short day-night cycle. This was because we were flying in the same direction as the rotation of the earth, so that daylight that lasted 10 hours on the ground below passed by in about half that in the air. If we'd been flying westbound, especially near the poles, we could have stayed in daylight for the whole trip by "chasing the sun."

I was glad I woke up when we landed. Since it was winter in Alaska, even though we were on the ground for a short time, we needed de-icing before takeoff. The sound of all that saltwater against the fuselage would have made it impossible to sleep.

Since I was refreshed from a good night's sleep, the rest of the people on board looked tired to me, not exhausted but lacking a good night's sleep. Even a first-class fold-down seat wasn't the same as a bed.

I decided the only political thing to do was ignore their lack of sleep, that, or have the plane redesigned. Now that is a thought.

I had breakfast in my conference room where I was joined by a chipper Harold. I was puzzled then remembered he had a Pullman bunk in his room in the cargo hold. Thinking about it, I realized we could have made three more rooms like his down there.

Chicago was a quick stop, at least quick for Chicago. The weather was good so there were no delays. The ground crew wasn't on a slowdown, so things went smoothly.

Landing in Savannah early evening we went straight to The Marshal House. There was no special reception on this trip. It almost seemed like they wanted us here for as short a time as possible.

We were to have a two-hour tour in the morning, then a project review, and have us on our way by noon. We three talked about that. It smelled fishy.

The tour the next morning was all dog and pony show. Things were set up for us to see, and we weren't allowed to deviate from the path. Jim, Todd, and I had discussed this in the morning. We decided to go along with them for the half day. From there we would see.

Chapter 52

The project review was all rah-rah and had little substance. Once it was finished the project manager thanked us for coming and stood to see us out the door.

I told him we were not done; we would be here for another two days going over the site. In the meantime, Jim was on the phone arranging for our accountants to fly in from LA.

Talk about seeing someone break out into a sweat.

To make a long story short, we had fraud and embezzlement charges filed against the project manager. We ended up replacing over half the supervisors. It was a grand mess. Instead of the half-day scheduled, and the two days we thought it would take, Jim and I were there for two weeks. Todd had to get back to run his plant.

We found that the breakdown in financial reporting was due to the accountant who checked the Savannah books being the project manager's niece. She ended up in jail with him.

Between Spain and Savannah, it led to a revamping of hiring procedures. We decided that we had left too much power in the hands of the project manager.

We came up with a shortlist of positions that Jackson Transportation headquarters would interview for and hire. There was no chance of recovering the money.

The project manager had a gambling problem. Prison would be hard on the ex-manager as he still owed a lot to his bookie. There was a good chance he wouldn't survive the experience. I left word that if anything happened to him in prison it was to be shared around the company. It was for the encouragement of the others if you will.

It is a bit ironic that his niece was using her share to support her church. I didn't think her minister would take out a contract on her while she was incarcerated, but you never know.

When all that was done it was time to head to LA for Christmas. The flight was ho-hum and over before you knew it. I was now so used to having all my conveniences at hand that it didn't even seem like I was flying. That would change if I decided to take a walk outside.

My plane dropped me off in LA and the crew couldn't get it turned around fast enough to get back to England for the holidays.

Dad was waiting with the limo. I updated him on the Savanna fiasco. He thought I was lucky to only lose a couple of million. All in all, my businesses were doing pretty well. He asked me if I had learned anything on the trip.

I told him that I now realized I had to pay closer attention than I had been. If I let things go it would only get worse.

I shared with him how Jim and Todd thought I was a man of the world, able to speak other languages, be comfortable in other cultures, and deal with world leaders.

"Rick, what part of that isn't so?"

"That I'm comfortable in other cultures."

"Did you get by enough that there was no embarrassment?"

"Yes."

"Then you did better than most."

I still had a hard time accepting the title, man of the world.

Dad had met me to specifically debrief me before I got home. He didn't want talking business to ruin the family gathering.

Grandmum had come from England accompanied by Mr. Hamilton. Aunt Sybil and Uncle Popeye were there. Harold had stayed on the plane back to England to spend time with his family.

I had planned on Christmas presents well before my trip. At each stop, I had asked to be taken to a high-end store that dealt in local products.

The only place that didn't work was Spain where we had to hightail it out of the country. I did have time in Rome to make up for it.

On Christmas Eve we had a luncheon for family and close friends. Christmas day would be family only.

For the luncheon, I provided poppers or "crackers" for the table. Two people would each pull an end of the cracker, tearing it apart. In doing so a small cap inside would pop or crack.

With Mr. Hamilton's help, I found a specialty store in London that would make a cracker with whatever contents you provided. I had a common cracker made up and a couple of special ones.

The common ones held a gold bracelet for men and a small diamond tennis bracelet for women.

I had to snigger when I realized that Denny had invited his girlfriend to lunch. I had just raised her expectations of Denny.

The special ones were for Mrs. Hernandez and her date who reminded me of Caesar Romero. A double-take, and I realized it was Caesar Romero. She was traveling in high company.

Her present was an antique set of turquoise inlaid hair combs, Spanish style. For the guy whom I was guessing at, I had included a white silk scarf with a very high thread count. I don't know who counted all those small threads, but I had been told the more the better.

Later Mr. Romero thanked me for the present. Several years later I saw that scarf in one of his movies. Mrs. Hernandez was in heaven with her combs. They became a trademark of hers.

For Mum and Dad, the cracker contained a tiara worthy of Countess Jackson. Dad got a certificate for a safari in Kenya and a license to take one bull elephant.

Eddie was sitting with Patty, who had made up with Mary. They had the common bracelet.

Grandmum sat with Mr. Hamilton. They seemed rather chummy. I had gotten her a smaller tiara so she wouldn't feel out of place with all her high friends.

While I had no way of knowing that she would be sitting with Mr. Hamilton, I was glad that I had put a diamond stickpin in his cracker.

Aunt Sybil got another tiara. I mean why should her sister have one and not her? It wasn't as big, but she was still thrilled. Popeye was the hardest. I bet he was the only guy in town with a pearl-handled blackjack in Sharkskin. I could see him thumping it against his hand as though he couldn't wait to use it.

Saving the best for last, I handed Mary hers. When taking it she remarked that it was too small for a puppy. Missed opportunity!

What it contained was a Lady Mary-sized tiara. The diamonds were real. Take that, Patty! She was sitting with a young man I didn't know. He was a friend from her school by the name of Eddie. He couldn't keep still. I think that Van Halen kid had ants in his pants.

Not knowing who she would have with her, I had a men's Bulova watch with a small band for her date.

The crackers were the hit of the day. The one I got the most kick out of was Denny's girlfriend. Even though she wasn't the only one to get a tennis bracelet, you would think she was engaged. Denny looked scared to death. Score!

My date for the party was Nina. She had come from Switzerland to spend Christmas with her parents. Her mother was staying with her father here. Nina didn't say anything, but you could tell she hoped they would get back together.

My gift to her inside the cracker was a sheet of paper with a phone number and code on it. Once she opened it, she gave me a quizzical look.

"It's the air charterhouse where I keep the 707. The sale has been completed and I now own it outright. Call that number and give the code, and then you can schedule the plane whenever and wherever you want.

Being rich is good. It certainly can keep you in your girlfriend's good graces. This was demonstrated by the yelp, hug, and kiss I received.

Since many around the table didn't know about my jet, it required an explanation which Nina was glad to give. She knew the plane better than I did from all the tours she had given at her school.

Christmas day was a quieter affair. The presents were on the order of fuzzy slippers and smoking jackets. Mum and Dad had gotten me a red velvet jacket, and Nina gave me a white silk scarf. I had to put them on at once.

They looked spiffy. All I needed now was a pencil mustache and a monocle.

The week between Christmas and New Year's was low-key. Nina invited me to dinner with her mother and father. From the way they paid attention to each other, things were looking up.

Nina and I found plenty of time to be alone.

On New Year's Eve, Mum and Dad threw a big charity ball. Nina and I made a short appearance for propriety's sake and then went to a party at one of her high school friend's houses. Since these were all Hollywood kids, we spoke on a level playing field.

Maybe my field wasn't as level as theirs, but we could still talk. In describing what I had been doing for the last year I realized I had been taking care of business.

Finished for now.

Back Matter

To be continued in Book 11: Interesting Times[1]
enelsonauthor.com[2]

For information on hiring Janet E. Rupert to edit your fiction project, email:

janeteditorrupert@gmail.com

---

1. https://www.amazon.com/gp/product/B091ZC9Q2D

2. https://enelsonauthor.com/

Other books by Ed Nelson

The Richard Jackson Saga

Book 1 The Beginning

Book 2 Schooldays

Book 3 Hollywood

Book 4 In the Movies

Book 5 Star to Deckhand

Book 6 Surfing Dude

Book 7 Third Time is a Charm

Book 8 Oxford University

Book 9 Cold War

Book 10 Taking Care of Business

Book 11 Interesting Times

Book 12 Escape from Siberia

Book 13 Regicide

Book 14 What's Under, Down Under?

Book 15 The Lunar Kingdom

Book 16 First Steps

In the Richard Jackson World

Mary, Mary

Stand-Alone Story

Ever and Always

Cast in Time Series

Book 1: Baron

Book 2: Baron of the Middle Counties

Book 3: Count

Book 4: Earl

Book 5: Earl of the Marches